ECHO KILLERS

A DICKIE FLOYD DETECTIVE NOVEL

DANNY R. SMITH

❀ Created with Vellum

Every day a special breed of men and women throughout this great country place themselves in harm's way for the greater good of our society. They are the peacekeepers, and this is for them.

I would like to extend a special thanks to Scott Helbing, a longtime friend and former colleague who now flies helicopters for the Los Angeles County Sheriff's Department. The cover of this book was created from a night vision photograph he took while flying over the City of Angels.

FOREWORD

A young foster child in South Central Los Angeles witnesses a thrill kill and then steals a puppy—or did he? As a team of investigators hunt for the killers, the killers hunt the child. Make certain your lap belt is tight and your seat is in the full upright position, as you are in for a ride. This is the third, and in my opinion the best, of a series of crime novels by Danny Smith.

Danny Smith is a retired Los Angeles County deputy sheriff. During his early career he worked exclusively in South Central Los Angeles as a patrol deputy, field training officer, and detective. For much of his time there, I was his watch commander. He was selected to work at the prestigious Major Crimes Bureau, one of only 25 personnel who handled every "in progress" crime investigation in Los Angeles County, including kidnaps for ransom, embezzlements, murders for hire, escapes from custody, threats against public officials, and "specials"—those crimes involving political or law enforcement personnel that required discretion and a critical expertise. I headed that unit.

I know well and have worked with both of the men characterized in *Echo Killers*. Dickie and Floyd worked for me as patrol deputies in the inner city as well as in Major Crimes. Their real history is as colorful as the one portrayed in these books. Their dark humor and dogged determination always set them apart in units that were themselves set apart. The relationships these men and women maintained with the people they served in South Central Los Angeles are not well known but a very real part of their success.

Danny and his partner, Floyd, were selected to go to the Homicide Bureau, considered by many to be the absolute pinnacle of any investigative position. Homicide only takes the very best, and they were considered a couple of the best among them.

All cops have stories: tales of human evil and depravity that, thankfully, most sane people cannot even imagine. Many cops have tried to capture these horrors and adventures in books. Most, unfortunately, fail. Danny Smith is a rarity. He combines believable stories in a fluid, compelling manner and with dialogue that is spot on. His works are on par with Connelly, Wambaugh, and Leonard.

In *Echo Killers*, the author toggles back and forth from the killers to the cops, illustrating the deadly game of chess they have all begun. Cancel your plans for the afternoon when you begin this book, as the story will keep you glued to your seat turning pages. It is truly a fast ride.

Danny's characterization of those tasked with solving these crimes and dealing with the most vicious and depraved criminals—while trying to maintain a *normal* private life—provides a rare window into the private conversations, thoughts, and minds of these men and women. Their interaction with one another is raw, terse, and honest. Their self-doubt is real, yet well hidden from the public. Danny exposes these things, and with this unmasking, reveals the human toll these cases take on those whose lives are forever altered by them.

Echo Killers shares those experiences and relationships and lets the reader ride alongside during this fast-moving read.

Dennis "Deac" Slocumb, Detective Lieutenant, Ret.
Director of Legislative Affairs
International Union of Police Associations
Washington, D.C.

The dead never leave. Their spirits take refuge in the minds and souls of those who have both the honor and the burden of seeking justice for them. Their presence evokes a range of emotions: frustration, heartbreak, anger, resolve. Of these, it is the resolve that matters.

1

THE KILLERS WALKED in dressed in black boots, pants, turtleneck sweaters, and ski masks. Only their eyes were visible to the witness, but he insisted both were Caucasian. *"You could just tell."*

The larger of the two carried a "machine gun," the young witness said, which hung from a sling over the man's right shoulder. The other cradled a sawed-off shotgun, the barrel resting in the crook of his right arm, his left hand holding the grip. This second man appeared small next to the other, the two of them filling the doorway as the glass doors closed behind them. The big man swung the rifle up and fired. *"Pop-pop-pop!"*

The witness, Cedric, continued: "The other one pointed his shotgun at the *chino,* and shot. *Bam, bam!"*

Floyd turned to look at his partner, Mongo, who stood silently against the wall behind them, his shirt collar unbuttoned and his tie hanging low. He offered a noncommittal shrug.

Turning back to face the kid, Floyd tossed his pen onto the table next to his notebook. He leaned back in his chair, frustrated, and waited. Staring into the sparkling hazel eyes of the young boy, he asked, "And you saw all of this, little man?"

The boy licked his lips. "Yessir."

"You said, '*chino*' . . . they shot the *chino*. What did you mean by that?"

"You know, *chino*." The boy then placed his index fingers at the outside corners of his eyes and pulled the skin back, making both eyes slanted. "The people who own the liquor stores."

"Did they see you, these two men with the guns?"

Cedric straightened in his chair. "Sure they did. I kicked the big one in the nuts on my way out the door."

Floyd glanced at his partner again, the big Hawaiian-looking Mexican named Diaz whom Floyd and now everyone else at the Homicide Bureau just called *"Mongo."* Always one to limit the expenditure of unnecessary words, Mongo only smiled.

Back to Cedric: "You're telling me that while these two guys are shooting the place up, you kick one of 'em in the nuts. I hate to say it, young man, but I think you might be stretching the truth a bit."

Cedric rubbed a hand back and forth over his short-cropped natural hair and ran his tongue across chapped lips. "I'm tellin' ya, mista, it happened. All of it, just the way I said it did. When I tried to run out, the big one grabbed me, got hold of my shirt, and I kicked him in the nuts. He cursed, said something to the other'n about gettin' me. I ran out, and when I was goin' 'round the corner of the building, *BAM!,* another blast from the shotgun.*"*

"They shot at you?"

"Yup, the littler one did."

Mongo sighed.

"I ran up the alley till I heard 'em peeling out, and then I jumped over a fence and hid in a yard, under a boat."

"Underneath a boat?"

"One of them metal ones. It was upside-down on the grass, and there was like an opening at the back, a part of the metal that's cut away where I think a motor goes. Anyway, there was plenty of room to crawl through there, so I did. Stayed there for a couple hours, me and Snuggles."

"Snuggles?"

"He's my puppy. I found him under the boat, and he followed me when I left."

Mongo surprised Floyd when he said, "You stole the puppy?"

"He di'nt have no food or water in there and he was on a chain. He snuggled with me while I was hiding out from them killers. He likes me, so I kept him."

Floyd shrugged, no big deal. "Okay, so you kept Snuggles."

"Yeah. You want, I can show ya him."

Floyd stood and Mongo and Cedric followed suit. They stepped out of the interview room into a tiled hallway where a steady stream of uniformed deputies passed in both directions, their police radios crackling, leather squeaking. Floyd put his arm around Cedric and led him toward the public lobby where a woman waited to take him home.

Floyd, guiding him through the door, said, "Alright, little buddy, I'm going to look into all of this, and then I'll be coming down to your house to see you. Deal?"

Cedric smiled, and Floyd raised his hand for a high-five.

"Will you come tomorrow?"

Floyd chuckled. "Maybe, buddy. We'll see. Okay?"

The boy stepped next to the woman and turned to make eye contact with Floyd once more. His head sagged and his eyes seemed less bright now. "Okay, sir."

Floyd retreated into the station hallway, pulling the lobby door closed behind him. Mongo stood grinning.

"The fuck are you grinning at?"

ACROSS TOWN A BIG MAN SAT DEEP IN THE CUSHIONS OF A WORN SOFA chair blowing smoke rings at the dim light above him. But gusts of air from its whirling fan blades turned the puffy circles into a stretch of thick haze that hung in the flickering light of a television.

"We have to find that green-eyed little bastard, and kill him."

His partner glanced over but didn't respond.

The big man stabbed his cigarette out in an overfilled ashtray while searching his partner's eyes, waiting for an answer. None came. He only saw apprehension, reluctance. The pussy.

The big man grunted as he rose from his chair. Turning toward the kitchen, he said over his shoulder, "Do you want a beer?"

I was working late, which never surprised anyone, especially Floyd, who walked to my desk with his suit coat slung over his shoulder and a weary look on his face.

"New suit?"

"Do you like it? Cindy picked it up for me at the Rack. Nice, huh? Four bills. Would've been eight or better at Nordstrom's."

He could have modeled it, my former partner who maintained his athletic build—a small waist and broad shoulders—by running, crossfitting, and training in mixed martial arts. Though part of the effort would be offset by the consumption of massive quantities of beer, he approached middle age gracefully. Twenty years ago, I had named him "Pretty Boy Floyd."

"Yeah, it looks good with the pastel tie."

"Well yeah, Dickie, it's the summertime look. How's the doc?"

I felt myself smile, unable to contain my delight when thinking of Katherine. Katherine James, M.D., my former shrink with whom I was intimately involved, negotiating the gray areas of doctor-patient relations.

"She's great. We went up to Bridgeport for the weekend, and I think we're going back next week. We like it up there, and we've started looking at some properties and talking about maybe making an investment. Maybe a vacation place or retirement."

"Where the hell is Bridgeport?"

"Hour and a half north of Bishop, up in the mountains near Mono Lake. Nice and cool up there."

"Wow, serious shit, Dickie. Are you two shacked up now? Is that why I never hear from you anymore?"

I chuckled. "Not shacked up, but we spend most nights together, her place or mine. The reason you never see my ass anymore is because me and Ray can't catch a break. We've picked up a case in each of the last four rotations. We're buried. How about you guys? I haven't noticed your name on the board lately. Do you still work here?"

He pulled a chair from the adjacent desk and made himself at home, propping a foot on my partner's unoccupied desk. "Are you kidding me? Shit, I'm working Firestone again. Seems like the last six cases I've picked up are Firestone, Lynwood, or Compton. And as much as I love Compton, I've got to say, I'd give anything for a real murder about now. All I get are these dead gangsters with no witnesses and nobody knows nothin'. I don't think I've solved a case since that serial killer case I solved for you."

I smiled.

"And you should see the shit I've gotten myself into now."

"Yeah?"

"It's the typical luck of Floyd. I'm working the desk when some goddamn fireman out of 16 calls. This hose-jockey starts telling me all about where he works, and I interrupt him and say, 'Yeah, buddy, I know where the hell Station 16 is, I worked patrol down there when you were still riding your skateboard to school.' Anyway, you remember there was that lady who lived a couple doors north of their firehouse when it was still on Holmes? Always had a bunch of foster kids."

"Yeah, of course I do. We handled a runaway or two there over the years."

"Well, she's got a kid now who has spun this wild tale about a murder he witnessed. She loads his ass up and takes him over to Firestone to talk to a deputy, and sees the station is now a community center. She didn't know they closed it down fifteen years ago, apparently. But she sees the idiot firemen out in front of their brand new firehouse across the street, washing their little red firetruck. So she stops in and asks what happened to the sheriff's station across the street, Firestone, and who should this boy talk to about a murder he saw."

"No shit?"

"Yeah, no shit. So that's when they call here—how they got our number, I have no idea—and I tell Biff the Fireman to send them to Century Station, and we would meet them there. So me and Mongo go down to Century and pull this kid into an interview room and he tells us this big whopper."

"You're not buying it, this kid's story?"

Floyd shook his head. "It's a wild-ass tale, and here's the kicker: the kid had run away from his two previous foster homes, so this is his last chance before they throw his little ass in juvie and lock him up as an incorrigible. So he can't afford to catch any more beefs; know what I mean? He'd be a three-strike foster kid with one more incident, and if you remember old Mrs. Nathan, the foster mom, she doesn't play games with these kids. She'll whoop their asses once or twice, but then she ships them out and says send me a new one."

"She's a tough cookie, I remember. Drags those kids to church every Sunday too, I remember that."

Floyd nodded. "Yeah, so that's my point."

"Well, what's his story?"

"He comes home with a puppy and Mrs. Nathan has a fit, wants to know where he got it. He says he found it on the way home from school. Because that's where he was supposed to be that day when this murder happens."

"This murder is during the day?"

"In the morning. But anyway, Mrs. Nathan, God bless her pointed head, is all upset about the goddamn dog. She says someone out there somewhere has lost their puppy and it's their civic duty to find its rightful home. She tells the kid that some other little boy is probably crying because his puppy's been lost. So they start looking all over town, trying to find Snuggles' rightful owners."

"Snuggles?"

"That's what he named the puppy. *Snuggles*."

He dropped his foot to the floor and sat up in the chair. I waited while he sipped his coffee.

"This goes on for a week, them looking for the puppy's owner by going around the neighborhood knocking on doors, checking the local markets. Have you been down there lately? They've put a strip mall on Firestone Boulevard where that liquor store used to be, Griff's Liquor, where winos and gangsters congregated day and night back when we were there. Now there's clothes stores, fast food, and a toy store, what else? . . ."

"Ruining a perfectly good ghetto."

"Exactly. Where was I going with that?"

"The puppy."

"Yeah, so they check all the stores and after a few days with no luck, they make fliers and put those up. Still no luck. So, Mrs. Nathan has just about had it, and she's convinced the little bastard's lying. She probably marched him by the ear down to his room and whooped on him for half an hour trying to get to the truth. Then junior comes up with this wild-ass story about two white guys with ski masks doing a murder right in front of him—"

I raised a brow. "In the ghetto, two white guys."

"—and he kicks one of the two in the nuts while trying to escape. Then, they try to kill him. The one with a shotgun blasts at him while he's running away. But they miss, and he runs down an alley and hops into someone's yard to hide. Under a boat, he says. And that's where he finds the puppy."

"Snuggles."

"Uh-huh. And so he stays under the boat for a few hours, afraid to come out. When he leaves, he takes the puppy with him. That's his story, anyway."

"Jesus. You think a kid's going to make up that kind of a story, just to keep a puppy? I mean, that's a wild imagination for a kid. How old is he?"

"I don't know what to think, Dickie. He's ten. Cute little kid with green eyes."

"Black?"

Floyd nodded.

"Remember that redheaded kid on Elm Street? He was a blood gang member. A redheaded, freckle-faced, Eastside Bishop."

"Yeah, I remember him. He was an asshole too. But an easy one to nail when he committed a crime."

We both chuckled.

"Anyway, I don't know about this deal. I want to believe the little shit, but I can't find any murder memos that match his story. Have you heard anyone brief anything that sounds remotely similar, two guys in ski masks? Some type of market or maybe a liquor store robbery? I haven't seen anything on the news either. You would think something like that would make the news."

I shrugged. "South L.A., bud, not many murders make the news. But no, I haven't heard of any cases like that. Nothing even close."

"I wonder if he didn't see this shit on some movie, or came up with it while playing video games. I mean, two white guys doing a number at a South L.A. stop-and-rob? When have you heard of that happening?"

"He couldn't tell you where it happened?"

"No. He said he had never been out of the neighborhood before. He had run away and only confessed to doing so on the condition we not tell Mrs. Nathan. He doesn't want to go to juvie."

"How'd he get back home?"

Floyd frowned at me. "Mrs. Nathan. She's who brought him in."

"No, jackass; how'd he get home that day, after the murder?"

"Oh, right. Well, ya see, that's the other thing; he says he took a bus back. He sat at a bus stop until one arrived that had *Watts* displayed above the windshield. The driver let him on for free when he told him he was lost and needed to get back to Watts."

"With Snuggles."

"Right."

"I always thought that was interesting, how you'd see buses that advertised going to Watts. I mean, where do they come from, and why would you ride a bus to Watts?"

"That's the key: where did it come from? I need to work on that, but you know what a fun puzzle that will be. I have a feeling I'm going to be chasing my damn ass in circles trying to prove it *didn't* happen, all because some goddamn hose-jockey had to call when I'm on the desk. Do you see why I hate firemen?"

"Did he say how far the ride was, or how long it took?"

"I asked, Dickie. Don't be thinking I'm missing shit just because I'm not partnered with Dickie *Clouseau* Jones anymore. He doesn't know, crazy as that may sound. I think he said he fell asleep on the bus or some bullshit."

"You've checked with LAPD, right?"

Floyd nodded.

"What about Long Beach?"

"No, not yet." He pulled a notebook from his briefcase, thumbed to a blank page not far from the front cover, and made a note.

"How did he get to where he went, when he ran away from the foster home? On foot? Bike? Did he steal a car or what?"

"Shit, I don't know. I assumed it was nearby, you know, walking distance."

"Right, but he rode a bus home. If it happened."

"*If* it happened. I just assumed it wasn't too far away from his house. We always found them somewhere nearby."

"I don't miss handling the runaways and missings."

As I said it, a few names and faces popped into my head, kids I'd gotten to know while working station detectives on those very streets. Some of the kids I had tried to help; others I had been dispatched to confiscate and relocate from abusive homes to state custodians. Many of them would never make it out of the ghetto alive; we all knew that. Those who had outlived their life expectancy generally didn't make much of their lives. Every once in a while you'd hear a success story, but it seemed those were rare.

I thought about a boy named Prince who had been one of Mrs. Nathan's fosters. He had been born to a crackhead and was immediately taken away from her and thrust into the state's custody. *The system.* Like this kid Floyd was dealing with, Prince was ten years old when we met him. Floyd and I were working station detectives and handling a runaway juvie case. Mrs. Nathan had reported it. One of the foster kids was missing, presumed to have run away. Prince volunteered to show us all the places we might find him. He took us the long route to each location, savoring his time riding around with two detectives. He was an enthusiastic, bright boy, and I had taken him under my wing after that night, to an extent. I had tried to mentor and guide him along the right path in an effort to give him a chance in life. But one day, he too was gone. Mrs. Nathan had said she was unable to deal with him anymore, so he was moved to a new "home." Sent off somewhere else in the system.

"Remember Prince?"

Floyd grinned. "I thought of him during this ordeal, and damn near asked Mrs. Nathan what had ever come of him. Didn't think I'd want to hear the answer though, if she even knew. I liked that kid."

"I checked on him from time to time after that night he rode around with us. Even took him a Christmas present that next year. Not long after, I stopped by and Mrs. Nathan said he'd been moved. Said she couldn't deal with him anymore, that he was getting into trouble at home and at school. I thought I told you about that."

Floyd didn't respond; he just gazed at nothing for a moment and I could see the anguish in his hazel eyes. We were like that, able to read each other; we had been that way for years. He was likely wondering what became of Prince, and maybe wondering what would become of this boy with the green eyes who says he saw a murder, but might be spinning a wild tale.

My phone vibrated against the desk. I looked to see it was Katherine calling in. As I pushed the button to send the call to voicemail, I noticed the time; it was nearly ten already. I broke the silence a few moments later. "What's this kid's name, your would-be runaway?"

"Cedric. Cedric Stanley Staley, the third. How do you like that?"

I smiled and stood from my desk. "Well, good luck with Cedric the Entertainer. I'm out of here."

"Yeah, well, thanks for all the help, asshole."

2

Lt. Joe Black asked if I would join him in the kitchen for a cup. I felt my eyes narrow as I instinctively questioned the motive. "Sure."

I set my briefcase on my desk and glanced at Raymond Cortez who sat watching and listening. We had been partners for the last six months, ever since I returned to work. I had been off for a year, recovering from being shot during the arrest of a killer in East Los Angeles. When I returned, my long-time partner and friend, Floyd, had been assigned to work with a new guy. *Mongo*. And Floyd was no longer available to be my partner. I had hated the idea of returning and having so many changes in my life. I was going through my second divorce, Floyd was no longer to be my partner. I had been reassigned from Team Two to Team Five. I don't do change well.

As if that wasn't enough, I had begun dating my shrink, Dr. Katherine James.

Though I missed being partnered with Floyd, it had been a delight working with Ray. We worked well together, and it would be difficult to find a nicer man in the office. The only challenger might be Joe Black, the lieutenant of Team Five. The move to Five also seemed to have changed my volatile relationship with my captain, James Stover. That was an unforeseen benefit. I wasn't sure if it was the fact that me and Floyd were split up, or whether Joe Black ran interference for me with the captain. Or both. Either way, the captain wasn't on my ass all the time as he had been in years past.

Ray only shrugged to indicate he had no idea why Joe had invited me back for coffee. I shrugged in return and followed Joe to the kitchen.

I stopped next to him at the coffee station and he poured me a cup. I accepted it without speaking, my mind racing. The possibilities seemed endless, none of them good. Floyd and I were defendants in a federal lawsuit that was about to begin, litigation involving the man I had killed 18 months ago. Six months ago, I was involved in two other shootings, one of which resulted in the death of a serial killer. But the last five months or so had been relatively quiet. No shootings, no wrecked cars, no fights, riots, or confrontations with the brass. I couldn't guess what this was going to be about.

Joe Black poured a cup for himself and suggested a nearby table by nodding in its direction. We took seats across from one another. Joe watched me as he took his time with his first sip, his eyes giving me no indication of the direction we were about to go.

"What's up, Joe? What did I do now?"

He smiled. "Why, Richard, you haven't done a thing wrong. No, no, quite the contrary. I'm very pleased with your performance, and I really enjoy having you on my team—"

"But?"

He took another sip, and again took his time with it. He sat the steaming Styrofoam cup on the table between us and watched it as he ran his finger around the brim. After a moment, he looked me in the eyes. "Richard, how would you like to take on a new body?"

"A new guy?"

"Not exactly."

"Someone from another team."

"No, a new body, but not a guy."

Jesus. "Oh, a female."

He nodded.

"It wouldn't be the best thing for me right now, boss, to be perfectly honest. I've really gotten comfortable with Ray, and I enjoy working with him. Also, well, I'm in a new relationship—"

"The doctor. Doctor James."

I wondered if he were reminding me of the precarious situation that I was in as a way to gain the upper hand in the conversation. I nodded. "Yeah, Katherine. Look, Joe, it's not just that. I mean, yeah, it can be tough on relationships when a guy has a woman for a partner, we all know that. We've seen it time and again."

He didn't agree or disagree. He waited for me to continue.

"I don't know that I'd want to work with a woman just now, in part because of that—my relationship with Katherine—and because I don't want to lose Ray as a partner. Who is she, anyway?"

"Josefina Sanchez."

I laughed. "Are you kidding me?"

"Do you know her?"

"I know of her. Everyone does."

He cocked his head.

I continued. "She's the one responsible for the sheriff's department's version of Rodney King."

"What do you mean?"

"I can't believe you never heard of it. She was caught on film beating some dude with her baton. It was broad daylight. The dude was on the ground but not complying, kind of like King. Her partner was trying to handcuff the guy and was on top of him, covering his torso. So all she really had access to was his legs, and the guy was wearing shorts. A huge black guy with legs as big around as telephone poles. She teed off on him like she was chopping wood. Must've hit him fifty times, alternating from one leg to the other. Well, of course there's a lawsuit, and the department probably paid out a couple million. You never heard about that? It was on the news non-stop back then, a few years back. The media compared it to the Rodney King beating."

Joe Black shook his head and waited.

"Another time, she runs over a guy in an alley—"

"She did what?"

"Runs over a guy. She's got a ride-along with her, some kid who's looking to get on the department. But he apparently changed his mind after eight hours with her. Anyway, they're on patrol down in North Long Beach, and she goes to drive through an alley, but there's a mattress on the ground. The alley's too narrow for her to go around it, and she doesn't want to back out. I guess she doesn't want to get out and move the goddamn thing either, so she runs over it. The kid riding with her—he tells the papers this later—says he hears a muffled scream. As they continue driving away, he's watching in his mirror and sees the mattress moving. He says something to Deputy Sanchez and she stops the patrol car. Now this old black guy is stumbling to his feet, holding his head and groaning. She stops the car, jumps out, and yells at the guy. 'Frazier, get your fucking ass out of this alley or I'll take you to jail.' And they drive off.

"The kid—this ride-along—is beside himself, but doesn't say anything at the time. He's probably just trying to survive the shift, thinking the broad's crazy. A few hours later, a 902R call comes out, *assist rescue*—"

"I realize it's been a few decades, Richard, but I do remember my radio codes."

"Well, she takes the handle on this 902R and they roll code three. When they get there, there's a couple of paramedics and a handful of firemen surrounding some guy sitting on the curb. This is several blocks from the alley where she had run over this Frazier guy, so she doesn't even think about it being related. Sanchez and her ride-along walk up and she sees it's Frazier. He's still holding his head, but now the whole side of it is matted in blood, and his shirt is soaked too. He looks up at her and starts to say something, but the paramedics tell him not to talk, they tell him to be real still. Well, she apparently knows what he's about to say, so she turns and heads for the car, tells the kid, 'Let's go,' and they get the hell out of there. The patient ends up telling these paramedics what happened, that he had been sleeping in an alley when the crazy lady cop ran over him."

Joe Black watched with disbelief in his eyes. "You're sure about all of this?"

"You can't make that shit up, Joe. I'm telling you the God's honest truth. I'm just telling you because if I have to work with her, I don't want Stover blaming shit on me. That's all I need, to be partnered with some crazy, half-cocked female partner who stirs shit up. I'm surprised sometimes that I have lasted this long just working with that idiot, Floyd."

"If what you say about her is true, how did she keep her job?"

I shrugged. "Hispanic female. What can I say?"

"But even then, I mean, it just doesn't make sense. How did she make it here, to Homicide? Something doesn't seem right, Richard."

"You're asking me, Joe? You guys are the ones who put these transfer lists together, you and your fellow lieutenants, and that genius captain of yours."

"That's for the deputies; she's a sergeant, and there is no list. We were just told she's coming."

"A sergeant?" I chuckled while shaking my head. "Where the hell is she coming from, anyway?"

"Compton Gangs."

I swigged the rest of my coffee and stood up from my chair. "Well, Joe, I have to be honest. I don't want her, and I don't want me and Ray split up. That's my feeling on the matter, but I'll do whatever you ask of me. I want to stay on your team, Joe. You've been good to me, so I'm not going to fight you on it. But I really don't want to take her if you can figure anything else out."

Joe's brows crowded his eyes as he nodded, clearly troubled by the information he had just received. I thanked him for the cup and began to walk out as my old partner Floyd glided in with his ever-present ear-to-ear grin.

"What are you doing, Dickie, kissing your lieutenant's ass again?"

I wasn't in the mood. "Yeah, that's it, you know me," I grumped.

We stopped to face each other, and his grin was gone. "What's up your ass?"

I glanced over to see that Joe had gotten up from the table but was taking his time with moving out. I lowered my voice. "I guess I'm getting another new partner."

"No shit? Who are you getting?"

"That crazy broad, Sanchez. Josefina Sanchez."

He laughed. "Oh, dude, that is outstanding! *Josie.* She rocks. You know her, right?"

I turned to walk back toward the squad room and Floyd followed my lead. "I know *of* her."

"She's hot. But don't make a move on her, I heard she kicked Kevin Greinke's ass at an off-training party for making some moves on her. She's supposed to be kind of badass."

"Badass? Really?"

He chuckled. "She kicked Greinke's ass."

"Yeah, whatever."

"What are you all uptight about, Dickie? I think it would be cool to have a hot chick as a partner."

"I just don't want a new partner, period. I enjoy working with Ray, and you know me and how much I love change. Also, with the things I've heard about her, seems to me she's a bit of a loose cannon."

He stopped me with a hand on my arm. "You're a loose cannon, dick-head, and yet here you are."

"Was."

"Okay, maybe. But give the girl a break, she's a hero."

"*Hero?* Let's not get carried away. She beat some dude who was down on all fours and ran over some cluck in an alley, an old wino who never hurt anyone in his life. Oh, and kicked some drunk deputy's ass. That's not my definition of a hero."

"And saved an LAPD copper's wife."

I frowned. "What are you talking about?"

"You never heard about it?"

I shook my head. "Apparently not."

"Jesus, dude, it was legendary. There's a pursuit—I think she was working Lakewood at the time, maybe Gangs—and the bad guy bails out and runs into a supermarket, Albertson's or something. It was early in the evening and the place was full of shoppers. This asshole had done a robbery somewhere, jacked a car, and was armed with a rifle of some sort, some sawed-off job with pistol grips. He runs into the store and she's the first through the door after him. She follows the eyes and fingers of all of these terrified shoppers, indicating which way the asshole went. She chases him through the store, up one row and down another. She rounds a corner and this guy with the rifle has grabbed a hostage, some broad who turns out to be an LAPD cop's wife. He's got the gun up to her head. Sanchez draws down on him. He's yelling for her to drop her gun, but she's walking straight at him telling him, no, you drop your fucking gun—just about like that, too, from what I remember hearing. Yates and Brown handled the shooting, you can ask them about it. Anyway, the cop's wife—who had probably been schooled by her old man—sees this is likely to go hot, so she drops as far as she can with him still holding onto her, kind of slumps like dead weight in his arms. It gives Sanchez enough of an opening—a split-second target opportunity—and she takes her shot. Two shots, actually, a quick little double-tap. And the asshole is down, DOA. Now *that's* big balls in Cowtown, Dickie."

There was a pause as I processed what I was just told about the crazy woman who was likely going to be my next partner. "How'd I not hear about that?"

"Maybe it's when you were off last year, I don't know. It hasn't been that long ago. The point is, that's probably how she got here. She got her ticket punched with that one, that's for sure. Promoted to sergeant and probably isn't going to stop there. Word is, she's a good gang detective. Give her a fair shake, Dickie, you might be surprised. Plus, she's easy on the eyes and probably smells good."

"Smells good."

"Yeah, dickhead, she emits a pleasant aroma, unlike yourself."

3

Traffic through the conglomeration of intersecting freeways known as the East L.A. interchange—the San Bernardino, the Long Beach, the Golden State, the Hollywood, the Santa Ana—never looks worse than it does on an afternoon when the Dodgers are at home. I tuned the radio to KLAC AM 570 so I could listen to the game while using surface streets to avoid the worst of the congestion. I was headed north, but it wasn't the most direct route to my home in Burbank. This was reason enough to stop in for a cocktail somewhere and wait while Katherine finished up at the office, telling *other* crazy cops they're nuts. I'd send her a text and ask her to join me. She would read it between patients or at the end of her day, which would hopefully be soon. I decided on Buck's in Sierra Madre and signed off with a line of heart emojis; I was becoming proficient with my texting skills.

I had drunk one beer and just received another when Katherine walked in and plopped her purse, a set of keys, and her cell phone on the bar next to my beer. I pulled it a few inches away from her belongings as she leaned down and kissed me lightly on the lips. Her brown eyes focused further down the bar, and I turned my head to follow her gaze.

"Is that Marilyn Monroe down there?"

I looked to see the woman with heavy makeup and bleached hair that was short and wavy. "Marilyn Monroe? Is it even a woman?"

"Legitimate question."

"How was work?" I asked.

As she settled onto the stool, she said work was okay, that it was more of the same old thing, trying to figure out who's more nuts, the cops she sees at work or the one she sees at home. And then she added: "Or in a dive bar in Sierra Madre."

"I'm comfortable here, surrounded by pirates. And Moby."

"Moby? As in Dick?"

I shook my head and then nodded to draw her attention to the other end of the bar. "The bartender. He looks like Moby, the musician."

"I've never heard of him."

"You don't drink here enough."

"I mean the musician."

"Well, this guy, the bartender, looks like him." Moby worked his way down the bar, swiping at rings of moisture left along the bar from the bottoms of glasses. "Complete with the bald head and horn-rimmed glasses."

He paused across from Katherine and asked what she would have. She paused for a moment, looking past him toward the shelves of liquor that sat beneath a wall which featured a painted pirate scene complete with swashbucklers and their wenches, some of whom were exposing their breasts for the patrons. The mural and several paintings throughout the lounge had been created back in the sixties by a local artist named Frank Bowers, a native Californian who had become an Angeleno during the Great Depression. He specialized in just this type of art, risqué murals in bars and clubs throughout Southern California and down into Mexico, where it is said he painted bullfights and bullfighters, with touches of randy Hispanic ladies showing their wares. According to modern lore, much of the painter's labor was payment for all of the drinks he had consumed.

Moby waited. His eyes were locked on Katherine and his brows were lifted in anticipation, a tight-lipped smile across his face.

"I'll just have a glass of water for now, please. With a wedge of lemon, if you don't mind."

Moby pulled a glass from somewhere beneath the bar. He scooped it full of ice and used his soda gun to fill it with water.

"Are you concerned I need a driver?"

"No, of course not. You have your cop car, so you're free to drink and drive, right? You can bounce off parked cars while leaving Buck's."

"Wow, that was a little judgmental. Did you have a bad day?"

Moby stabbed a straw through the ice and tucked a wedge of lemon onto the rim of the glass. He set it on a fresh napkin and, as he slid it in front of her, he nodded toward my beer as if to ask if I needed another. I quickly chose my answer based on Katherine's last statement and shook my head. He sauntered back toward Marilyn whose eyes appeared fixed on the two of us.

Katherine drank her water and took a moment before answering. "No, I was mostly kidding. But today I had a client who—and this is confidential, I shouldn't be telling you—was sent to me because *your* department wants to correlate his bad behavior with the stress of the job."

"There's something to that."

"There's also something to just being a drunk, Richard," she snapped. "This guy has had two DUIs. The second one involved his hitting a car in the parking lot while leaving a bar. A cops' bar, of course. Thankfully, he didn't hurt anyone. I just think it's irresponsible and a bit audacious to blame it on the job."

"Bounced off cars in the parking lot, did he?"

She sighed and took another drink of water without replying.

The phone rang, and Moby picked it up. He barked "Buck's" into the mouthpiece, over the music and conversation and laughter that filled the dark room. He waited, listening, and then he looked up and down the bar before speaking into the phone again. "Not here, haven't seen him." He slapped the phone back into its cradle and yelled toward a booth where two elderly men sat sipping some type of whiskey. "Lou, your old lady's looking for you again." The man called Lou waved him off as if it were the same old story which interested him not.

I thought about what Katherine had said as I slowly sipped my beer, suddenly feeling a little self-conscious. I thought about the cop who hit the car and all the others who had done the same or worse over the years yet had remained on the job. Many were top brass. The commander of Men's Central Jail, one of the most populous jails in the country, housing over

10,000 inmates, had actually crashed his unmarked county sedan into a black and white police car from another jurisdiction. Then he tried to flee. After being arrested and booked for drunk driving, the department sent him off for 30 days at the Betty Ford clinic, after which he was deemed fit for duty. Another executive who had had several alcohol-related mishaps —all of which had been swept beneath the department's lumpy rug— finally crashed into a CHP unit, injuring two officers. The department had to do something, so he was retired.

"Well, what do you say we blow this place and go grab some dinner, somewhere nice."

Her eyes showed fatigue or disinterest. "I don't know, Richard. I may just have an early and quiet evening. Would you hold it against me?"

It was equally clear that something was wrong, and that she wasn't going to divulge to me what it was. Not yet. Not here and now.

We had been dating for six months and were accustomed to spending a couple of nights a week at one or the other's apartment. Granted, we had had a rocky start. Our first social outing ended in a gunfight when a man who had been stalking me made his last stand in a bar in Chinatown. Up until then, I had been Katherine's patient. But the events of that night both ended our professional relationship and launched our romantic affair. At the time, we were both separated from our spouses and in the processes of divorce. Like two drunks trying to be sober together, we were probably the last thing either of us needed at the time. Maybe she was pulling back now. Or, maybe she just had a bad day. I tried to not overthink it, but that seldom works for me. It's the way I'm wired.

"I thought you looked tired when you walked in. Go home, take a bath and have a quiet and early evening. I'm going to head out of here after one more beer, unless I can spend a buck in the jukebox and talk Marilyn Monroe into a dance."

She glanced down the bar, disinterested. I expected a punch on the shoulder or at least a dirty look. "Okay, I think you're right, I could use an early evening. You don't mind?"

I shook my head.

She reached over and placed her hand on my forearm, the first offering of affection this evening since the peck on my lips. "What do you have planned tomorrow?"

"We go on call at six, so I have no plans but to wait and see how his day goes."

"*His?* Who's that?"

"The asshole that's going to start pissing someone off at some point tomorrow and become my next source of overtime."

She rolled her eyes and stood, collected her belongings and leaned in to give me a parting kiss. It was less passionate than the first, if that was possible. I watched her walk past Marilyn, who scanned Katherine from head to toe and seemed to scowl as she passed. When the door closed behind her, I signaled Moby for another beer.

After that one, I switched to gin.

IT WAS MIDNIGHT WHEN I LEFT THE BAR AND SAW THAT KATHERINE HAD sent a text saying goodnight. It had come in two hours earlier. I opted to ignore it so as to not reveal the time of my departure. *Deny everything, admit to nothing, demand proof, and make counter-allegations.* Floydism. I pulled out of the lot noting that I hadn't struck any parked cars, and suddenly I felt anger directed at Katherine. My tires squealed against the asphalt as I accelerated toward the freeway, pleased to see the streets were nearly empty, the quaint town of Sierra Madre all rolled up for the night.

Out of curiosity I phoned the desk and asked how things were going, and was there a chance our team would come up early. It made a difference as to whether I would shower and put a suit out tonight or wait until morning when Team Five officially went on call for murders. The detective on the desk said her name but I didn't catch it or recognize it. There were eighty detectives assigned to Homicide and we'd had such a turnover in the last two years, there were plenty I still didn't know since my return. She said nothing had gone out since yesterday and Team Four had a full line-up. That meant it wasn't likely Team Five would come up early. I thanked her, disconnected, and settled into my seat. I removed my hat, turned off the air conditioner, and lowered my window to allow the cool night air to flutter against my face.

And protested my displeasure into the wind, *"Women!"*

4

It was half past seven when I awoke, heart racing, my body damp from sweat under the covers. I stared at the ceiling for several minutes, reliving the Chinatown shooting incident that regularly visited me in my sleep. Six months had passed since the evening Katherine and I first met outside of her office where she had seen me as a patient for many years, off and on. Most of those visits were the results of other shooting incidents; she was one of several shrinks the department used for counseling. After my wife left, the sessions with Dr. Katherine James began feeling different. Where I had previously resented having to meet with a head doctor and talk about my feelings, fears, and the type of recurring dreams I had just experienced, I found myself looking forward to our time together. Eventually I convinced myself that she felt differently about me as well, and I took a chance and asked her out to dinner. She met me for a drink instead, and of all the nights she might have done so, on this night there was an attempt on my life. A serial killer who had a contract to kill me had walked through the doors, intent on taking me out in front of dozens of witnesses. Fortunately, there had been a surveillance detail assigned to cover me after the first attempt several days before. They saw the suspect enter, and two of the team's members, along with my old partner, Floyd, came in behind him. The shooting started, and amazingly, only the suspect was killed. But in my dreams Katherine is mortally wounded and all of the patrons at the bar between me and the killer are exploding from my errant bullets, complete parts of bodies—heads, torsos, and arms—disappearing in red mist as portrayed in video games. I've never played video games, and fortunately, I've never hit an innocent bystander during a shooting incident. But for some reason, this had become my greatest fear and it played out time and time again during deep slumbers.

I sat up and stared at a digital clock and remembered it had been nearly three a.m. before I stopped drinking and crawled into bed. After coming home from Buck's, irritated at Katherine, it seemed a couple more beers were in order. Fortunately, there were plenty in the refrigerator, and it was comfortable on the balcony in a sweatshirt. The streets were empty and the stars hovered over the nearby mountaintops, making it a perfect time and place for contemplation. I sat and drank in silence while trying in vain to figure out women. Soon those thoughts were replaced by memories of the man who had stalked me and tried to kill me, the man who had spent an unknown number of hours sitting on the street below watching me.

As I stepped into the shower, I realized that as long as I lived here there would be recurring memories and nightmares about the man named Leonard Freeman and the night that my partners and I put him down in Yee Me Loo's.

Though it was the first time it had occurred to me, the thought resonated, and I pondered it all the way to the office. But where would I go? I loved my little apartment in Burbank with a view of the mountains and a relatively easy commute to the office. The fact it was a short drive to Katherine's in Pasadena was an added bonus. But I now knew I'd never enjoy that balcony in the way I had prior to Freeman. It was time to move on.

For a brief moment, I pictured myself at Katherine's place. Then I dismissed the thought. Something wasn't quite right with us at the moment though I couldn't put my finger on what it was. I also didn't think I was ready for that type of commitment yet. My divorce from Valerie wasn't even final, but it would make strike two. I needed to be very careful about the next pitch I swung at, and make sure it wasn't going to be a curveball, something I couldn't possibly manage.

I WALKED INTO THE OFFICE HUNGRY AND HUNGOVER, FACING AN ON-CALL period where Ray and I sat second up in the rotation for murders. That meant we were likely facing a long day and sleepless night. Possibly long days and sleepless nights, plural. You never knew what the next case had in store and where it might take you. Most of the cases were gang- or drug-related, routine investigations that didn't keep you awake at night worrying about their outcome. Every once in a while, however, the murder gods would slam you with a dead cop or a dead kid and life would cease to exist outside of work for weeks on end. I sat my briefcase on my chair and walked directly to the office kitchen for coffee, hoping for a little luck during this on-call rotation.

But the second I saw her sitting in the kitchen talking to my lieutenant, I knew my luck had been expended over the last year and a half; I had used it all up surviving two shootouts and two wrecked marriages. Though we had never personally met, I knew who she was. By the way she watched me, I had to assume she knew who I was also. Lt. Joe Black followed her gaze and when his eyes met mine, he smiled widely. "Richard, come meet your new partner."

FLOYD MET ME IN THE HALLWAY AS I HEADED BACK TO THE SQUAD ROOM, a fresh cup of coffee in my hand and a scowl on my face. "What the hell's wrong with you, Dickie?"

I shook him off and glanced over my shoulder. The table where I had left Joe Black and my new partner, Josefina Sanchez, sat empty, though I hadn't seen where the two went. Turning back to Floyd, I said, "I got to meet my new partner just now."

"She kick your ass?"

"Not yet."

"Well, it's coming, I'm sure. With your shitty attitude and her propensity toward violence, it's bound to happen."

"You're one to talk."

"About?"

"Propensity for violence. What did Sloan used to say about you, you've been in more fights than most bikers?"

"It was after that little misunderstanding down at the Western Connection—"

"Misunderstanding."

"—when Donnie got us in a fight with about four or five wannabe cowboys. Lieutenant Marks was on my ass about it, as if it was my fault, and you jumped on his side, saying I *do* get into more fights than most grown men. Then Joe chimed in and said, 'Floyd gets in more fights than most biker gangs.'"

"Yeah, I remember."

"But that was a case of self-defense, like all the others."

"Right."

"So what'd you two talk about? Did you tell her you're a workaholic asshole and she will no longer have a personal life?"

"What I told her, is I looked forward to working with her. I mean, what the hell do I care? Couldn't be any worse than working with you. Though I do think I'll miss Ray."

"I do realize you're just grumpy and you don't really mean that."

"It's not that I'm grumpy; I just happen to have a splitting headache this morning. And so far, this day has been a piece of shit."

We stopped at my desk and I noticed the one next to it was cleaned off. There was nothing on top to indicate it had been occupied by Raymond Cortez up until the last few hours. I assumed the drawers were empty too, that Ray had stayed late or come in early and moved back to Unsolveds. Nobody liked moving when the office was full. Like driving in L.A., there was too much traffic to negotiate. Plus, everyone wanted to ask you what you were doing. Desks were cleared out during the hours of darkness around this place.

Floyd said, "Hung over?"

"Huh?"

"Are you hung over?"

"I don't really think so. I mean, I had a few last night, but it's not as if I was drunk. I did however make the mistake of switching to gin. I think Bombay gives me a headache; Hendricks doesn't seem to do that."

"It's the quinine, Dickie, not the gin."

"The what?"

"Quinine. Something derived from African tree bark, I think. That's what gives you a headache. Don't blame the gin."

"How do you know this shit?"

"Make it up, mostly." He turned to walk away. "Good luck with *cha-cha*."

THE KILLERS SAT CONCEALED IN THE BACK OF A PANEL VAN WATCHING through the windshield as a Korean store owner unlocked the front doors of his market and propped them open. He seemed busy, in and out for several minutes, the little man wearing brown slacks, a green polo, and dress shoes. The pants were too short on the small storeowner, revealing red, white, and black Argyle socks.

The bigger of the two killers pulled a ski mask over his face, a final touch to the head-to-toe black dress. He looked through two holes and saw his partner was following suit. "Looks like it's just him," he said. "Are you ready?"

His partner nodded, two beady eyes looking back at him.

The big man flung the side door open and out they went, the big man leading the way with his AR-15 rifle. The smaller of the two sported a sawed-off shotgun. Nobody was in the parking lot. It was too early in the day for most of the people in Compton to be moving about, just as the big man had predicted.

They stepped through the door and stopped. Big man saw nobody behind the counter. He scanned the store but didn't see the owner or anyone else. He walked further in, toward the counter, and as he glanced around the interior once more, the Korean walked out through a door at the back of the shop. They stood staring at one another, twenty feet apart. Big man raised the rifle to his shoulder. The Korean raised his hands and stepped back. Once, twice, and then the silence was shattered by automatic gunfire followed by two blasts of a shotgun. The big man looked over at his partner and smiled, though he realized the smile couldn't be seen beneath his mask.

The big man emptied the register while the other moved quickly toward the man crumpled on the floor, a pool of blood spreading beneath him. The next time the big man saw his partner, they were both headed for the front door. "Did you find the safe?" He was shown a bag that appeared full but not too heavy. "Good job. I guess he had a key." As the two crossed the parking lot, the big man stopped and leveled his AR-15 at an old black man with a gray beard who had a slow, unsteady way about him as he staggered toward the store. The old man didn't look up as the sounds of automatic gunfire and a loud bang shattered the morning stillness; he just folded quietly to the asphalt below him.

The big man looked from the dead wino to his partner, and he laughed.

5

The squad room is configured in a manner which allows the front desk personnel to look through a window and clearly see Teams One and Two lined up directly behind their station. Teams Three and Four are mostly in view, but there would need to be a fair bit of moving around by desk personnel to view all of the fourteen members of each of those two teams. Teams Five and Six are around a corner and completely out of view, so the desk crew would have no idea who from those two teams was in the office and who wasn't. I was sitting at my desk when my cell rang, and I saw that it was the front desk. My good friend Rich Farris was on the other end. "Dickie, where you at, my brother?"

"I'm sitting at my desk, Rich. And you're sitting around the corner at the front desk."

He chuckled. "Yeah, my turn in the barrel. You might as well come see me, we've got a murder for you down in Compton."

I glanced at my watch. Not even ten yet. The crooks weren't usually awake before noon. The desk next to me still sat empty and I hadn't seen my new partner since we had been introduced a half hour earlier in the kitchen. Maybe Joe Black was giving her a tour of the bureau, or maybe the captain had her in his office warning her about what an asshole I am. Whatever. I might handle the case on my own just to piss everyone off.

I rounded the corner into the front desk lobby only to run into Lieutenant Black and my new partner, Josefina Sanchez. In our previous meeting at a table in the break room, I couldn't help but notice her almond-shaped, light brown eyes. Outlaw eyes. She was sexy and dangerous, and her gaze dared you to further appraise her assets. But now as I saw her standing near the front desk, I couldn't help but appreciate her lean and shapely physique, her soft brown skin, and silky black hair. She stood poised, exuding confidence. She glanced over her shoulder as I approached, and I looked away.

"What do we have, Rich?"

"Hey, Dickie, I just met your new partner, Josie."

I glanced from Rich to the outlaw eyes and back. "Josie, huh?"

He chuckled. Chances are, he had already laid the smooth talk and charm on her before I walked up. Rich was a player, a lady's man, though somewhat of a catch-and-release type. He had already divided his pension by three and hadn't yet learned the skill of releasing sooner, or fishing in a different pond, or not fishing at all. He said, "Yeah, man, the outlaw Josie Wales. Or, in this case, Sanchez. I mean, look at those eyes, brother."

I glanced back to see she was all business, having none of it. I tried to get us back on track, and quickly. "The case, Rich. What do you have for us?"

"Liquor store robbery in Compton. Two dead, the owner and an old grape who's apparently part of the landscape there. He was going in for his breakfast bottle when the assholes were on their way out, from how it looks, according to the deputies on scene."

Rich handed me a Dead Sheet with the basics: a case number, an address, and the times of various notifications thus far. The details of victim names, death notifications, coroner's case numbers, et cetera, would be filled in later, once verified. The Dead Sheet is a form used by the desk to track assigned cases, by the lieutenants to complete their murder memos, and later, by the secretaries who enter all of the data into our computer system. I took the sheet and copied the location and file number onto the front cover of a fresh notebook, and then turned the notebook over to again write the file number and location, along with additional details: investigator names—me and my partner—the lieutenant, Joe

Black, the time I received my notification and by whom, and where I would be responding from, the office.

Rich Farris spoke as I continued jotting notes: "You know the store, right, Dickie?"

Without looking up, I said, "Yes."

"That's the place used to be run by Ho and his brother. They always took care of the coppers. They were Vietnamese, as I recall. I wonder if they still run it, if that was Ho who got killed out there."

"I know who you're talking about." I finished a note and looked up. "He was a good guy, I remember that. And nobody messed with him during the riots as I recall. In part, because he treated people with respect, and in part, because he popped for the cops and always had a steady stream of black and whites parked out front."

"Uh-huh. Well, I hope it wasn't Ho."

"Me too, Rich. I'll keep you posted."

I handed the Dead Sheet back to Rich Farris, and turned to my new partner who stood quietly, waiting, Lieutenant Black standing behind her. "You ready?"

"Yes sir."

Joe Black smiled and nodded at me, seemingly giving me his approval.

"I like each of us having a car in the event we need to split up during the investigation. Do you want to follow me, or do you know your way to Compton?"

She didn't bat an eye. "I grew up in Compton, if you want to follow me."

HO'S LIQUOR IS WHAT WE HAD ALWAYS CALLED THE NONDESCRIPT WHITE building that sat on Compton Boulevard a block from Atlantic Avenue. Compton Boulevard is a four-lane major street that runs east-west. Atlantic Avenue runs north-south. The two major east-west boulevards that run either direction from Compton are Rosecrans to the north, and Alondra to the south. Both have easy access to the Long Beach Freeway that also runs north and south, a short distance east of Ho's Liquor. The name on the building said Easy Liquor, and the numbers were 14622. I made a note of both as I sat in my car just outside the yellow tape at the edge of the parking lot. Josefina pulled in behind me, and I met her at my trunk.

"We use fresh notebooks for every case, and never mix notes from one to another. It's not like patrol or gangs."

She plopped a blue notebook next to mine on the trunk of my car. I saw she already had the same information I had written in mine, other than the name of the business and the address. I wondered if she copied it quickly from the Dead Sheet before leaving the desk after I had walked away. I glanced at my watch and added the time of our arrival, and she followed suit. A uniformed deputy walked toward us with a clipboard in his hand.

"We'll sign in, then find out who the handling patrol crew is and take their statement. Then we will probably have them give us a walkthrough before we start documenting the scene. When we start, we'll come back here and begin with the overall scene description, and work our way in. I'll dictate the first couple of scenes we process, and you'll get the hang of it. In other words, you'll write in your notebook what I say as I describe the scene for our report. Any questions?"

"No, I think I'm good."

"Okay." I turned to the deputy who now stood waiting, and he handed me the clipboard. I wrote *Jones/Sanchez, Homicide, 1022 hours, I/O's* across the next available line. It was the crime scene log that would memorialize any and all persons who entered an established crime scene, without exception, and the reason for their entry. We were the investigating officers. The names ahead of us were sheriff's deputies and fire/EMT personnel. All but the handling deputies already had times indicating their departure from the scene. I handed the clipboard back to the deputy and said to Josefina, "If we arrive together, one of us can sign us both in. Most of the time, we won't be arriving at the same time, and you'll sign yourself in."

She nodded.

"Is this your handle?" I asked of the deputy.

"Yes sir. My training officer is inside."

I offered my hand and he shook it. "Richard Jones, from Homicide, and this is my partner, Josefina Sanchez."

"I go by Josie."

I nodded, and the deputy reached over to shake her hand too. "Pleased to meet you both."

"Are you going to run this by us, or do you need your training officer?"

"I can run it by you, sir. This is my ninth murder."

"Ninth? How long have you been out here?"

"This is my sixth month, sir. I'm off training at the end of next week." He smiled after he said it, as if the words sounded good to him as they crossed his lips. His smile was bright against dark skin and short-cropped hair. Trainees seldom wore mustaches, by tradition, but I didn't think this young man could grow one if he tried. He looked familiar to me. He also looked like a Marine. There was always something about the deputies who had served in the military that made them stand out from the others, and usually it was their command presence. But especially those who were Marines.

"Where did you work custody? It seems I know you."

"MCJ, sir."

"Men's Central Jail, huh? Did I meet you there, maybe on an inmate death case?"

"I don't recall if we met there or not, sir, but we've met."

"I think so too."

"I know so." He smiled again, knowingly.

I left that hanging because I wasn't sure I wanted to know. I glanced at his name tag. *Nelson.* It didn't ring any bells. There had been a few young deputies over the years who had known me from my patrol days, usually black or Hispanics that grew up in South Los Angeles where I spent a decade working patrol and station detectives. They were usually the kids who had been in a bit of trouble but somehow made it out okay and ended up in law enforcement. Sometimes they were explorers, and once they'd grown up, you didn't recognize them. We had had quite a few black explorers when I worked Firestone Station, and I wondered if that was where I knew this kid from. But there was an equal chance I knew him from somewhere else, a situation that maybe wouldn't be best to bring up. "Okay, Deputy Nelson, why don't you run this by us."

"Yes sir."

Josie and I each wrote the time, Deputy Nelson's name and employee number, his partner's name and employee number—which the trainee knew from memory—and their station and unit designation in our notebooks. Once done, I nodded, and Deputy Nelson provided a summary, which I recorded in my notebook, and Josie did the same:

Deputy Nelson and his partner received a two-eleven, shots fired call at this location at 0905 hours. They arrived at approximately 0910 hours and found one victim (Victim #2) lying in the parking lot. (He pointed out the area adjacent to the building where paramedic debris was scattered.) Deputies cleared the interior and found the other victim (Victim #1) on the floor in a pool of blood near a door to the back room. Paramedics from Compton City Fire, Station #1, responded and treated Victim #2. He was transported to MLK via Adams Ambulance. Victim #1 was pronounced dead by Paramedic Lowe under the command of Chief Harvey.

The location was secured, and Homicide was notified at 0935 hours.

"Any witnesses?"

"None to the shooting itself, that we have been able to locate. We canvassed the neighborhood and found several people who heard the shooting. One lady reports seeing the suspects flee in a white van, west on Compton Boulevard. She didn't see if they turned on Atlantic or not. We put out a broadcast and had units canvassing the area and watching the freeways, but nothing came of it. Lakewood Station set up to watch the ninety-one eastbound, and East L.A. was supposed to keep an eye on the Long Beach north. Long Beach PD was notified also. So far, there's been nothing."

I removed my fedora and wiped sweat from my forehead with a bare hand. Nelson smiled again and said, "Yes sir, now that I see you without the hat, I know for sure we've met."

So it was before I worked homicide, I thought. I'd worn fedoras as long as I had been assigned to the bureau. Where did I know him from? His smile made me think it might not have been a good situation, like he was going to tell me he outran me one night or I arrested him or maybe worse yet I arrested his mama or something. "What's your first name?"

"Roger."

"You a Marine?"

"Yes sir."

I remembered there had been several explorers from Firestone who had joined the Marines, blacks and Hispanics alike. There had been a female explorer who also joined up, and I heard she had made sergeant.

"Okay, Roger, what else do you have for us?"

"There are two-twenty-three casings inside the door and again out here in the parking lot." He pointed toward the area where the second victim had been found, and said the casings were about halfway between him and where we stood. I could see yellow chalk on the asphalt, and an occasional reflection off of brass on the ground.

"Who chalked it?"

"I did, sir. In case the paramedics kicked them around. I don't think they did though; it seemed they noticed the yellow circles and were careful to avoid the casings."

I nodded. His partner, a thin, blonde-haired deputy named Johnson whom you might expect to find at the beach, but not in Compton, walked out of the liquor store and came to us. After introductions, he said, "There's surveillance video equipment in the office, but it appears to be digital. I haven't touched it and wouldn't know how to review it if I wanted to."

"Good deal," I said. "We'll probably have the Tech Crew come down and take care of that for us. I can't get Netflix to work on my TV; I'm not messing around with technology on a murder scene. Anything else I need to know about before we get started?"

"The victim inside is a friend to most of the deputies here. His name is Ho, and he always took good care of us."

I nodded, somberly. "I wondered if it was still his place. I've been here a few times myself over the years. Didn't it used to be called *Ho's?*"

"No, it's always been Easy Liquor." Deputy Johnson smiled. "We used to call it Easy Ho's."

"How long have you been out here?"

"I've worked Compton Station six years, but I was at Lynwood before that."

I frowned. "How have we never met?"

"We have, sir. Several times."

35

I felt embarrassed and now I had to wonder if something was seriously wrong with my memory. I also realized that his partner, Nelson, who had handled nine murders in his six months of training, was just another deputy whose face seemed familiar, but the name and situation of our acquaintance escaped me. Maybe this is what happens when you get old. Though I was only 46, the odometer seemed to have rolled over once already, and they say it's the miles that really count.

My partner had her notebook and pen ready, watching quietly and waiting attentively. Other than the fact she seemed to distract all the males in her presence, so far, she seemed okay. Paying attention and working quietly without any questions, she got it. All of it. This might not be so bad, if she didn't go off half-cocked.

I thanked the deputies and told them we were going to start documenting the scene. "Crime lab should be here any minute. Depending on who they send us, we'll either stop what we're doing to get them going in the right direction, or let them go on autopilot. Hopefully we get Gentry, and then we just wave and say hello."

"Okay, sir, let us know if you need anything."

I ducked under the yellow tape and paused to hold it up for my partner. She barely lowered her head and walked under the tape. I had it lifted for her convenience, but not high. I looked down at her shoes and saw they were low-heeled women's dress shoes. Practical. Something you could run in if you had to and they wouldn't give you too much trouble in a fight. Unlike the high-heeled shoes you saw TV cops wearing while they kicked ass and solved crimes in their skintight slacks and low-cut tops, all in an hour. I put my partner at about 5-05 but wasn't going to ask for confirmation. I also wasn't going to ask her weight, but I'd have to guess a buck-thirty.

"Okay, I'll describe the scene and you can write it down. No sense in both of us filling our notebooks with it. Normally, a new guy—"

"Gal."

"—will have several trash runs before they get a murder. Suicides, accidental deaths, industrial deaths, cases like that. One-man responses—"

"Or woman."

"—usually, but when I have a new guy—*or gal*—I like to buy as many of those I can get, for practice."

She smiled, and for the first time, she appeared friendly.

"Sometimes, I will dictate a scene into a recorder and let the secretaries type it. I've done that when it's raining, when writing notes doesn't work well. It's a bit of a gamble in that if something goes wrong with the recording device, you're screwed. It also takes a lot of scenes to be able to do it that way and not miss anything. You don't have your notes to look back at. Anyway, you get to start with a big one right off the bat, robbery-murder, maybe a double. This is a death penalty case, but you should already know that."

"Right, sir. I'm ready when you are."

I looked at her and considered for a moment whether or not I was ready to be on friendly terms with the new guy—*gal*. Ultimately, it came down to not wanting to be called sir. "You can call me 'Richard.'"

She smiled again and said, "Okay, Dickie."

6

The scene investigation consumed the bulk of the day, and it was late in the afternoon when we began our canvas for witnesses. The patrol deputies had knocked on doors shortly after the initial wave of commotion had calmed. But murders are like earthquakes and airstrikes, from a law enforcement perspective; the initial shock and awe settles and only tremors remain throughout the following hours and days. Once a scene has been secured and the victims are either pronounced dead or transported to hospitals, for patrol deputies, everything slows to a halt; they make their notifications and wait for Homicide. The primary function of the handling patrol unit, from that point forward, is to maintain the integrity of the crime scene. Make sure nobody enters who doesn't have a legitimate reason to be there, and log in and out anyone who does cross the yellow tape. When the paramedics, firemen, and our department executives clear out, the handling unit will often ask assisting deputies to look for witnesses by talking to gawkers and knocking on doors. It was my practice to conduct an additional canvas of my own—sometimes more than one—because people tell detectives things they won't tell patrol deputies. There are two reasons for this: trust and approach. As for trust, the uniform often represents the focus of collective grievances in high crime neighborhoods. Many of the citizens don't see the police presence for what it is, a fine line between civility and chaos. Riots should help them to better understand that concept, but they don't. As to approach, all too often a deputy is task-oriented, which can cause him to be abrupt and narrow-focused in these situations. It is the nature of working in a violent community. Triage. Do what you can and move on to the next victim, the next call, the next violent encounter.

While the deputies maintained control of the scene and Phil Gentry from the crime lab finished up his final documentation, Josie and I walked toward the neighboring homes as I explained my theory on this. I gave an example of a case that had occurred not far from where we stood, on another street where cops were not warmly welcomed. After the scene investigation, my partner and I had canvassed for witnesses and a newly assigned homicide lieutenant trailed along. His background consisted mostly of patrol functions, though he had had a very brief assignment working internal affairs—which doesn't count as investigative experience to anyone other than house-fairies. It was late in the evening and dark when one of the neighbors we contacted at his door looked past me, scanning the surrounding with concern before inviting us in. I knew he had something to say but wasn't comfortable talking to the cops. We went inside, and he asked us to have a seat. My partner and I did. The lieutenant stood impatiently at the door, fidgeting. The resident was a black male in his fifties who had two German shorthaired pointers. Before asking the man what he might know about the killing that had happened a hundred yards from his front door, I spent ten minutes talking to him about his dogs and about bird hunting. The man was passionate about both, it turned out, and we had a nice chat before getting to the business at hand. The lieutenant had rolled his eyes and sighed repeatedly, to the point I nearly asked him to leave. After obtaining pertinent information about that murder case, we departed. Once outside and away from the witness's home, I explained to the lieutenant—as politely as possible, given my opposition to diplomacy—that if he paid attention, he might learn something, and if he was in a hurry, he was at the wrong assignment.

Most of the people Josie and I spoke with at their front doors had the standard line that they hadn't seen or heard anything. But once I told them that Ho had been killed, their demeanors would change and soften, and many showed genuine concern and regret. They would ask questions, and

I would answer to some degree. That was how you established a rapport. Though few reported having seen anything, we learned of Ho's generosity. He had provided diapers or milk to mothers in the neighborhood when they didn't have the money to pay. He paid an old wino to clean up around outside. He had caught kids stealing, and rather than calling the cops, he had walked them home and told their mamas.

We also learned Ho's brother had been killed in a carjacking somewhere in Long Beach several years prior. Josie made a note of it. We spoke to the woman who had seen the van, and we were able to obtain a few more details about its description. There were no windows on the cargo section of the van, and the windows in the front and on the rear doors were tinted dark. Also, the muffler was loud.

The last door we knocked on provided valuable information, once we broke through to the young mother. She had spoken with deputies earlier, and she had told them she didn't hear or see anything. I took a chance that she might have, at some time in her life, been the beneficiary of Ho's kindness, so I told her how he was gunned down in cold blood as he prepared to open his store for the day. I lied and said he was restocking diapers when the gunmen barged in and filled him full of lead for no damned good reason. I saw her choke back tears and glance behind her where a playpen held one baby and a highchair held another. She asked us in and begged us to forgive the mess of empty beer containers and fast-food wrappers strewn about a couch and coffee table, both stained and dirty with cigarette burns and the stench of stale beer.

We talked for a minute about her two young children. Their fathers didn't help with money or love. That led into a conversation about Ho, and then came tears from a woman named Latisha whose heart lay beneath a hard shell, born from a hard, impoverished life. She felt bad that Ho had died before she could repay him his charity and kindness. I doubted she would have ever been able, but that she recognized a debt owed is what mattered, and provided a glimpse of her true character. She wiped at her tears, lit a cigarette and said, "I saw the two men who did it."

Latisha Carver had been up since seven feeding her babies and watching cartoons. She was often one of Ho's first customers as she seemed to always need something when he opened at nine. The market was conveniently located two doors down, which allowed her to leave the babies in the playpen if she hurried. She needed formula for the babies and truthfully, she said, she could use a beer. She didn't normally drink this early in the day, she said, glancing at Josie. Latisha straightened in her chair and quickly teased her hair with her fingertips. She said she was aware of the time as she waited for nine and that's when she heard the rumbling of the loud van pass by her home. She noticed because it sounded like a car owned by the father of one of her babies, who gets pulled over all the time because of the noise it makes. She walked outside and looked down the street to see a white van with tinted windows pulling into Ho's. She didn't give it a second thought, and walked back in. But then it was almost nine and Ho would be there opening up and another customer—whoever was in the van—was probably going in, so she decided she would as well. She secured both babies in their playpen and began walking toward the market when she saw the two men in black walking out, carrying "rifles." She hadn't heard gunshots up to that point. But then she saw old man Frazier—a local wino who lives on the streets and alleys and can always be found hanging around Ho's—walking toward the store. The two gunmen turned and fired, gunning Frazier down in cold blood before casually walking away.

Latisha had seen other people shot and some killed in her lifetime; death was a part of life on the streets of Compton. She said, "But to blast a harmless old man like that, and walk away? I ain't never seen anything like that before. I ran back inside, back to my babies, hoping those men hadn't seen me and weren't gonna come kill me and my babies next."

"Could you tell their race?" I asked, thinking of the story Cedric told Floyd and Mongo.

"Theys was all covered up. Head to toe, like terrorists. Theys prolly Muslim."

"Did you see which direction they went when they left?"

"I didn't. I stayed in my house with my babies. I'm sorry." She swiped at wet eyes again. "Did they kill Frazier too?"

"He's still holding on, the last we heard," I told her. I looked at Josie to signal I didn't have any other questions, so if she had thought of something to ask, now would be the time. But she wasn't Floyd who could read my mind and once I realized that, I asked if she had anything for Latisha.

She shook her head. We stood and thanked Latisha for her time as we stepped around clutter on our way out. Babies cried behind us.

At the door, I handed Latisha my business card with a fifty-dollar bill folded behind it. I said, "You'll have to go to another market today. Here's a little help for the kids."

She took it and didn't bother wiping at her wet eyes. "Thank you."

Down the walkway, Josie whispered, "That was nice of you."

"I'll blue it out. It was nice of the county."

"Blue it out?"

I stopped at the sidewalk. "We spend a lot of money at Homicide, paying informants, moving people, traveling, buying meals. There's a safe in the bureau and there's always a few thousand in cash. Lieutenants have access. You need money, fill out a blue slip with your case number and reason. I'll write 'Witness fees' on this one."

She nodded, and we started walking. The truth of it was, we were reimbursed for less than half of the cash we spent. I didn't push it. I'd fill out a slip for some of the expenses, but there were many that I hadn't bothered with. My tax man allowed a grand a year for miscellaneous informant fees and other cash transactions where receipts were not generated. I figured it worked out in the end. More than anything, those babies needed something to eat and dry diapers, and mama needed a beer. If there were better causes, I couldn't think of one at the moment.

After a moment, I added: "Floyd and I always keep a couple of fifties in our wallets for these types of situations. The hard part is remembering to replace what is spent in bars."

PHIL GENTRY HAD BAGS OF EVIDENCE SITTING ON THE TRUNK LID OF HIS county-issued Ford Taurus. He had parked outside the crime scene tape behind my charcoal gray Crown Victoria and Josie's Toyota. We headed toward Phil as it appeared he was finished with the crime scene.

As we passed Josie's car, I asked, "They didn't give you a county car yet?"

"No, Lieutenant Black said to see Darlene when I had a chance and she'd get something assigned to me."

I glanced at my watch. "She might still be there when we get back to the office. I don't see what else we can do out here today. We can see about getting you a county car, and then check on Frazier's condition before we decide what else needs to be done. We'll need to figure out a next of kin for Ho and make a notification."

Phil put the evidence bags in his trunk and closed the lid.

"Done, Phil?"

"I think so. Do you need anything else?"

"No, I don't think so. Not now. Maybe if you can get some aerial shots in the next few days, that might be a good idea. I'm thinking wide shots that show the freeway accesses also. I don't think these killers are local."

"Sounds good."

"We'll see you up at the lab tomorrow, when we bring in the firearms evidence."

"Do you want me to take that with me?"

"We'll bring it in. I want to find out if they can identify the weapon from those expended two-two-threes. My guess would be an AR, but who knows?"

Gentry nodded and smiled. "See you guys tomorrow then."

"Guy and gal," I said.

Josie shot me a look.

I let the deputies know we were finished, and that they could break down the scene. As a patrol deputy, a murder scene is hectic at first and then it settles and becomes boring for hours while detectives and coroner's investigators and crime scene technicians methodically document and collect evidence. It wasn't unusual for a patrol crew handling a murder to have no other entries on their daily activity log and still be able to put in for overtime. A single notation on their journal, one call that stretched beyond their eight-hour shift.

Before parting company, Josie stopped me with a hand on my arm. She said, "I don't expect special treatment or consideration. I don't need coddling or handholding. I expect my partner to treat me with respect and to have my back, on the streets and in the office. I will always have a partner's back. Is that fair?"

I smiled and nodded. "Fair enough, Josie."

"Thanks, Dickie."

As I opened my car door she said at my back, "I'm honored to work with you. I know a lot about you."

"I've heard a few things about you as well."

"Yeah, well, don't believe everything you hear."

I smiled. "Likewise."

The smile remained as I pulled away from our Compton crime scene and worked my way through the *Hub City* via Atlantic to Rosecrans to the Long Beach Freeway north. Josie stayed glued to my tail. The phone rang and the display showed Katherine's cell. It was a little after four, much earlier than she usually finished her day of counseling crazy cops. "Hi, honey."

"Are you busy?"

"I'm just headed back to the office; your timing is good. We picked up a new case."

Her voice crackled. "I'm on my way to Burbank Airport. My mother has gone into the hospital and it doesn't look good."

"Oh no, what happened?"

"I don't know. Dad is a mess, and he seems overwhelmed, confused. He needs me there for sure. It sounds like maybe she's had a stroke. I need to be with her."

"Absolutely. What can I do?"

"Nothing, Richard."

"If I hadn't just picked up a new case—"

"It's okay. There's nothing you can do. I'll keep you posted."

Silence lingered for an uncomfortable moment before she said, "I'll call when I can, okay?"

"Okay," was all I could say before the line was dead. I frowned at my phone and snapped it into its cradle mounted on the dash. In the mirror I saw my new partner tracking behind me, on my tail, peering through her windshield in her designer eyewear, all business.

Women.

7

While Josie was being assigned a car, I wandered over to Floyd and Mongo who sat at their desks typing on computers.

"What are you two assholes doing?"

Mongo glanced up but went back to work without replying. Floyd spun his chair to face me and grinned. "Dickhead, how about we go out back for a few minutes?"

"I'm not going to lie; I could use a good ass-whoopin'."

I pulled an unoccupied chair over next to him. "You get anywhere on that deal with the kid, Cedric?"

"No. Why do you ask?"

"I just picked up a liquor store murder in Compton. Two shooters, both dressed in black, head to toe. Some type of two-twenty-three and a twenty gauge shotgun."

Mongo spun around to show his large face puckered into a frown. Sweat beaded on his forehead and his tie was loosened. His jowls hung over an unbuttoned collar, and his sleeves rolled up to his elbows.

Floyd said, "You've got to be shittin' me."

I shook my head.

"Why didn't you call us out there to have a look? You too busy sniffing your new partner's ass?"

I glanced over my shoulder. Floyd laughed and said, "You're not scared of her, are you?"

"No, dipshit, I'm not afraid of her. But I sure don't need you starting stupid rumors either. That's the *last* thing I need. The reason I didn't call you down is I didn't know anything about the suspects until an hour ago. After we finished with the scene, we found a witness who saw the shooters gun down one of our victims, an old grape in the parking lot."

"What was that about?"

"I don't know. Eliminating a witness maybe? Although he wouldn't have been much of a witness, to be honest about it. Poor old cluck was barely getting by. I wondered if it wasn't more of a thrill kill."

"Fucking savages."

"Uh-huh."

"Any evidence?"

I smiled.

"Video?"

I nodded.

"Let's see it, Dickie. I might have to arrange movie night with Cedric the Entertainer."

"That's exactly what I was thinking. The tech crew came down and took the digital hard drive from the recorder. I didn't mess with it, so I don't know if we have footage or not. But I'm hopeful. I could use a little good luck on a case, for a change."

Floyd's eyes drifted beyond me and he nodded slightly to draw my attention. I turned as Josie walked up behind us. "Victim two is deceased."

"Well shit, that sucks. I guess we picked up a double. Did the desk notify you?"

"No. I called Killer King and checked his status."

Killer King. I was starting to like my new partner. Not only had she taken the initiative to call and check on our other victim without being prompted to do so, but it seemed she was unconcerned with political correctness. Martin Luther King, Jr. Medical Center was commonly called Killer King by cops who worked the area and were familiar with their lackluster care. Everyone knew about a particular deputy who died as a result of their incompetence back in the early nineties. He had come in with multiple gunshot wounds, and the emergency room doctors saved his life. You had to admire their ability to treat gunshot victims. The military certainly did; for years they would send medics to intern there as there were no other hospitals in the country that consistently treated the volume of high-velocity, military-caliber type gunshot wounds seen at MLK. However, we deputies had always said that if you go there, get out as soon as you've been stabilized, and go somewhere else. The deputy who died there had seemed to be pulling through, then suddenly took a fatal turn. Lawsuits followed, and experts testified that the care he received post-op had been criminally negligent. He should have been moved. Several years before, there had been a well-respected Firestone deputy who made a stand against a protocol stating that deputies would be taken there for treatment. He had dug in and fought with the department brass, stating no deputy sheriff should ever be taken to MLK, and declared he would never comply with the order. But as often is the case, his legitimate concern and righteous battle was ignored by the department executives. The deputy was rolled up to West Hollywood Station for his sin, taking a stance against Killer King.

I smiled at Josie. "Nice. Thanks for doing that."

"No problem. I also updated the dead sheet at the desk, notified the coroner's office, and pulled another coroner's case number. Do we need to update the lieutenant?"

This girl had done her homework and was able to handle some of our clerical duties without being prompted to do so. I had not yet mentioned these tasks to her, much less shown her how to take care of them. The fact she took that initiative endeared her to me that much more and added to the good impression I had of her thus far. "Yeah, just let Lieutenant Black know so he can reflect that in his murder memo. Thanks."

"No problem," she said.

Floyd watched her walk away and then turned to face me. "She rocks, dude."

I smiled. She was definitely growing on me. "Yeah, you might be right about her, but only time will tell. Listen, we need to find your crime scene. I have a feeling that your boy, Cedric, wasn't bullshitting you about what he said he saw."

"How do you propose we go about doing that, slick? It isn't as if I haven't tried."

"Wanna go for a ride?"

Floyd glanced at his watch, no doubt thinking he'd already stayed longer than he had hoped today. He was probably about to tell me he missed his workout or needed a beer, or the kids had games or Cindy was on his jock again about the long hours. "Jesus, dude, seriously? I haven't been to the gym all week—"

"You can go tomorrow. Come on."

I stood and waited. Took a step away, stopped and waited again. "I'll drive, and I'll buy you a steak and beer after."

He huffed as he stood. Mongo had again turned from the work on his desk and sat watching. Floyd said to him, "I'll see you Monday, partner. Apparently, my dickhead needs a dinner date tonight."

I smiled and walked briskly to my desk to grab my briefcase. Josie sat with files strewn over her otherwise tidy desk that sat next to mine. She looked up from her notebook and lifted her brows in a questioning gesture.

"Why don't we call it for tonight?"

"Okay, I was just catching up my notebook."

"I'm going with my old partner—"

"Floyd?"

I grinned. She was fast. Fast to learn the job, fast to pick up profiles and personalities, and seemingly very aware of some of the office dynamics. "Yeah, Floyd. We're going to take one of his witnesses out for a bit, see if we can find a crime scene."

"Is that the kid, the one who might have seen a murder similar to our case?"

"Yeah, how do you know about that?"

"Reading teletypes and murder memos. I stayed late last night and spent some time familiarizing myself with recent cases. I saw the request he sent out to local law enforcement to see if he could identify a case where two gunmen dressed in black with ski masks did a robbery murder of a market. Sounds similar to ours, I'd say."

I was speechless and for a moment felt guilty for not asking her to come along. "Right, you nailed it. But so far, he hasn't found any cases that match what the kid described. He wants to take the kid out for a ride, see if maybe we can at least narrow the area down where it might have happened, and go from there. Probably a long shot, but worth a try. Plus, I owe him dinner."

She smiled. "I heard you two were inseparable."

I broke eye contact first, feeling overpowered at the time. As I gathered my belongings I suggested we meet at the office tomorrow around nine. It would be quiet on a Saturday morning and we could catch up on our reports and then hit the streets for follow-up on our case. Then I told her goodnight, and turned to see Floyd waiting at the back door in his suit and shades, a smirk on his face. As I drew near, he said, "You don't want to bring cha-cha along?"

"I wouldn't let her hear you call her that, partner. You might be tough, but I don't think you're that tough."

<hr>

ON OUR WAY THROUGH BELL GARDENS AND SOUTH GATE HEADING TO OUR old stomping grounds in the Firestone District of Los Angeles County, Floyd called Mrs. Nathan to let her know we'd like to take Cedric for a ride to work on his case. When he disconnected, I looked over and said, "We set?"

"Set, Dickie."

"Right on. Dickie Floyd, ten-eight in Firestone."

"It doesn't get any better than that, does it? I better call the wife, let her know I've once again fallen in with a fast crowd."

I smiled and turned onto Holmes Avenue, feeling alive and charged in South Central Los Angeles with my old partner, Pretty Boy Floyd.

Cedric the Entertainer stood outside his foster home under the watchful eyes of Mrs. Nathan as I swerved my Crown Vic toward her driveway and left it half in the street. Floyd introduced me to Cedric and asked Mrs. Nathan if she remembered the mean guy in the hat. She smiled and said, "That big teddy bear? He's not mean. Of course I remember Detective Jones."

We drove off with Cedric leaned over the seat between us, anxious to get started. Floyd said, "Sit back and put your seatbelt on, Cedric."

"Y'all don't have all y'all's seatbelts on."

I glanced over at Floyd and grinned. He grinned in turn, and then said to Cedric: "Yeah, well, me and Dickie might have to get out and kick someone's ass. You never know."

Cedric didn't hesitate to reply: "Yeah, well, me too."

I looked at Floyd and said, "It's hard to argue with that."

He shrugged. "The kid's got a point."

8

Travis Hollingsworth sank comfortably into a worn couch and plunked his scuffed black boots onto a coffee table. Dirty ashtrays, empty beer containers, a Soldier of Fortune magazine, and a cocked and locked .45 caliber pistol sat on its tinted glass tabletop. A shotgun sat propped against the wall at one end of the couch, a Colt AR-15 rifle mirrored its position on the opposite end. On the carpeted floor there were several green military surplus duffle bags, all of which contained various tools, equipment, and supplies used by *operators*.

That was the preferred term for killers of men, he would say: *operators*.

A man appeared in the hallway, buttoning the fly of his black tactical pants. He nodded as a manner of greeting Hollingsworth. "I hoped it was you I heard out here."

Hollingsworth shook a cigarette from its package and offered it to the man in the black pants and t-shirt. His name was Carlos. He accepted the smoke and took a seat at the opposite end of the couch, placing a pistol of his own on the table before him. He leaned toward Hollingsworth who struck a flame on a Zippo lighter and met him halfway. Carlos leaned back and blew a plume of smoke at the ceiling fan.

"Where's *mi hermana*?"

Hollingsworth frowned at his friend, a young operator in training. Someone he had taken under his wing and had committed to teaching all he had learned as "an operator."

"Don't talk like a fucking cholo, Carlos. You ain't in Compton anymore."

Carlos sat silent for a moment, sulking. He then stood and started for the kitchen. "You want a beer?"

"Yeah."

He returned with two cans of Budweiser and again took his seat on the couch. After handing a beer to Hollingsworth, Carlos opened his and took a long pull. Hollingsworth could see he was butt-hurt again. Carlos always got butt-hurt when Hollingsworth made comments about Mexicans, or *cholos* or *beaners* or *greasers*.

"The fuck's wrong with you? You get your feelings hurt again?"

Carlos took another sip of beer, keeping his eyes straight ahead, maybe looking at the television that sat muted with news showing on the screen.

"She's watching the gook's place, to answer your question," Hollingsworth continued. "She's convinced he's alive. I don't know how the fuck he could be alive, all the lead we sent downrange. I know I hit him, and I think she did too. How could she miss with that sawed-off boomer?" He chuckled and continued. "You know, it's funny, her and that little shotgun. She packs it everywhere we go and always has a pocket full of shells. Two shots at a time, and then she reloads. *Blam, blam.* But she never takes the first shot, or at least she hasn't so far. It's like she's unsure of herself, so she just follows my lead. I shoot, then she shoots. *Pop, pop-pop-pop-pop—BLAM, BLAM!*" He laughed and shook his head, and had a gulp of beer. "I swear to God, it's every fucking time, too. *Pop, pop-pop-pop—BLAM, BLAM!*"

Carlos was smiling now.

Hollingsworth, the big man, tipped his beer back and held it until the contents finished draining down his throat. He crushed the can in his big hand and laughed until he coughed. "Like having a gun parrot, repeats everything I say. *Pop—blam!* Like a fucking echo."

"That's cool, man."

Hollingsworth looked off across the room for a moment, then came back to Carlos, who seemed to be waiting for more. "You know, I seen my share of action, man, and I seen some funny-ass shit happen along the way. But I don't know there's nothing funnier than Tina lighting off with that sawed-off boomer of hers after I start shooting. It's almost distracting. I've stopped and looked at her and thought, '*What the fuck?*', and her eyes pop out through those little holes in her mask when she looks over at me laughing at her. Then I laugh more, cause the fucking mask is usually crooked on her little face by then, and she looks like a little kid playing cops and robbers. Bonnie and Clyde, or some shit. We can't find anything small enough for her at the surplus. Even those britches she wears are twice her size, and they don't do anything for that killer little ass she's got. You'd think with all the bitches they got going in the military now, they'd make britches for bitches." He coughed through his laughter. "Bitches and Mexican midgets."

Hollingsworth continued laughing. He found himself hilarious, and he didn't care whether or not anyone else did. He didn't bother to look and see if Carlos was butt-hurt again; he was certain the sensitive little wetback would be.

"So, she's watching the store?" Carlos asked. "Alone?"

"Yeah, she's sitting down there in her little car trying to get a glimpse of the slope, see if he's still alive or if they got a new gook running the joint. She thinks he's alive. I told her if he is, he's a lucky sonofabitch, but not for long."

"What are we going to do, if he's alive?"

"What are *we* going to do?"

Carlos nodded.

"We're going to get your hands dirty, Ortiz. That's what *we* are going to do. It's time you put in some wet work, so we know we can trust you."

Carlos went to the kitchen and came back with two more beers. "I'm ready for some action."

Hollingsworth was skeptical about whether or not Carlos could put in the work. Sure, he says he can, but Hollingsworth had heard that before.

"You say you are; we'll see. I seen plenty who'd freeze up when it happened, especially during their first contacts. I seen it more'n once. When I was with the Cav, and we was overseas, you'd see what a guy was made of when the shooting started. Once the rags started popping their AKs at you and shooting rockets under your fucking Humvee, that's when you found out what you were made of. Not when you were sitting in the living room drinking fucking Budweiser."

"I'm ready."

"We'll see about that when I put the gook on his knees in front of you. And after that, I might let you cap a little green-eyed nigger kid. That's if your sister figures out the gook's still alive, and if we can find the kid."

Carlos glanced at the watch on his wrist, a bulky plastic beveled piece with dials and buttons and an olive-drab cloth band. "When's she gonna be back?"

"After they close, I guess."

"She shouldn't have gone alone."

Hollingsworth looked over at the young operator-in-training. "Your sister's fine. Like she said, she fits in down there, doesn't draw no attention. I guess we could have sent you with her, but you don't know what the fuck you're doing."

TINA ORTIZ WATCHED AS THEY CLOSED THE STORE AT NINE. A WOMAN came out first, made two trips back and forth to the car. She seemed to be looking around the parking lot as she did.

Tina felt comfortable across the street; the woman never looked in her direction. Other than an occasional crackhead passing by and eyeballing her car, nobody seemed to notice Tina at all. Even those who did take a look—the crackhead, a gangster or two—were not likely able to see her sitting low behind her tinted windows. No matter, she had her shotgun across her lap.

A flash of light drew her eyes back to the front door where the woman appeared again and the man followed, limping along behind her with a pair of crutches tucked under his arms. Tina could tell by their body language they were arguing, the woman waving her arms around and the man shaking his head. The door closed, stealing the bulk of light that allowed Tina to see clearly, and moments later the two were loading into their car.

Tina Ortiz had just started her car and was about to turn on her lights when the detectives passed her and then jerked their unmarked police car into the lot. Tina shut off the ignition, not wanting to draw their attention. She sank deeper into her seat and became aware of her heart pounding beneath her black hoodie. Her finger stroked the trigger guard of her sawed-off coach gun—that's what Travis would sometimes call it—and her thumb caressed the two hammers that she knew rested on live rounds of 20-gauge #6 shot. Travis called the shells *duck shot,* and he had told her when she was big enough to shoot a 12-gauge, she'd move up to buckshot.

The cops were out of the car talking to the storekeepers. She thought about her cell phone and wondered if she should call Travis, or her brother. But why? What could they do? Why would it matter? It was news that the man was still alive, but it wasn't news that the detectives would be calling on him and his wife. After all, their store had been shot up in a botched robbery attempt. By the appearance of the owner, he had been shot up too. But not killed, just as she had thought and had told Travis.

She waited, breathing slowly while processing all of the possibilities and what her actions would be in response to the various scenarios she imagined. She pictured the cops suddenly turning and focusing on her, pulling their guns and running toward her. But why would they? She had to relax, this was all routine and nobody knew that it was she who had stood in that doorway just a few days ago, firing at will. Now she was just another Latina in a car in Compton, and nobody could see her anyway. Still, she caressed her coach gun.

The one detective wore a hat and looked like a cop out of an old noir film. The other had the physique of an athlete—you could see it through his suit—and she pictured him in a movie you might see now, the type of movie where a beautiful woman would fall for the dark-haired, handsome cop. Maybe a Mexican woman from the barrio who falls in love with a local cop, a white guy who has a blonde wife and a couple of kids at home. He takes them to dinner on Friday nights but keeps a girlfriend in the ghetto where he works. But tonight was Friday night and this good-looking cop wasn't home with his wife and kids and this wasn't a movie or a love story either.

Tina thought about Travis and how she'd often ask him to take her to dinner, but he'd send her out instead. He'd tell her he can't be out in the neighborhood with all her people because most of them were fucking savages and he didn't want to have to kill everyone he met, not that he was opposed to doing so. He'd remind her of his combat experience and how, as a Ranger, he had learned to kill men a hundred different ways, with or without a weapon. She knew, though, that he'd never been a Ranger. He had failed Ranger school, but in the civilian world, he'd never mention that part. Travis would usually be drunk by the time they finished eating whatever it was she had brought home, and that's when he'd go through his stages from being happy to getting mean to wanting to make love. That's what he called it, making love. Until he was good and drunk, and then it would be humping or fucking or tearing a piece off.

Sometimes she would make love to him, but other times she'd go into her room and lock the door and sleep with her gun at her side, the way she had when she was a teenaged girl living with a sexually abusive father and four brothers who at times forgot she was their sister. The longer they were together, the less she felt for Travis and the more she realized what a terrible mistake she had made. But now she was trapped, with no way out of the deep hole the two of them had dug for themselves.

They had been on the run for a couple of years, hiding their identities and living off of the grid because of the intense search that had continued for them both. She didn't know, maybe they were still looking for them. To make matters worse, now they had become murderers, which meant there was a whole other collaborative effort underway to identify and locate the two outlaws. Maybe this handsome cop and his friend with the hat, the one that looked mean and wouldn't fall for her smile the way the other would, were the ones heading up that effort. She wondered if that was the case.

The cops were back at the car, but now someone was getting out of the back seat. Jesus, it was the kid, the little black kid with the green eyes who saw it all that night. He had run off through the alley, and Travis had told her to take the shot. She had purposely waited until he was nearly around the corner, and even then, she aimed wide to the left and missed the kid completely. How could she kill a little boy?

She and Travis had driven behind the market and down a couple of alleys but had not been able to find the little boy. Tina had been relieved that they didn't. Travis said they needed to go since the cops were likely coming, and she had been happy to hear him say it.

And this was him, right here in front of her again. He was with the cops now and was likely telling them all about the robbery and the shooting. Maybe their vehicle too. How much did he know?

The boy was returned to the back seat of the sedan, and the detectives gathered once more with the storeowners at the rear of their car. There was conversation and then the group gravitated toward the front door of the building, the man bringing up the rear, hopping on his crutches. Light spilled onto the sidewalk once again as the door swung open and the group crowded through the doorway. A moment later, darkness replaced the light and the cops and storeowners were out of view.

"We have to find that green-eyed little bastard, and kill him."

Travis's words echoed in her mind as she stared at the boy alone in the backseat of a detective's car, parked in a dark parking lot in Compton. This was the time and place to do it. Travis would insist on it.

Tina started the car and sped into the night. She made a right on the first street she came to, and halfway down that block she flipped on her headlights. She knew to leave the lights off so that nobody could see her license plate, at least until she got away from a crime scene. Tina turned the car left and right, alternating at each intersection until she came out of the neighborhood and back onto a major street. She glanced in her mirror and settled down once she was comfortable that nobody had followed her.

As she headed south to Long Beach, she powered up her phone, scrolled through her favorites past Carlos and Dre and Emmy and so on until the entry labeled only as 'T' was highlighted. She pushed the phone button and waited to tell him the news. Part of it, anyway.

9

Cedric the Entertainer seemed certain this was the place. A little neighborhood market in Compton, five miles south of where he lived. Floyd turned to look into the back seat; I found Cedric's eyes in my rearview. Floyd said, "How sure are you?"

"This is it."

We had taken a shot at heading south from Watts toward Compton, eyeballing the various markets and liquor stores on the main drags along the way. We were driving past this one that appeared abandoned or closed, all the lights off in the early evening. Cedric startled us both by yelling, "There!"

I slowed to nearly a stop in the southbound lanes. "Hey partner, there's someone in that car." A sedan stood alone in the parking lot. I had caught a glimpse of movement inside.

I glanced over to see Floyd leaned forward, looking past me toward the parking lot. "Let's talk to them," he said.

We pulled in behind the parked car. Floyd was out quickly. As I exited, I looked back at the excited kid in our back seat, and told Cedric to stay put.

An older silver Mercedes sat idling not far from the front doors to the market. Walking up, I saw there were two occupants. I had approached on the driver's side, Floyd on the passenger's. I motioned for the woman who sat in the driver's seat to roll down her window.

"Hi, how are you?"

"Fine," she said.

She was Asian, forty to fifty, rather petite and dressed nicely in business-casual attire.

"Is everything okay?"

"We own the store," she said, and glanced toward the man sitting in the passenger's seat. "We just closed for the night. Can I help you with something?"

It occurred to me she might not know we were the cops. In the ghetto, we were accustomed to everyone knowing who we were, no matter how we presented. I was convinced I could walk through the projects in drag and get the "Hi Po-lice" from half of the kids, and the "Five-oh" warning from all of the adults. But some of the foreigners-turned-entrepreneurs would surprise you at how unaware they were of the life outside of their immediate little worlds. It amazed me they weren't killed more often. Killed for their Mercedes or payroll that probably sat between them on the front seat.

"I'm a detective with the sheriff's department, ma'am."

"Oh?"

As if I could be anything other, a white guy standing in a dark parking lot in the middle of Compton wearing a suit and dress hat. Not to mention I had walked up on a stranger's car.

"My partner and I are investigating a robbery, maybe a shooting that might have happened here a few nights ago."

She shook her head and looked away.

"Nothing like that happened here?" I asked.

"No, you have wrong store, I'm sorry. We have to go now, okay?"

I looked across the top of their car. Floyd's brows told me all I needed to know; he had the same gut feeling I had, that something wasn't right.

"I'm going to have to ask that you turn off your car, ma'am, and step out for me."

"Why?" she asked, now in a very unfriendly tone, "I tell you already, nothing happen."

Floyd opened the passenger's door and began speaking to the man seated there. The woman exited the driver's door, and expressed her displeasure. "I talk to Mayor. She set you straight."

"Can we have a look inside?" I nodded toward the market.

It had crossed my mind we were in the wrong place, but then her demeanor told me we weren't. It wasn't unheard of to have uncooperative victims—especially in the ghettos—and it had been my experience that some of the foreigners were distrustful of the police. Many of them had learned to handle matters as they might in the countries from where they came. Koreans had a reputation throughout Los Angeles to be quick to resort to gunplay when protecting their property. Like everything else, there was some truth to it, but it was also an overgeneralization. The inner-city residents felt the Koreans were rude. Many of the markets were set up similarly to high-end jewelry stores and low-end pawn shops, fortified with bullet-proof glass and configured for impersonal transactions. Some of the citizens were resentful of the attitudes and the prices, and over the years, the tensions had grown between some of the entrepreneurs and their customers. There were no cultural sensitivity classes for the citizens of Los Angeles who were unaccustomed to the ways of some of these storeowners. Although some of them could be abrupt, maybe unfriendly, the truth was that many of them had been victimized many times and had grown fearful of a large sector of the communities they served. Storeowners had killed and been killed. The media would generally exploit such tragedies in a one-sided fashion, favoring the victim class and seldom giving an honest reporting of facts. During the riots, most of the Korean-owned markets were looted and burned to the ground, for all of these reasons and for sport. Or in the name of "justice."

Other than Ho's. His market had stood untouched while the city burned around him. In part, because of the relationships he had with many of the residents, and in part, because of his relationship with the local cops.

Floyd had now asked the man to exit the vehicle as well, and when our eyes met again, we were still on the same page.

"What do you say we have a quick word with Cedric, partner?"

"Good idea," Floyd said.

We left the two storeowners standing at the back of their car. We returned to our vehicle to find an excited witness perched against the back of the front seat, closely watching the action.

Floyd asked if he recognized either of the two who stood in the glow of our headlights.

"Yes ma'am, that's the chino I told you about."

Floyd saw me grinning and said, "*Ma'am?*"

"Sorry, sir. Yes, sir, that's the chino they killed, that man right there on his crutches."

I burst into laughter and Floyd followed suit. It was one of the problems we had never been able to overcome in our partnership: untimely fits of sick, twisted humor.

Once we were meeting with another detective and the family of a missing person who was presumed murdered. The detective was bringing us up to speed on the case, explaining that the last person to see the woman alive was a man she had only recently met and to whose apartment she had gone. The detective then, for reasons still inexplicable, said he could only imagine what they had been doing in there, and as he said it, he pumped his fist and made a grunting sound. This detective was much older than we were, and he had worked at the Homicide bureau for a very long time. Which meant he had many more years of experience than we did, along with much more wear and tear and the toll of the job. One could easily argue, based on those facts alone, that he was crazier than us too. To strengthen that premise, it should be known that the detective in question had actually experienced a mental breakdown due to the stresses of the job. In other words, he was a certified nutcase, and everyone knew it. Not that anyone at the bureau was completely sane, but even grading on the curve, this guy was off the charts. I had immediately begun emergency attempts to suppress the laughter I could feel boiling over inside me. The critical part would be to avoid eye contact with Floyd. I knew if I looked across the conference room table at him, we both would lose it. *Don't look at your partner. Don't look at your partner.* The room had stood silent for what seemed an eternity, and suddenly, in the silence, Floyd made a tiny snorting noise as he too fought to suppress his laughter. When he did, I completely lost it, and I began laughing so hard I started crying, which of course made Floyd start laughing out loud as well. I looked up to see tears in his eyes. I glanced over to see the detective in question chomping his gum with a smirk on his face, as if wondering what the hell was so funny. The family members were all stone-faced. Once I was able to get control of myself, I apologized profusely, but it was a moment I could never forget nor forgive myself for either. But I also still laugh until I cry when I recall it.

Now standing in this parking lot in Compton, I again found myself with tears in my eyes. I said to Floyd, "You want to ask the dead guy if we can look inside his market?" and we both lost our composure.

———

WHEN WE CAME OUTSIDE NEITHER OF US WAS LAUGHING. THE TWO storeowners continued to insist that no crime had occurred. When we pointed out bullet holes in the wall behind the counter, they said those had been there a long time, longer than they had owned the store. When asked about the injury to the man's leg, the storeowner said he had hurt himself playing golf. When pressed, he said he fell out of a golf cart. Floyd and I nodded at that, both having firsthand experience with similar experiences.

"What do you think?" I asked on the way to our car.

"I think Ballson Chin is a lying bastard. That's what I think, Dickie."

"I think you're right."

We stopped at the front of my sedan and each turned back to study the building and its surroundings. There was an alley that ran behind it, and it would be accessible from either side of the store. But on the far side, the storeowners' car sat parked to the side, twenty feet away from the opening that led to the alley. The owners had just entered the vehicle again and were preparing to depart.

Without speaking, I walked over to the Mercedes and shined my light at the back of it. There were two small holes—one in the trunk lid and another through the right rear taillight. Both appeared consistent with 20-gauge shotgun pellets. I turned and shined my light on the front door of the market and estimated the distance to be twenty-five feet.

Floyd watched as I walked back.

"Well?"

"Didn't you say he told you the one with the shotgun took a shot at him as he ran toward the alley?"

"Yeah."

"I think a couple pellets hit that car. My guess is they park in the same spot every day."

Floyd nodded and then looked around the lot once again. "If she was parked there, and Cedric was running around the corner of that building, the shooter is either a terrible shot, or they have a hell of a scatter on that shotgun."

I considered it for a moment. "Or the shooter didn't want to hit the kid."

Floyd squinted, deep in thought. "What would make them want to miss? That doesn't make sense."

"I don't know, maybe because he's a kid. Even killers have standards."

"Some do, maybe. If these are the same people who did your murder, killing Ho and then gunning down that harmless grape, I'd argue that these two assholes have neither standards nor consciences."

I silently agreed, though the thought lingered as I took my time walking back to my car. The Mercedes backed out and began to pull away. I stood appraising the outside scene of an apparently unreported attempted robbery and shooting, maybe a murder.

We settled into my Crown Vic where an anxious Cedric waited with adventure in his eyes. "Did you see what happened in there? Is there blood everywhere?"

Floyd turned in his seat. "You're a hundred percent sure this is where it happened, right?"

"And that Asian man on the crutches is the one you saw get shot, right?" I added.

"Yup. I seen the whole thing. I can even show you where I hid behind the store, down that alley. I'll show you where it was I stole that dog from underneath the boat."

———

THE OFFICE WAS DESERTED LATE AT NIGHT AND JOSIE TOOK THE opportunity to walk about and look at the various desks of her new colleagues. She enjoyed seeing the family photos, the various news clippings, cartoons, and gimmicks that littered the desktops and defined personalities. Some desks were cluttered beyond belief and had the appearance of having been in a hurricane. Others were organized and tidy and clean with all the photos aligned and arranged so that they were square to the angles of the desk and their other trimmings. Her partner's desk was of the latter classification, indicating he was an A-type, tightly-wound old soul with a bad case of OCD. It was just as he had been described. She pulled his chair out and sat at his desk as she continued to study it. The blotter on the desk was free of clutter and dust and family photos too. There was a photo of a bulldog that appeared to have been taken in a driveway next to a trailer that held a boat. The only other photo was of his old partner, Matt Tyler, the one he and almost everyone else called Floyd. In the picture Floyd stood shirtless at a barbecue with a beer in one hand, tongs in the other, and a wide smile and dark sunglasses on his face. There was a phone list of the 23 sheriff's stations spread throughout the county, the various custody facilities, all detective divisions and bureaus, and all of the other pertinent department functions including Special Enforcement Bureau, Aero Bureau, and the various sections of the crime lab. Another list had all local law enforcement agencies, fire departments, and hospitals. There was a Homicide Bureau roster with all of the detectives' cell phone numbers listed alphabetically. She wondered why anyone would have printed copies of all this material when everything was now at the touch of a few keys on your mobile devices.

She looked around the office to be certain she was still alone. Convinced, she began checking the desk drawers. She knew a lot could be learned by routine integrity checks, as she liked to call them. She hadn't coined the phrase, and in fact, it was a phrase she heard from cops quite often, usually in reference to their spouses or lieutenants. She knew it was probably because cops don't trust anyone without verification. That's all she was doing, verifying she could trust her new partner. Did he have a bottle concealed in the desk? What about a secret phone book with phone numbers of wild women and bookies and strippers?

Josie's ex was a bit of a player and it was just this type of routine integrity check that had ruined her best shot at being married—thus far—while at the same time saved her from a lifetime of grief and likely health issues. The macho, body-building jail deputy she had dated for a year turned out to be bisexual and had since been diagnosed HIV positive. Josie tested for the next five years to be certain she was free of infection, and for many of those years she had all but avoided romantic interludes. Instead, she focused on her career and her family: two sisters, two brothers, and an aging mother whose body was worn from a lifetime of labor. Josie didn't need a man in her life. Most of the time, anyway.

Satisfied there was no evidence to be found in the desk, she carefully lined the chair back into its position with the arms perpendicular to the front edge, just as she had found it. She double-checked each drawer to make sure she hadn't left anything open half an inch, and she adjusted the desktop blotter a sixteenth of an inch to make sure it was square and that everything would be in order when Dickie returned. Then she decided to slip out before he did return, so that he wouldn't know how much time she put in at the office today. On her way out, she stopped at the desk and signed out, listing her hours as nine to five for an eight-hour day. She glanced at her watch as she walked away. *10:45.*

WHEN FLOYD AND I LEFT THE OUTBACK THEY WERE CLOSING THE DOORS behind us and sweeping the floors beneath our feet. As I drove us back to the office, we recapped all of the brilliant ideas, conclusions, and planning that had been born over many pints of cold draft beer and a couple of medium-rare steaks smothered with grilled onions and mushrooms and accommodated by a loaded baked potato for me and fries for my idiot.

"Well, I guess you better get cracking on that search warrant, Dickie."

"Wait, why would *I* write the warrant? This is your case, pal."

"I don't have a case. You heard what the dead man told you, he and his lovely bride. Nothing happened there. Speaking of lovely brides, do you ever hear from Val anymore, or are you two never speaking again? And what's the status with you and the shrink, what's-her-ass? Also, are you hot on your new partner?"

"Katherine. Doctor James to you, asshole. No, I never hear from Val, and that's probably best. Katherine is out of town; her mother is in the hospital and it looks bad. Dad's not doing well either, I guess. I'm not even entertaining your other question."

"Sorry to hear about the shrink's mom."

"Thanks. And it's your warrant because the only way you prove Cedric ain't lying is to pull bullets out of that wall and compare them to the bullets from Ho's place. And that is *your* obligation. You swore an oath pal, an oath to the County of Los Angeles and its citizens, so stop trying to weasel out of doing your job."

"Have you ever been partnered with a broad before?"

I looked over at him. "What?"

"Have you ever had a chick for a partner?"

"Yeah, I heard what you said, I meant *what,* like, where the hell are you going with this?"

"The odds are very high that in mixed gender partnerships a romantic interest will grow over time."

"I think you're a mixed gender if we're going to be honest about everything."

"I'm just trying to warn you, Dickie. I know you're not up on these social situations and changing times, and I don't want you to be surprised when you catch yourself admiring her ass, or her eyes, or whatever it is that draws you to a woman other than a well-stocked liquor cabinet."

I glanced over and shook my head. "You're such an asshole."

Floyd, straight-faced: "Don't say I didn't warn you."

WE ARRIVED AT THE OFFICE TO PICK UP FLOYD'S CAR. BOTH OF US needed to make a recycled beer deposit down the hall, and we each wanted to grab a cup of coffee for the road. On the way out, I checked my desk to see if I had left anything behind or if there were any notes or phone messages or if I had any reports returned from dictation that needed their final touches. There were none, so I turned to depart but caught something from the corner of my eye. My computer's keyboard was not located in its assigned position. Close, but not exact. Someone had been at my desk.

This I pondered for part of my drive home and concluded it had been my partner. Often someone will pull your chair from your desk to visit with somebody else nearby. That was to be expected. I didn't like it, and I had marked my chair so that I would always get mine back if it did in fact accidentally get switched with someone else's. But when something like that occurred, there would never be an attempt to return the chair to its perfect positioning at my desk in the manner in which I would always leave it. So, whoever it was that caused my keyboard to be slightly askew on my desktop, didn't want to leave any evidence of their visit and had tried hard to conceal their intrusion.

Which meant it had to have been Josie.

No doubt it had been a routine integrity check, and I didn't blame her for it. In fact, I admired her for it. She was a smart girl.

I was reminded of what Floyd said about partnerships and romantic feelings. For a moment, I could see his point. It wasn't uncommon to see partners of the opposite sex becoming involved personally. But I dismissed that thought and knew I'd never admit to Floyd that I had even considered it. Nor would I admit it to myself, or anyone else.

Floyd. Jesus, this guy.

10

Tina Ortiz arrived at the house in South Long Beach to find her man, Travis Hollingsworth, and her brother, Carlos, preparing to flee. At least that was how it appeared to her. She closed the door and stood looking around a living room cluttered with half a dozen military duffle bags. All of them appeared to be full, and some appeared heavy, the shapes of large and bulky items poking at woven fabric from inside.

"What is all of this?"

Travis sat down on the couch and picked up a beer from the table. Carlos stood with his hands gripping his slender hips, looking around the room as if trying to figure out what she was referring to.

"Are we moving out?"

Travis took another swig of beer before answering. "We were getting ready to go, in case you didn't make it back."

"I called and told you I was on my way back, and that I didn't have a tail."

"As far as you knew. Did you look up? Besides, we weren't going to take a chance after you said the detectives were right there. Jesus. Then Carlos tried calling you back, and your phone went straight to voicemail."

Her dark eyes darted around the room. "It was off."

Neither Travis or Carlos responded.

Tina hadn't thought to check for helicopters as Travis had previously cautioned her to do. He had told her about the various types of surveillance she needed to be aware of—more than once. He called it counter-surveillance tactics, and he would teach her maneuvers such as making several turns on side streets before getting onto a main boulevard, and crossing through parking lots or driving down dead-end roads and stopping to watch for a few moments; that was how you spotted a tail. For a moment she felt stupid for not even thinking about aerial surveillance, and she could tell by the silence that Travis was irritated with her because of it. He likely knew from the look on her face when he asked if she had looked up.

"Nobody followed me and there weren't any birds up either. They aren't looking for us, Trav; they're investigating a robbery. That's what they do when someone gets robbed. Detectives go and talk to the victims."

Carlos turned to walk into the kitchen and Travis Hollingsworth called out for him to bring another beer.

"Besides, I was right. The *chino* is still alive."

After she said it, the boy was on her mind. She fought the urge to tell him. It would gain favor with Travis if she came back with a positive report, but then she would have to answer as to why she hadn't tried to take him out, or why she hadn't tried tailing the cops to see where the boy lived. She decided nothing good could come of mentioning it. Besides, she was completely against the idea of killing a kid.

Travis got up from the couch and walked over to her. She tried to read him but wasn't sure if he was drunk or sober, mean or horny. The closer he got the more she had to look up. He towered over her at nearly six feet, four inches tall, compared to her five feet, four inches. Finally, he grinned, which told her he'd had just enough booze to still be nice, but that meant he'd also be wanting to be with her soon. His small, tobacco-stained teeth barely showed through the wiry brown mustache and beard that concealed his face. Scraggly hair framed the whole mess, and Tina had often thought back to when she met him and how he was clean cut, clean shaven, and lean. A good-looking man in a rugged way, which she liked. Now he looked like a mountain man, or a biker, and she didn't like it at all. In fact, she was generally repulsed by him, and that was a feeling that seemed to grow daily.

"What do you say, little woman, that you and I spend a little time alone tonight? Maybe go have a shower and then some drinks in bed."

He reached for her hair, but she pushed his arm away and walked past him. "Maybe later. Right now, we need to clean this place up. We aren't running again. Not yet. Not unless we have no choice. I like it here and if we don't have to go, we won't. This is the first time in two years the three of us aren't crammed into a one-room apartment."

The big man raised his voice. "Yeah, and how do you suppose we can continue to pay the rent here if we keep fucking these jobs up? How hard is it to whack a fucking gook and take his fucking money? I used to slit throats for fun, for Christ's sake. Now we can't kill 'em with a rifle and a sawed-off shotgun."

"The last job was good."

"What, two grand, that's good?"

She didn't answer.

"Your brother needs to pick up the slack, get his hands dirty. No more pussy-footing around."

Tina glanced over at Carlos. "He's just a kid."

"I was in Ranger school by time I was his age. He's old enough."

He'd failed Ranger school by that time, he meant, Tina thought.

"I'm ready," Carlos added.

Tina shook her head and disappeared into the hallway. She closed the bedroom door behind her and leaned her back against it, pausing to collect her thoughts. Carlos was her little brother, the only family she stayed in touch with. The only family she claimed now, besides her grandmother. She didn't want her little brother killing. She wished there was another way for them to live, she and her brother, but the choices she had made with Travis had cemented a certain lifestyle that offered no future. There were few options available to them.

She locked the door and took a seat on her bed.

Life seemed almost unfair, how one decision would completely alter the course of your life. And then another decision shortly after would spin you off in another direction. But never did it seem you could look at a map and chart your course and find your destination. As a kid, all she thought about was being a doctor. She did well in school and felt she had a legitimate chance. She avoided gangs—she was the only one in her family who had—and she was the first to graduate from high school. The first in all of her family, ever, as far back as anyone knew.

But college was a dream not easily realized by someone with no support from family. Even with all of the grants and scholarships that were available to her, it didn't seem to be enough. Someone had told her about the military and free school, and three months after receiving her high school diploma, she was in the army and on her way to earning free college.

Tina loved the white boys; she always had. After joining the army, she found herself surrounded by them. Most were fit and sharp and motivated. Some were cocky and had the respect of younger soldiers for their various accomplishments, the rewards for which they wore on their chests. The more ribbons a soldier wore—*chest candy*, they called it—the more action that soldier had seen. And everyone seemed to be enthralled by those who had seen combat.

After completing Advanced Individual Training (AIT) at Fort Leonard Wood, Missouri, Private First Class (PFC) Christina Ortiz shipped off to Fort Hood, Texas, home of the legendary 1st Cavalry Division. That was where she had met Travis Hollingsworth, a salty sergeant whose swagger had caught her eye. His stories of combat and his propensity for violence excited her greatly. Her MOS (military occupational specialty) was a motor transport operator (88M), and she found herself driving for Sergeant Hollingsworth, who never stopped telling her and the others about his adventures overseas. The first night they were together socially, he had scared her so badly she nearly had a panic attack. It was in a pool hall not far from base where military personnel would oftentimes mix with bikers, cowboys, and farmers. There would often be tension, and sometimes the nights would end in disaster. That night, Travis found himself in a disagreement with a biker after gambling on a game of pool. The two went out back to settle their differences. Tina had followed them outside as did several of the biker's friends. In the very first moment when the biker had begun to posture, Hollingsworth struck out with lightning speed and punched the man in the throat. The biker dropped to the ground, grasping his throat as blood spilled from his mouth. One of the other bikers had started to step up but stopped when the barrel of a small pistol was shoved into his face. She was sure she was about to witness a killing. Perhaps she already had, it occurred to her, as the first biker was on the ground gurgling blood. The bikers backed off and Travis took her by the arm and they were gone.

They stayed off base that night in a dingy motel and the love making was passionate to a degree she had never experienced. It occurred to her in the following weeks and months that she was addicted to danger; she was an adrenaline junkie. Suddenly all she would think about was violence, and at times she made sure it would happen. Travis was the jealous type, and it didn't take much for her to get him into fights. She loved it, and the passion continued. But she also discovered that fights were not nearly enough to satisfy her craving. She often thought back to the biker they had left in the alley and she wondered if he had lived or died. The idea of it stimulated her sexually, and she needed more of it, more of the violence. She also became aware of her desire to partake in the violence, and slowly, but surely, she did. One night, Travis had knocked a man down in a barroom with a single punch to his face. She had no idea what came over her, but Tina began stomping the man's head as he lay unconscious on the floor. She found that to be more exciting than anything she had ever experienced, and she had insisted Travis make love to her in their car before fleeing the scene. Fortunately for them, when the cops arrived, they went straight into the bar and never bothered with checking the parking lot. Travis had insisted they flee, but the presence of the cops sent her further into ecstasy, and she was having none of a premature departure.

While assigned to Echo Troop, 1-7 Cav at Fort Hood, Tina had been attracted to a commissioned officer but hadn't intended for it to go anywhere. Initially, it had been the excitement of Travis's jealousy that spurred her on. Travis hated the lieutenant, and the lieutenant clearly had an interest in Private First Class Ortiz. There had been endless flirtation and then a chance meeting in town—away from the base, the army, the jealous boyfriend—that led to drinks and a night of dancing. She slept with him that night and found something she hadn't expected to find, something she believed may have been her only encounter with true love. But she would never know, and it could never be. Not after a decision made on the second day of June, two long years ago.

A knock on the bedroom door startled Tina. "Who is it?"

"It's your daddy, little girl. Now open the fucking door."

11

Saturday morning the sun rose over the San Gabriel Mountains, casting an orange tint across the Southland from the Mojave Desert to the Los Angeles Basin. Many Angelenos slept while others were just beginning their days. Some of those whose day had just begun embraced the crisp morning air as they jogged or rode bicycles for exercise. Others sat on patios and decks sipping coffee or tea, embracing the short reprieve from the sounds of a busy metropolis. But for some, it was just another work day.

Such was the case for cops and firemen, nurses and doctors, cooks and waitresses, and a host of others including Jimmy Ortiz, a two-strike convicted felon who made his living primarily by burglarizing homes during the day and businesses and cars by night. He was an equal opportunity thief who did not discriminate as he strove to feed his methamphetamine addiction.

This morning he pedaled a stolen bicycle while packing a .38 Special; he had lifted both the day before during a residential burglary not far from his North Long Beach home. He had also picked up some jewelry which he fenced for thirty bucks, and used that to score some meth. Now he had been out all night—*tweaking*—and riding through alleys and quiet streets with some new ideas about scoring his dope. Jimmy knew it would be more beneficial to use the gun to get cash from a variety of individuals than it would be to fence it once for fifty bucks, or maybe twenty. After all, either way—just one more felony conviction—he was going away for good. Why not live large until that day came?

It was in North Long Beach that he saw his first target, a young lady walking away from a car left running at the end of a driveway, parked in a manner that blocked the sidewalk. Jimmy slowed as he approached, and finally stopped in front of the adjacent property in the shadows of a maple tree. He thought about dropping the bike and taking off in the car. It was black and shiny and probably not very old, and he figured he could get a couple grand for it, or at least a couple hundred. That would give him a week off from his work. He looked around to see empty streets and the quiet homes of still sleeping neighbors. Just as he made his decision and started to drop the bike, the woman returned to her car.

She was young, an attractive Latina with her hair pulled back in a ponytail. She wore black yoga pants, bright white tennis shoes, and a gray windbreaker with red and black accents and some type of logo over the left breast. She carried a purse over one shoulder and what appeared to be a gym bag over the other. She seemed focused, maybe in a hurry, as she walked to the rear of the idling car and opened the trunk. Jimmy started peddling toward her, and as he did, he made up his mind. This would be his first robbery. An easy target.

In those brief moments between the time he decided to make his move and when he arrived at the would-be victim's car, Jimmy saw himself sticking his gun in her face and demanding her purse. He knew with the gun, she wouldn't resist. There would be fear in her eyes and she would want to scream, and he would have to tell her to be calm. He'd get her purse and pedal away before she could fully grasp what had just happened. Or maybe he'd drop the bike and drive off in her car, taking her purse with him. Or maybe he would put the bitch in the trunk and take her, the car, and the purse, back to the detached garage behind his grandmother's home where he lived just a few blocks away. He wished he had more time to consider it all.

But he didn't. It all happened very quickly.

Still leaning into the trunk, she turned her head and locked eyes with him as he stopped. He planted his feet on the sidewalk while still straddling his bike only a few feet from her. She narrowed her eyes as if to question his purpose or intent, but as Jimmy reached into his pocket her expression of question turned to that of an angry and resolute woman. Jimmy fumbled with the gun that had hung up halfway out of his pocket.

Finally, his gun came free of his clothing. As he raised it toward the woman, there were brilliant flashes of light against an otherwise subdued morning sky. Jimmy Ortiz felt a burning sensation in his chest, and the pain and pressure took his breath from him. He knew he'd been shot, but he couldn't believe it. This was it, he thought, as he succumbed to the pain and the weakness and dropped to the ground. The lovely woman stood over him and he held onto her gaze as a wave of darkness rolled over him.

I WAS HORIZONTAL ON THE COUCH WHEN I WAS AWAKENED BY MY PHONE vibrating against the coffee table. The TV was on, showing a man in a suit who appeared to be preaching from a podium. The volume was muted, so I had no idea if his message was for me or all of the other sinners waking up on their couches late in the morning.

The display showed it was Katherine calling, not the office. That was a relief. Though Josie and I had picked up a murder yesterday morning, our teams—Teams Five and Six—would be tasked with getting the bureau through the weekend. It wasn't uncommon for teams to have to recycle partners through the rotation in order to hold their own until Monday morning. This was, after all, the City of Angels.

I tried to sound awake. "Good morning."

"Did I wake you?"

"No, not at all. I was sitting here watching church."

"Watching church? On Saturday?"

That puzzled me; I hadn't thought of it being Saturday. As I frowned at the television a message began scrolling beneath the man in his suit, apparently offering a discount on his course of how to live a purposeful life. "I thought it was church, but I guess it's a commercial."

"Ah, you're sleeping on the couch still."

"Just last night. I must have fallen asleep watching the news."

"Uh-huh."

"I wasn't even drinking."

"I didn't say you were, Richard."

Maybe I had a guilty conscience.

"What are you doing? How's your mom?"

She sighed. "Mom's going to have to go into a home. Dad too. Both of them need constant care, and, well—"

"Are you okay?"

"It's just, I feel awful about this, but what can I do? My life—my career, is two-thousand miles away from here—and they are unable to care for themselves. I feel terrible about this situation. Putting them each in a home. Then there's the estate—"

A tone beeped in my ear and I pulled the phone away to see *unknown* displayed across the screen. That meant it was likely the office, as caller ID is blocked on the office lines. I also figured with our teams being on call, it was nearly a certainty. "Honey?"

"If my brother wasn't such a loser—"

"Babe—"

"Yes, Richard?"

"I hate to do this—"

"You have to go. Fine, goodbye."

The line went silent. Dead. There was a chill that accompanied the disconnect. "Shit!"

I switched over and growled, "Jones."

"Dickie, it's Ramirez at the desk."

"Yeah?"

"There's a D.I.S. in North Long Beach, off-duty female deputy dumped a dude during an attempted robbery."

"Jesus. When did this happen, last night?"

"No, just a half-hour ago. Team Six is handling it, but Joe thought you might want to come out with your trainee to assist."

Deputy-involved shootings could wipe out a team due to the intensity of the ensuing investigation. It has been said that a tent and three rings should be erected at the command post because the circus is coming to town. There would be a dozen or more homicide detectives accompanied by at least one of our lieutenants, and even the captain would be out there getting in the way. An area or duty commander would be driven there by some lieutenant who was bucking for captain's bars, and a host of cheese-eaters from Internal Affairs Bureau would descend upon our crime scene. Our department's Force Review board would be represented, and one or more prosecutors from CAPOS—Crimes Against Peace Officers Section —would make an appearance. Then there would be members of the Sheriff's Information Bureau there to handle the press coverage. And last, but not least, Civil Litigation would send someone with a checkbook and an authorization to spend the taxpayers' money. Their job was to pay off the next-of-kin without admitting any wrongdoing on the part of the sheriff's department, and to do so before the lawyer sharks smelled blood in the water.

"I'll give my partner a call. Where are we going?"

"She's in the office," he said. "I'll let her know you guys are rolling."

I frowned across an empty living room. "Okay, thanks. Tell her I'll call when I get on the road."

BY THE TIME I ARRIVED AT THE SCENE, HALF OF THE AFOREMENTIONED circus performers had arrived and were mostly huddling with their own, hesitant to approach the lion tamers. It didn't matter if the sheriff himself arrived, homicide detectives were in charge of the scene and nobody—not even the sheriff—entered or exited a cordoned area without tacit approval from the assigned investigators, and only with good reason. It had become a tradition to gather the entire crowd and conduct one walkthrough of the crime scene so that all of those involved could be briefed and would feel that they were part of the process. Only the prosecutor, whose job it would be to review the case after the investigation was concluded, mattered. All of the other suits at the scene were irrelevant to me. Most homicide detectives felt the same way. We were there to investigate the killing of a human being, and on the law enforcement food chain, there is nothing more profound. Whether or not a deputy used proper tactics and a departmentally approved off-duty weapon meant nothing to us. We couldn't care less. The deputy could have used a bazooka and our focus would still be the same: Are the circumstances surrounding her use of deadly force legally justified? We would gather the facts and CAPOS would make the determination. Or, in a worst-case scenario, a judge or jury would. But first, CAPOS would declare it a justifiable homicide, or a murder, or something in between, perhaps manslaughter. Ninety-nine percent of deputy- and officer-involved shootings are justified, and no further legal action is taken against the shooter or shooters.

Because Josie and I had not been assigned to assist on this particular case, the handling detectives asked that we make the next-of-kin notifications and start a background on the decedent. We were given the short version of the events as provided by the shooter deputy in a preliminary statement to the first units on the scene. The deputy said she was placing her bag in the trunk of her car, preparing to leave for work, when the suspect approached and attempted to rob her. Her backup gun was easily accessible to her—easier than her everyday off-duty pistol that was located in the purse slung on her shoulder—so she pulled her weapon from the bag as the suspect struggled to retrieve a revolver from his pants pocket. She could see the grip of his gun, and though she didn't recall him saying anything, she knew he was trying to rob her. Before she could give any commands for him to stop, he had freed his gun and was bringing it up with the muzzle coming toward her. She fired two shots at center mass and he had dropped.

We were all relieved it turned out the way it did, and not another way. In the recent past our department had lost a deputy in a similar situation, and years before that, a female LAPD officer had been shot multiple times in an eerily similar situation. This one had a happy ending, as far as any of us were concerned.

Before we departed the scene to carry out our assigned tasks, Josie gazed for a moment at the dead man lying on the sidewalk with his legs twisted awkwardly around the frame of a bicycle. When she saw me watching, she said, "I know that asshole."

12

At seven o'clock Monday morning my cell phone vibrated on the kitchen table as I sat eating a bowl of cereal, some type of granola with dried fruits and nuts topped with yogurt and low-fat milk. I found my desire to cook had dwindled quickly after Valerie had left me a bachelor again, so it was back to fast and simple for me. The caller ID said *private number,* so I assumed it was the office, though I hoped it was Katherine.

"This is Richard."

"Good morning, Dickie." It was the office, an investigator named Jason Campbell whom everyone called Jay. His high-pitched voice was easily recognizable, and the nature of the call predictable. Having just picked up a murder, the odds were that one of my two victims—or maybe both—were scheduled for a postmortem examination. Also known as an autopsy.

"Morning, Jay. I take it there's a post this morning."

"You guessed it. Eight o'clock with Doctor Strickland on your victim, Nguyen."

I asked if my partner had been notified, and was told no, they called me first. I told them I would take care of notifying Sanchez, and then I disconnected and called my new partner.

"Have you ever seen an autopsy?"

"Only on TV," she said, "*NCIS, Criminal Minds*."

"Well, you don't get the sights and sounds on TV; this is one of those things you just have to experience firsthand to fully appreciate. Did they issue you a respirator yet?"

"Yes."

"Good. Bring it with you and meet me at the coroner's office."

"Where do I go?"

I glanced at my watch. "Can you be at the office by seven-forty-five?"

"I think so."

"Okay, let's meet there and we'll go together. We'll need to go to the crime lab afterwards anyway."

<hr />

WE ARRIVED AT THE CORONER'S OFFICE AND ENTERED THROUGH THE BACK, where white vans with blue stripes would be backed to the docks in order to have their cargo unloaded. This morning seemed fairly routine with two vans at the dock and swarms of flies buzzing under the covered shelter that is the loading—or rather, *unloading*—dock. The putrid smell of decaying flesh mixed with a strong chemical odor welcomed you each and every time. Josie had her nose turned up long before we breached the doorway.

The entrance marked *Employees Only* is where cops enter, and on most mornings, you will find a receptionist who sits behind a counter answering phones and working with a computer while visitors come and go. There is a sign-in sheet for guests but nobody to verify ID or your purpose for entering. Homicide detectives are regular visitors and probably easily recognizable. Besides, it wasn't as if people were dying to get in here. Well, actually . . .

Before turning into the hallways of the service floor, I paused briefly to make sure Josie had time to admire the gigantic fish tank. Big, ugly fish swam about lazily in the murky water, bumping the glass at the sight of new onlookers. Josie frowned and turned away from it.

"Trust me, you don't even want to know what they feed the fish."

"Gross."

I slid my respirator over my mouth and nose. Josie did the same, then followed me into the supply room where visitors and staff alike don protective clothing prior to entering the examination rooms. As I pulled various items from shelves and bins, I indicated with a motion of my head for her to dig in. "Cover everything you can," I said, speaking slowly as the words labored to break through the apparatus covering half of my face. "You'll be glad you did, once we're standing table-side and shit is splattering everywhere while the techs wash the body down."

She began opening items of clothing and holding them against her petite frame to see what would fit.

"Also, you'll want to keep a pen and your notebook handy because once you put all this shit on, you'll never find either one if you leave them in a pocket. Make sure you have a business card handy too. It's easier to hand a card to the doctor than to try talking to each other through masks."

We donned blue paper gowns, booties, and hats, and I told her the eye protection was a good idea too, but I had never gotten into the habit of wearing it. Finally, we put on thick nitrile gloves and continued our journey into the house of horrors through hallways lined with stainless steel tables on wheels, some with bodies, some without. Some of the bodies were wrapped in plastic, others were not. Some were bathed and awaiting photographs, x-rays, and their final medical examination, others had just arrived, and still others had completed the process and were prepared for departure. Josie took it all in silently, though the plastic face shield she wore did little to conceal the disgust in her eyes.

I leaned toward her and raised my voice to speak through my respirator. "You don't want to go horizontal here, ever. You get tired, sleep standing up."

My smile faded as I noticed the solemn look on her face. "You okay?"

She nodded, unconvincingly.

The examination rooms are on opposite sides at the end of the hallway. Both rooms have swinging doors with small 12x12 glass windows at eye level, and there is room for about half a dozen examinations in each. I looked into one room and then the other before I recognized Ho Nguyen on one of several occupied tables in the second room.

The doctor and an assistant had started before our arrival a little past eight, and I could see that their charting was just about completed. I stepped close to Josie and lifted my respirator slightly. "When we're finished here, I'll walk you through the process that precedes the actual autopsy. You should be familiar with all of the stages, and hopefully we'll see them prepping other bodies. If not, maybe we'll come early for the next one so that you can see the whole process. But basically, before they get to this part of it, there's a lot that takes place. Notice how the body is relatively clean?"

She nodded.

"The body is first taken for photographs in a room down the hall, in just the condition it arrived. Head to toe, front and back. Then they collect the clothing and carefully preserve it in the event there is trace evidence. After that, they wash the body, and the photoshoot is repeated with him—or her—naked. They get height and weight and run him through x-rays. The techs will also fingerprint him unless that was done in the field. That happens on occasion; it just depends. Same with nail scrapings and the collection of the victim's hair: sometimes it has been done in the field by a coroner's investigator, and other times they do it here. There's a few variables, but the point I'm trying to make is that it's ultimately your call out there. You're the one who sees this case through to the end, all the way up to an execution if you're lucky. It's not the coroner or the crime lab or your idiot captain or any other host of people who become involved through the process. Not even the D.A. That's one of the things that pisses me off, these cases get to trial and all of a sudden this deputy District Attorney who only leaves his office to play tennis during lunch acts like the case is his baby. But the truth is, they're an uncle at best. They weren't there when it was born and they didn't walk it through every stage of life. They don't know the case the way you do, and they haven't stood over the body at the scene or sat in the living room with the grieving mother. At the very best they've seen the photos and showed up for the birthday parties along the way. I guess this might not be the best metaphor for dead people, huh?"

I could see she smiled finally; it showed in her eyes.

"But you get my point."

Josie nodded.

"Out there in the field, you own the scene. There is a reason we call the coroner when we're ready, not the other way around. Yes, the body is theirs, and we don't physically touch it at the scene until a coroner's investigator is there with us. But, the scene is ours, and the victim's body is part of that scene. If you want nail scrapings out there, ask the coroner's investigator for it when he examines the body. If you want him printed out there, ask for it. There's very few coroner's investigators who are hard to work with, and it won't take you long to know who they are."

It appeared Doctor Strickland had finished his charting and notes and was close to cutting. He acknowledged our presence during the break that naturally occurs between all of the preparation and the physical act of dissection. He greeted me with a simple nod and a three-syllable utterance: "Detective." Then he leaned close to Josie and spoke to her, though I couldn't understand anything he said as it was garbled through his mask. She handed him a business card, and he examined it before placing it on a table with his notes. He jotted her name onto his notes and glanced at me once more before making note of mine. He wouldn't require a card or introduction from the only blue-clothed man with a fedora.

He set his pen down and looked each of us in the eyes, alternating from one to the other as he held his respirator an inch or so from his face to speak. "This poor bastard looks like he was killed in war." He stepped around to the side of the table, still holding his respirator away from his mouth as he pointed out the various gunshot wounds that stretched from head to toe. "I've charted sixteen gunshot wounds, though some of those are exits."

I nodded. "How do the x-rays look? Anything stay in him?"

He motioned for me to follow and I nodded at Josie to extend the invitation. The three of us stepped a few feet away from the table and Doctor Strickland flipped a switch to light up an x-ray film illuminator that hung on the back wall. He flipped through the images, snapping one sheet of film after the other into the clips that hold them against the illuminated screen. Moving through them quickly, he pointed out white blemishes in the shapes of projectiles and fragments throughout the thorax, both legs, and the victim's head. Doctor Strickland lifted his respirator again and shouted over the noise of an electric saw two tables down, where the skull of a woman was being removed. "There were quite a few through-and-throughs, but I'd bet we get a couple of clean projectiles out of him, and probably another dozen or so fragments."

He pulled the films from the board and tossed them carelessly on a nearby table and went back to his work. Doctor Strickland pulled an overhead light closer and leaned over his subject with a scalpel, and without further conversation or consideration, he carved a Y across the front of Mr. Ho Nguyen by making two long, deep cuts from the shoulders to the sternum, and then one long cut from where those two intersected all the way down to the pubis.

Josie's eyes showed intensity, but not fear or loathing or excitement; the look seemed to be that of morbid curiosity. I leaned toward her. "It's not like surgery, or what you see on TV."

She glanced up and gave me a slight shake of her head.

"Wait till they remove the breast plate."

As I said it, Doctor Strickland retrieved the tool they use to cut through ribs, which is nothing more than small pruning shears. I watched Josie's eyes widen with anticipation. She glanced at me and I smiled, though I have no idea if she knew it. The doctor began cutting the breast plate away by clipping through the ribs at the far sides of the cage until the entire section could be removed as one piece. The snapping, popping sounds of the tool defeating each rib are similar to the sound of pruning branches that are on the edge of being too large to prune. It is a barbaric display never to be forgotten, and all too often recalled.

"It changes your appetite for ribs, too."

Josie lifted her mask. "Really, there's no other way to do this?"

There is, and I debated telling her at this time. Maybe it would be a conversation during our drive to the lab afterwards, or on a long night working the desk on Early Mornings, graveyard barrel duty. I was thinking about an autopsy of a deputy sheriff, the first of several I had attended. They were all similarly conducted, but the first is the one that made the greatest impression. It was the difference in reverence for which I am eternally grateful. All stages and aspects of the examination were careful, considerate, delicately performed. As if it were surgery, perhaps while a loved one watched. There were no other autopsies at the time of the deputy's; it had been scheduled for the afternoon in order to have a private room. Murdered cop posts are attended by a large and solemn audience, and all efforts to remove the usual horror house butcher shop atmosphere are made. When the breast plate was removed, each rib was carefully cut with a scalpel. The pruning sheers never appeared. All of the care and respect that could possibly be presented during such an awful procedure were enacted.

Josie leaned forward and stretched her neck to see inside what I call the canoe. It is a sight to see the first time, and then one to overlook thereafter. Doctor Strickland removed organs one at a time, carefully examining each for damage and evidence before weighing and recording the results of these observations onto his notes. Some doctors dictated, and others just called it out and a tech would write it on his notes. Doctor Strickland seemed to be more of a hands-on, orderly, and set-in-his-ways type. When an organ was found to be perforated, he would take his time to go back to the x-ray board and compare the image to the organ. This would assure him of where he might expect to find evidence, and how many items of evidence might exist, before the dissecting would begin.

The remainder of the body examination focused much on the recovery of projectile evidence. With each bullet or fragment thereof, careful notes were taken as to the location of the recovery and path of its travel. Sometimes this would require organs to be replaced and the use of rods to connect entries and exits and paths thereof.

"This is one of the reasons we attend autopsies," I told Josie. "There have been times when they get it wrong because they have no idea what happened out there. Our job is to fill in the blanks and provide clarity when needed. Sometimes, something as simple as knowing from evidence at the scene or a witness that a particular wound could have only happened one way, can eliminate excess prodding and mistaken assessments."

Josie nodded without taking her eyes off of the action.

Doctor Strickland had now stepped back to the cart where his notes and tools sat with an assortment of envelopes that were stained with body fluids transferred from soiled gloves. He thumbed through the envelopes and examined the contents of each to make certain the proper notations accompanied the evidence and corresponded with his notes. After a few minutes of doing so, he looked up and pulled the respirator from his mouth. "Are you taking the evidence?"

He saw my nod, but likely only heard the response through my mask as "Mmehn hmpf."

Doctor Strickland asked his technician to summon the evidence custodian to our table. I knew from experience—as clearly did he—that this could take some time, which is likely why he called for it before concluding his examination. The x-rays had clearly shown a projectile fragment in the victim's head, which had not yet been examined. Just as I reconciled the thought, Doctor Strickland called out to the back of his technician: "Tell him to give me fifteen minutes."

With that came the grand finale. I bumped Josie's elbow with mine and took a couple steps backward. She followed my lead. The doctor took only a moment to peel the victim's scalp by making a small incision and then skinning it back. The front was pulled forward and left covering his face. The back fell loosely against the block that held his head high off of the table. Once the top and back of his head were fully exposed, the sound of an electric saw buzzing through his skull crackled through the room. I had no doubt Josie could see the fine spray of flesh and bone matter misting beyond the safe zone of the examination, which truly didn't exist. She would likely be thankful that we had repositioned. Once the cutting was finished, a chisel and hammer aided in the removal of the skull cap, which was another procedure that had been handled quite differently during the deputy's examination. The brain was removed, and as with the organs, it was weighed and examined and then dissected until the evidence was recovered.

It had been nearly two hours since we had arrived. Some autopsies took longer than others. I had once attended a three-day autopsy, each day consisting of about four to five hours of examination. The decedent had been killed in a police-involved shooting that involved four agencies and two dozen shooters. I had left after the third session with 128 envelopes of firearms-related evidence. Two hours seemed long and I was looking forward to leaving, but I often reflected on the three-day autopsy to put all others in perspective.

Josie followed my lead on the way out, tearing away the protective paper clothing. She wadded it up and stuffed it, hard, into a nearby trash can that already overflowed with more of the same. It reminded me of a case to which one of my former partners and I had been assigned. I shared it with Josie as we walked to my car. Floyd and I had had an assist to El Monte PD. Our department investigates their homicide cases for them, as we do for many of the smaller agencies within our county, at their request. Some agencies will assign one of their detectives to act as a liaison of sorts. A female, new to detectives, was assigned to us and came along to the autopsy. It was her first. On the way out the door, she not only discarded the paper clothing, she also threw away her department-issued respirator. Grinning, I told her she might need that for her next case. I couldn't tell if it was more fear or revulsion on her face, but she spat, "I am *never* coming back to this fucking place."

When I finished telling Josie the story, I looked over at her from behind the wheel with a wide grin on my face. She said, "Yeah, well, that's some weak-ass shit."

I smiled. *The Outlaw Josie Sanchez.*

13

F loyd looked up from a magazine as I walked into the office carrying two 6x9 envelopes stuffed full of 4x6 photographs. Josie peeled off, turning down Team Five's row of desks, headed toward her seat. I continued toward my old desk on Team Two, now occupied by Mongo. When I got there, I pulled a chair from an empty desk and rolled it to a position between Mongo and Floyd, neither of whom looked up. Floyd had his nose in a magazine.

"What are you reading?"

He tossed the magazine onto Mongo's desk and said, "Bullshit."

Mongo chuckled, and his chest and belly shook. Floyd was shaking his head when he turned to me and said, "This dipshit seems to take pleasure in seeing how bad he can piss me off."

"Yeah? Let me see."

Mongo handed me the magazine and it didn't take any time to see what Floyd had been reading. There was a story on Bruce Lee featured on the front cover. The article was easily found inside by a creased page where the story began. Floyd had always admired Lee for his martial arts skills, and there was little doubt this story would be less than glorifying, given Floyd's reaction. I figured it was probably a hit piece on the martial arts legend.

It started with Lee's childhood, reporting that the young Bruce Lee had, at one point, formed a gang of sorts among his peers. Taking to the life of crime, he reportedly pulled a knife on his PE teacher. It went on to allege that Lee had forced a boy to pull down his pants and then painted the boy's genitals with red paint he had stolen from a construction site. Police had considered the boy Lee a delinquent, according to the story. Then, as a man, Lee was said to be a philandering playboy who cheated on his wife and had "cut a wide swath" through the female production of actresses, groupies, housewives, and hatcheck girls. It is said he underwent circumcision to be more like an American, and that many described Lee as vain and arrogant. There were reports that he had had issues with his temper and a craving for control, traits that were played out in his treatment of women. Martial Artist-turned-movie star Bruce Lee, the man who introduced the western world to his Taoist philosophy and had opened the door to martial arts in the west, who had been a kung fu instructor to the Hollywood elites such as James Coburn and Steve McQueen, was said to have died of heat stroke at 32 years of age.

I returned the rag to Mongo as Floyd watched me carefully, no doubt interested in my take on the report.

"Well?" I said.

"He didn't die of no fucking heat stroke."

Mongo snickered again.

What could I say? I didn't know if any parts of the story were true, and how he died seemed to be the least contentious part of it. But not for Floyd. I handed him the envelopes with his name on them. "These are from the lab. Gentry asked me to drop them off to you, said you had put a rush on them and that he had come in early to get them done."

Floyd took the two envelopes and thanked me. "He's a good man."

I agreed.

"But do you believe this shit with Mongo? This asshole is going to bring this blasphemous bullshit in here and present it like it's the *truth* about Bruce Lee. I ought to kick him in the head and show him the truth about Lee, the dumb bastard."

Mongo had turned back to his desk and his head was down, but his shoulders were shaking, and I thought I heard a snort. I was grinning widely myself at this point.

Floyd tossed the envelopes of photos onto his desk, staring at the back of Mongo's head. "Do you hear me, Mongo? Hey, asshole . . . *Fucking heat stroke.*"

Mongo turned to reveal a red puckered face with tears coming out of his eyes. I began laughing too, and Mongo turned away. Floyd stood up from his chair and walked away, mumbling something about kicking both of our asses. He hadn't smiled once during the conversation, and it occurred to me this had been a serious affront to him.

"I guess he was serious," I said. But Mongo couldn't talk. He never talked anyway, but this time he actually *couldn't* say a word as he fought to contain his laughter. I had nothing left to say, so I rose from my chair and left Mongo there snorting.

" '*HE PASSED AWAY PEACEFULLY.*' WORDS I'M SURE WILL ESCAPE ANY eulogy of mine."

I set the Star News down on my desk with other mail I had carried back from the front desk. Josie looked up. "Obits in the department rag," I clarified. She nodded and went back to reading from a stack of reports on her desk.

"What's that?"

She didn't look up. "Oh, just some robberies."

I pulled up my chair. "What robberies? What do you have going on?"

She stopped and swiveled her chair to face me. "Friday night before leaving the office, I called the crime analyst from Compton Gangs, Loretta. I asked if she could go back six months and pull all of the liquor store and market armed robbery cases in a thirty-mile radius from Ho's that involved two suspects. There aren't as many as you would think, to be honest, because I didn't have her put any other qualifiers on the search. I figured it would be best to have a big pile to wade through rather than taking a chance of missing something. After all, we don't know anything about our killers, even their race."

"Not bad, Detective."

She smiled. "Thank you."

"So your premise would be that there has been an escalation, that there would be straight robberies preceding those accompanied by killing."

"Yeah, I think it's a possibility."

I nodded. "I think it's brilliant. Have you found anything interesting yet?"

"I just started. She must have dropped them off this morning on her way to the office while we were at the autopsy."

"Speaking of, I'm getting sort of hungry." I glanced at my watch and saw it was nearing noon. My internal clock was right on track. "What about you?"

She stuck her tongue out. "I think I'll be losing weight around here, if I have to keep going to that awful place."

"Well, you do have to continue going, if you're going to stick around. But you won't lose any weight from the autopsies. You'll actually get used to them, believe it or not. There's just certain types of food I avoid when I leave there, like ribs. Maybe spaghetti too."

"I don't think I'll ever get used to seeing people carved up. I pray to God I don't."

I chuckled. "Let me know what you come up with from those reports. I'm going to see if my sister has powered through her hormonal imbalance and is ready for lunch."

Josie's brows narrowed. "Your sister?"

"Floyd."

She smiled. "Oh, gotcha. Mr. Pretty Boy."

IT WAS ALMOST NOON WHEN TRAVIS WALKED INTO THE LIVING ROOM, barefoot and shirtless with a cigarette dangling from his mouth and sleep in his eyes. His long brown hair was disheveled and his beard resembled a rat's nest. He wore the standard issue black tactical pants with a belt. The butt of a gun protruded from the waistline, pushing into his belly fat. Tina averted her eyes and focused on the book on her lap, a John Grisham novel about lawyers and murder. She heard him shuffle off, and glanced up to see his sagging drawers. The man had no ass, and a hairy back.

From the kitchen he called out to her. "Where's that little shithead brother of yours?"

She drew a deep breath and paused, careful not to react to his words. "He's out."

Travis Hollingsworth stuck his head around the corner to glare at her. "I know he's out, I can smell that much. Where the hell is he?"

Tina again broke eye contact as she answered. "He had errands."

"Well that's special. Why don't you call him or text him or whatever and tell him to bring back something to eat. There ain't nothing here to eat in this goddamn place, except beans and tortillas."

"He's casing some places. I'm not going to call him while he's working."

Travis had walked back into the living room. He stood rubbing his hairy belly and grinning until she glanced up again. "Well, then send him a text. Tell beaner-boy I need some fucking food, or I'm about to get downright unpleasant, and his big sister's going to pay the price."

Tina thought about killing him. It hadn't been the first time she considered it, and it wouldn't be the last. In fact, she realized it would be her only way out, an exit plan she might need to implement sooner rather than later, before it was too late. But the time and place had to be just right, and she hadn't worked out the details. She did know it would be imperative that his body was never found. His discovery would confirm her status as alive and well, and AWOL from the United States Army. She didn't want to have to flee to Mexico, so she would need to be careful in her planning. And she would have to get Carlos on board, but first she'd need to see that he could handle killing. She proffered a placating smile and said, "I'll make you a couple burritos while you shower."

MONGO DIDN'T JOIN US FOR LUNCH. FLOYD, STILL PISSED, SAID, "THAT jackwad started working out at a kickboxing gym a month ago—"

"Who, Mongo?"

"Yeah, dickhead, Mongo. He's trying to lose weight, and now all of a sudden, the guy is kung fu fuckin' panda. A roly-poly, J.D.-drinking, snoring-while-he's wide-awake, expert in the martial arts. Even though he can't kick higher than your knee. *Then*, he has a good laugh over badmouthing the godfather of martial arts. I swear sometimes I think God hates me."

"Josie's turning out okay, so far. You might've been right about her."

"Of course I was right, Dickie. Shit, just look at her. You're riding around with Jennifer Lopez and I've got kung fu panda taking up two-thirds of my front seat. You just let me know if you want to trade, pal."

"Jennifer Lopez?"

"J-Lo."

I guess I had never known her real name. Had I thought that was her name, *J-Lo?* I didn't know.

"She's a good cop, has good investigative instinct."

"Yeah, I told you as much," Floyd said, as his eyes wandered around the food court.

"She's got a stack of reports she's going through, looking at two-elevens with two suspects. Trying to find something we can sink our teeth into."

"There's got to be hundreds."

"Not as many as you'd think, surprisingly. She narrowed the search to only a couple of cases where two suspects hit markets and liquor stores in a thirty-mile radius of Ho's, our Compton murder. At least in the last couple months."

He frowned. "And you're telling me that's all there is? I call bullshit."

"I was surprised."

"Well, good for her, but I bet she missed something. There's got to be a shitload of robberies with two suspects."

"Right?"

"So, are you thinking these assholes started out doing robberies without killing?"

I shrugged. "It was her thought, and not a bad one. What's new with your deal, you and your boy, Cedric?"

"I was turned down for paper."

"Wait, what? You had a warrant rejected?"

"First time in my life. Went to the wrong judge, apparently."

"Who'd you go to?"

"Me and Mongo had court in Compton, so I just went with Moore.

He's usually so hungover or drunk he doesn't even read them, or at least that's what I thought. The sonofabitch read this one though, the entire affidavit. Then the bastard says, 'You want a warrant when you've got no crime?' I told him I wanted a warrant to prove that a crime occurred. He said to come back when I had a victim. You believe that shit?"

"You should have gone to Tracy."

Floyd was finishing his soda, tipping the paper cup up to get the last of it. When he set it down he said, "Banuelos?"

"Uh-huh."

"Shit, I forgot she was a judge now. She's in Compton?"

"I saw her last week."

"She still hot?"

"Uh-huh."

"Well, there ya go, Dickie. It's what I've been trying to tell you, I'm in a slump. Don't even know about hot judges and I get a warrant kicked back by a drunk. And it started with this goddamn kung fu panda partner of mine. We need to get back together, *Dickie Floyd*, before I lose all my mojo."

I laughed. "I've got to get back, check on my girl. Let me know when we can set up movie night with Cedric."

"You've got film?"

"It's not great, but he should be able to say if it looks like the same two blobs of black clothing, based on shapes and sizes."

"Plan, Dickie. Catch ya later."

14

W e moved along slowly in the Monday afternoon traffic while heading back to our latest crime scene for follow-up investigation. I asked Josie if anything had come from her search of robberies in the area.

She frowned. "Not what I had hoped. Couple of crackheads did one or two jobs in Compton, but one is in custody and the other is named. Two kids pulled a job over in the Vermont District, but both are midgets—"

"Midgets?"

She grinned. "Well, both are shorter than me, so we're not interested. And there were two robberies in Long Beach that looked good at first, but I don't think they're related."

"Why is that?"

"One of the two suspects was a female, at least on one of the robberies for sure. The other job there were actually three suspects, not two. The report only listed two, so that's how it landed in my pile, but when you read it, there was a getaway driver that wasn't seen by anyone, so he wasn't described on the face sheet of the report. But that makes it three suspects. The detectives have those two cases listed as being related."

"Interesting."

"What's that?"

"Well, could there have been a driver on our murder? I don't think we know."

"Yeah, you're right, we don't know. I guess there could have been."

It might have been a long shot, but I felt it was worth looking at anyway. "Who are the detectives? Do you know?"

"I don't know. They're both Long Beach PD cases. I'm not even sure how Loretta knew about them, or how she got the reports."

"There's some good dicks in Long Beach. We should probably look into those two cases a little closer, see if there's anything at all we like about them maybe being related to ours. Were the suspects wearing masks?"

"Yep, just like our case. That's what I liked about it from the start, but then the woman . . ."

"How do they know one of them was a woman?"

"Apparently she said something to the other suspect during the robbery. According to the witness, it was a woman's voice."

I thought about it for a moment. "Okay, then how do we know our suspects are both men?"

I had just rolled to a stop not far from our office, crossing through Bell Gardens on our way into Los Angeles. I glanced over and waited while Josie sat silent. She was looking at me and she seemed to be pondering the idea of it. Finally, she shook her head. "I guess we really *don't* know."

"Maybe the smaller of the two is a woman."

"That'd be one crazy bitch," Josie said, and returned her gaze toward the bustle on the streets.

"That is a fact."

A few minutes of silence followed. I could smell the freshness of a woman bathed in floral shampoos or soaps and not drowned by perfumes. The fragrance reminded me of Katherine, though her scent was a bit more subdued. I pictured Katherine taking care of her mother, tending to her father, putting all of her life's priorities on hold. Including me. But that was okay; I was at the point in my life where a short phone conversation, a quick note in the mail, or even a text or an email would suffice. It was enough to be thought of, to be considered. I wondered if she was thinking of me.

I looked over to see my partner still gazing through the passenger's window as we continued south into Los Angeles, on our way to Compton. I couldn't help but notice the sleek lines of her profile and her silky black hair that laid nicely on her shoulders. I inhaled through my nose to enjoy her fresh scent, and the next thing I knew, I had pictured her out of the shower. Fresh. Wet. The bouquet of wild flowers wafting through the car put me right in her most private of moments in my head. Maybe Floyd was right about this. Maybe men and women shouldn't spend the amount of time together that the job requires, at least not if either are otherwise involved. There is an intimacy between partners that is often unspoken, but always realized. And without malice aforethought, the seeds of lust and temptation can grow. I forced my mind back to Katherine and her ailing parents. To hell with Floyd.

She glanced over and caught me looking at her. "Wouldn't the freeway be faster?"

Probably, but who was in a hurry? Not me; there was nothing to hurry home to, and I had found myself enjoying every minute with my new partner. Was that inappropriate? I didn't know. I didn't think so, but Floyd was in my head now. I'd ask him—not Katherine—about it. My two counselors.

I had taken surface streets from the office, which was always my preference. The smog seemed hardly noticeable on this otherwise lovely afternoon in the County of Los Angeles. Somewhere, two ferocious killers sat in the comfort of their home, or maybe they still slept after a long night of terrorizing somebody's community or family. I often thought about killers and wondered what they were doing when not committing their heinous crimes. I would think about them while I enjoyed a cocktail on my patio or in my favorite watering hole, and I would wonder if they too were sitting on a patio somewhere with a cocktail. Enjoying a nice evening, speaking to the neighbors, playing with the family dog. I generally concluded that these killers and thugs didn't enjoy nice evenings, neither did they appreciate scenic views nor savor fine cocktails in a civilized manner. They had no appreciation for the finer parts of life, and they had no appreciation for life itself. These people were sociopaths, hell-bent on plowing through the world with no regret for the death and destruction they left behind. Once skunked on their cheap drink, they'd take their hostilities toward the world out on whatever life-hostage they had taken for a mate.

This train of thought would inevitably lead me to the next—one I had never shared with Katherine or with either of my wives—which was, killers like this duo who were gunning down innocent people, thugs like the Regalados and their mastermind, Donna Edwards, were soulless reptiles who should have their heads cut off and buried in separate holes, apart from the rest of their bodies. Public hangings should make a comeback; that's how you deter crime.

Josie seemed to be waiting for an explanation. I said, "You miss out on all the action from the freeways. It's like going through life looking at your cell phone. You don't see what's really going on in the world. You think you're up on everything, but you missed the good stuff while looking at Facebook."

"But it *is* faster."

I pondered that a moment. "Are you in a hurry?"

"No."

I glanced back and forth from the road to my partner and let that sit for a moment. "This isn't the job for people in a hurry. Nothing is fast here other than the pace of new cases. But the process is slow, methodical, carefully considered, and never rushed. It's why nobody really bothers to keep time records here; none of us wants to know how much of our lives we give to the county. But that's also why the lieutenants don't blink when you hand them overtime slips, and why they don't ask you to submit a time off request when you stay home because you're under the weather. They know we put in far more hours than we'll ever be compensated for, and that we never truly have time off."

She alternated between looking straight ahead and turning to look out the side window, taking in the street-view action, people moving about on congested sidewalks where street vendors populated every corner, making it feel more and more like the home most of them had left behind.

"When Floyd and I were together, we tried taking vacations at the same time. Inevitably, court cases would pop up or there would be a break in a case. There'd be someone new to talk to, or a suspect identified by DNA or prints or something, and we'd have to swing into action. We never seemed to get a true break from the job. Then we decided to take separate vacations so that one of us could handle such issues while the other enjoyed his family. Well, that didn't work either, because whatever one of us got ourselves into, the other seemed obligated to join in. It would start with a simple phone call, 'Hey, partner, just letting you know we had a break on the Smith case, a suspect in custody at Lennox,' and then the one on vacation would ask the other if he needed a hand, and there would be the, 'Ah, nah, I think I can handle it.' Then, before you knew it, the two of us would be strategizing over a fresh cup of coffee at one sheriff's station or another, or at some random police station where we would be summoned to investigate a murder, while a suspect sat sweating in the box, waiting for what he knew was coming."

"You and Floyd were partners for a long time."

She was looking at me now with some sort of expectation, or so it seemed. New partners will eventually talk about old partners in the way new couples eventually get around to talking about their exes. It seemed to me it was part of the bonding process, and no different from a budding romance, the fewer secrets the better. Though in some situations, it was those kept secrets that allowed the romance to continue; you had to find that balance. The light turned green and I turned onto Atlantic. The conversation would be delayed until another ride, another day or night, another time of intellectual intimacy between two cops testing the waters of partnership. There's a difference between working together and being partners.

"Yeah, we were. Keep your eyes peeled around here for that van."

CARLOS CAME BACK WITH MCDONALD'S AND TRAVIS SAID, "WHAT'D YOU do, get a Happy Meal?"

Tina was in the kitchen cleaning up after the two men in the house. There were empty beer containers and overflowing ashtrays and the remnants of midnight snacks strewn about the counters and table. She had finally given in once it was clear nobody else would lift a finger. She met Carlos at the table with a beer. He gladly accepted the beer and then tore open the McDonald's bag to reveal two wrapped burgers and an order of fries. He motioned to one of the burgers and she shook her head.

Travis said, "I'd take one."

"You've eaten. Let the poor kid have his lunch."

Travis laughed at her. "Well, the least you can do is grab your ol' man a beer too."

Tina returned to the fridge and grabbed two more. Soon the three of them sat at the small table in the dimly-lit dining room—their blinds remained closed at all times—and Tina asked her brother what he found out today. Travis rolled his eyes as if he didn't expect much from him.

Carlos didn't finish chewing before he started. "Well, that gook is still alive, as you said. I seen him today. And as far as other stores around that we might could hit, there's one or two."

"Fucking brilliant, I'll tell you."

Tina glared at *her man* for the comment.

"But I came up with a better idea anyway."

Travis plopped his beer down on the table. "Oh, I'm sure this is going to be good."

"Armored cars."

Tina watched for Travis's reaction but couldn't read him, which didn't happen often. He was rather simple to figure out and even easier to manipulate.

Carlos continued. "The guards are sloppy. I seen 'em. In fact, I started following one of 'em around after I seen 'em pick up money bags at that market with the gook you didn't kill. They left there, went to two other markets and then a check cashing place. Every place they stopped, they went in with empty bags and came out with bags full of money. Sometimes, they wheel it out on a little cart. Other times, the dude just carries a bag. It's alway just the one guy with a pistol though that gets out. The driver waits in the truck. It seems to me it'd be easy enough to take him."

Travis took a long pull on his can of beer and set it down resolutely. He nodded to Tina. "Get me another beer."

She wanted to tell him to fuck himself, but instead she got up and took another beer out of the fridge. Her brother was off his rocker. *Armored cars.* But as she considered it, she saw Travis being gunned down during the attempt, and thought maybe this would be the way to make it happen. Then she remembered he needed to disappear. She handed Travis the beer and looked at her brother.

"I don't like it, *hermanito*. Too much risk. They have guns and they will shoot it out. The guy in the truck shoots out the little windows. They won't open it up."

Travis was watching her, but he didn't respond for a moment. He looked at Carlos and smiled through his scraggly beard. "I like it."

15

Tina left the two men in her life sitting at the table discussing how to take down an armored car. She locked her bedroom door and started filling the tub in the master bathroom she shared with Travis. She watched herself undress in the mirror, slowly unbuttoning her blouse and letting it fall to the floor behind her, and then wiggling her hips as she pushed her jeans into a heap at her feet. Standing in her panties and a lace bra, she turned each direction and evaluated her body. She had gained twenty pounds since leaving the army, but she was by no means fat. She pictured herself standing naked in front of Morgan—Lt. James P. Morgan—and pictured him smiling at what he saw.

Jesus, had she messed up her life.

She wished now that she hadn't made such a hasty decision. She was driven by adrenaline, she had discovered, and that drive had brought her to where she is today. A wanted outlaw. A fugitive, *Absent Without Leave* from the United States Army. She unfastened her bra and slipped out of her panties, still appraising her physique. As she lowered herself into her bath, she thought back to the day her life had changed forever, just two years earlier.

They had been out on a training mission. PFC Christina Ortiz was driving an LMTV—Light Medium Tactical Vehicle—and Sgt. Travis Hollingsworth rode shotgun. He was the TC—truck commander—and there were five soldiers aboard, riding in the open-backed cargo area. In the preceding weeks, Texas had been pummeled by severe storms, resulting in saturated ground and swollen creeks, bayous, and rivers. All were susceptible to flash flooding. The governor had declared a state of emergency, with Central Texas receiving seven inches of rainfall in the first two days of June. The crew had been crossing the unusually swift waters of Owl Creek when their vehicle suddenly sank into the earth and became stuck.

The rain began pouring down, sending torrential waters through the already vulnerable creek. An unyielding current swept away the seven-and-a-half-ton military tactical vehicle as if it were a toy. Crew members were thrown from the back as the roaring waters flipped the truck onto its side. As water gushed through the cab, Travis took Tina by her arm and pulled her with him as he climbed out through the driver's window.

Tina had been petrified, sure she would drown in the rapid waters. Her swimming skills were substandard; there was a reason she had joined the army, not the navy. Without a life preserver, she wouldn't have stood a chance if not for Travis. When they finally found shore, what seemed like miles down river, they were alone. The two of them laid on the wet ground not far from the roaring waters and panted, and then laughed, and then they each stripped off their wet clothing and Tina made love to the man who had saved her life.

She had later read in the papers that one of the surviving crew reported seeing the sergeant and Private Ortiz being swept downstream ahead of him. He could see that both were alive and fighting to keep their heads above water. She remembered wondering, while she read that article and others, what the reports might have said if someone saw them on the shore making love.

The two soldiers huddled together, fighting against the cold. They were exhausted from nearly drowning and then making intense love, and they each fell asleep beneath an ominous sky. When they awakened, the water had risen and they were nearly back in the river. The wind blew dark clouds across the horizon, and both knew there would be no helicopters sent out to find them. They dressed and began walking out, and that was when Travis suggested they never return. "Presumed dead," he had told her. "Free of the bullshit for the rest of our lives."

Young and foolish at the time, she had no idea what lay ahead.

Days later, the waters had settled and the rescue teams had concluded their intense search efforts. Only four of the seven crew members had been recovered: the survivor who reported seeing Hollingsworth and Ortiz swept away, and three dead soldiers. Three were never found: 27-year-old Sgt. William Randolph Robinson, an eight-year veteran, 31-year-old Sgt. Travis Lee Hollingsworth, a 12-year veteran; and the crew's sole female soldier, 20-year-old PFC Christina Marie Ortiz, a two-year army veteran. The latter two saw the report on the news from a motel room in Ding Dong, Texas, where they had been holed up for three days.

The first murder had been unavoidable.

The motel clerk recognized the pair and made mention of it on the fourth day when Travis went into the office to inquire about bus schedules. He still had nearly two-hundred dollars after paying for their room, and they figured that would be more than enough to get them both to California where Tina had family who would help them. After all, she had told him, all of her family were outlaws. But when the clerk told Travis he'd seen him and his gal on the news, Travis had two choices, and one meant going to the brig.

He didn't choose the brig. When they left the motel, they were nearly a thousand dollars richer and traveling by car, not bus, courtesy of a nosy clerk.

In the months that followed, rumors that the army was investigating the possibility that two of the three MIA had actually gone AWOL had spread beyond the base and made much of the news in Texas and beyond. Tina read about most of it on the internet, and she checked daily for new reports. Sergeant Robinson was presumed dead, but the other two were thought to be alive and well. The persistent presence of Army investigators from the Criminal Investigations Command lent credence to the theory, said a writer for the online Army news website.

Tina turned the water off with her toes and lay back in a tub of a lukewarm bath without bubbles. She pictured the lieutenant she had fallen for with his boyish smile and pale blue eyes. She pictured him in his dress blues, the colorful ribbons over his left chest pocket, the name Morgan over his right, silver bars adorning each shoulder that by now were probably doubled, easily on his way to making captain. Lt. James P. Morgan, a southern gentleman, born and raised in North Carolina. Too much of a gentleman, she felt, to tell her what he knew about Travis. He had only hinted that the rough and tumble soldier she had hooked up with was not the soldier he portrayed himself to be. She had asked, pried, but all she could get out of the gentleman lieutenant was, "Twelve years in and he's a sergeant. It's all I need to say."

It didn't matter to her now. Her fascination for the rough and tumble sergeant had been left far behind, and had been replaced with contempt. She needed him out of her life, and there was only one way that would ever happen. She needed to formulate that plan.

WE MET AT THE BACK OF MY CROWN VIC IN THE PARKING LOT OF EASY Liquor, commonly referred to as "Ho's," and paused there momentarily. I looked around the neighborhood to see if anything popped out at me: someone watching, a viewpoint I hadn't previously noticed, a service truck, or even a mailman or paperboy—anyone who might visit the area regularly that we could talk to and find out if they had noticed anything the morning of the murders, or any time before. Maybe someone had noticed a vehicle that seemed out of place in the days leading up to the slaughter of a respectable merchant and a pitiful man. In this case, our victims were both truly innocents who did nothing to contribute to their deaths. That wasn't always the case in this part of town.

"I meant to ask you the other day and forgot; how did you know that guy who was killed by the deputy?"

"Who, Jimmy Ortiz? He was a burglar. Everybody knew him. Well, I should say, all the cops knew him. When he's not in prison, he lives right there with his grandmother who didn't seem all that upset when we told her about his death. The garage we searched has always been his crash pad. We'd get a burglary in the area, we'd go barge into the garage and find dumbass with the stolen shit. Every time. He was easy to pick up for burglaries, so he started working off his cases as a snitch. He'd give up dope houses and sometimes robberies and murders. All the gang detectives knew him; he was a real piece of shit. I guess he's rehabilitated now though."

"I guess he is. His grandmother seemed nice enough."

"Just ignorant. There were three boys—wait, actually, I think it was four—and a girl. All the boys were shitheads, and now that Jimmy's dead, I'd say they are all either dead or in prison. He was the last left in the neighborhood, living there with Grandma."

"Jimmy."

"Jimmy Ortiz. Jimmy, Johnny, and Jesse were the three oldest boys, all gangsters and dopers. I forget the younger boy's name, but it didn't start with a J, I remember that. The only girl in the family was Tina. Cute little girl who seemed to have a few things going for her, smarts and a personality."

I nodded. "Good for her. Did she make it out?"

"She did. She joined the army a few years back. I doubt she ever looked back. She wasn't an asshole like the rest of them."

"You know a lot of people down here."

"I grew up in Compton. Spent a lot of time in North Long Beach, and I've worked down here for the bulk of my career. I know the shitheads, and I know most of their families."

I looked off again and saw people mingling in front of their homes in the cool evening air. "What I'd like to do today is what I had planned for us to do Saturday until your burglar friend tried to rob a deputy sheriff."

"God rest his soul."

I smiled.

"Okay, and what would that be?"

"Re-canvas the neighborhood for witnesses. To me, you can't talk to the local people enough on any of these cases. Nobody talks easily down here—you know that—but in this job, we have the time to keep trying. If you take the time to build relationships and gain trust when you find the right person, it can be the difference in a solved and an unsolved. When I was new here, my partner used to say we solve murders by wearing out shoe leather, not staring at computer screens. I believe it."

A radio car glided toward us. Josie said, "Did you ask for them to meet us?"

"Nope. I prefer they're not around. Again, uniforms don't seem to get people talking openly. It seems they usually have the opposite effect. But if I'm not mistaken, that's the two who handled this call the other day, Nelson I think his name was."

"Nelson and Johnson," she confirmed.

They parked and left their car running while they approached us on foot. We greeted them, shook hands, and then I asked if they had just happened by. Johnson said, "We've been spending a lot of time over here since the murders, especially in the morning, from when we come on at seven until at least ten. Hoping to see some type of pattern that might help out."

I was nodding and probably smiling too. Some deputies seemed to be a cut above others, and it was refreshing when you would encounter the good ones. The training officer, Deputy Johnson, was a seasoned street cop with a lot of experience. But that wasn't all he had going for him. It was the hunter mentality, and he and his trainee each seemed to have it. They were the type who went out every day and put themselves in harm's way, and they did so because they loved being cops. It was their calling, and for those of us who loved being cops, there was nothing better than working a fast station with a good partner.

"We were going to do a little canvas ourselves," I told them, "see if we missed anything or anybody the other day."

Johnson said, "We can stick around until you've finished, sir, if you'd like."

I smiled. "I have her here if anything goes south. I think we'll be alright."

That got everyone smiling and once again I found myself searching the dark recesses of my brain trying to place where I knew this Deputy Nelson from. He seemed especially familiar to me when he smiled, and the otherwise sober Marine-turned-deputy sheriff trainee transformed into a lighthearted, jovial young man who showed a hint of boyish mischievousness. But I couldn't place him and wasn't comfortable revisiting the conversation.

"Good enough," Johnson said, "Call the station if you need anything. We're Unit 285 today."

"Will do. Thanks, guys."

With that, they departed, and Josie and I began wearing out shoe leather on the streets, walkways, and doorsteps of Compton.

16

Chief Warrant Officer 2 James P. Morgan (CW2) sat in a conference room at the 6th Military Police Group (CID) headquartered at Joint Base Lewis-McChord, Washington. Though his battalion headquarters remained at Fort Hood, Texas, he had been brought to the Group's headquarters at Fort Lewis to be briefed on developing information on an active AWOL case under investigation by the United States Army's Criminal Investigation Command. The case was of particular interest to CW2 Morgan, who had worked with the two suspected absconders while serving as a 1st Lieutenant in the 1st Cavalry Division. Morgan had been one of many who spent countless hours and risked personal safety in efforts to locate the two who, at that time, were believed to have been swept away in a flash flood.

PFC Christina Ortiz was of particular interest to him; he had been romantically involved with her, though briefly and discreetly.

Following her disappearance, Morgan spent many a sleepless night seeing her smiling face as he struggled to accept her presumed death. But within months of the tragic accident that had claimed the lives of at least four soldiers—deaths that had been confirmed by their recovered remains —rumors began circulating that two of the three MIA may have gone AWOL.

Morgan had since turned down a promotion to Captain in order to commission as a 31D, a C.I.D. Special Agent in the Warrant Officer Corps.

The Criminal Investigations Command, formerly known as Criminal Investigations Division, and still commonly referred to as C.I.D. due to the historic title, allowed Morgan to fulfill his desire to be a law enforcement officer and an investigator.

Wearing khaki-colored cargo pants and a long-sleeved buttoned shirt, Morgan sat comfortably near an open window that offered a refreshingly cool reprieve from the Texas heat and an unobstructed view of snow-capped Mount Rainier. But as he gazed off at the splendor of his surroundings, his thoughts remained with the beauty of one particular missing soldier. Chief Warrant Officer 2 James P. Morgan still had strong feelings for Private Ortiz, though if she was in fact alive, she was an outlaw now. Maybe even a killer.

Dark green portfolios marked *C.I.D.* and *Confidential* accompanied each of the five positions on the conference room table. The unit's commander, Colonel Sandra J. Parkinson, would not be a party to the briefing, but her name was prominently inscribed on each of the portfolios in gold letters. Also embossed on the portfolios were the C.I.D.'s emblem, the scales of justice teetering from the end of a sword. The words *SEEK THE TRUTH* were boldly displayed on a rocker below it.

Chief Warrant Officer 3 Charles Farley took his seat at the end of the table and looked around at his four investigators. CW2 James Morgan and CW2 Paulina Lazarevic sat to one side. Warrant Officers Roy Ridley and Mark Montoya sat on the other. It was a tight-knit, diverse group of soldiers with a proven track record of success, and whose ability to blend into various communities throughout the world rivaled that of many CIA teams. The camaraderie of the unit was unmatched, as far as Morgan had seen in his nine years in the army.

"We're all familiar with the case involving Sergeant Hollingsworth and Private First Class Ortiz," CW3 Farley started, "both believed to be AWOL since the flood incident at Fort Hood. Morgan and I have been actively monitoring mail and phone calls of a dude named Johnny Ortiz. He's a brother of Private First Class Ortiz, and he happens to be a long-term resident of the California Department of Corrections in Vacaville, in for armed robbery. He works as a metal fabricator and is apparently a model prisoner with no discipline problems. He receives mail from an attorney—which we are not privy to—and from a woman in San Pedro named Luciana Marten. She appears to be his significant other. She writes often and visits every other month or so. We have previously conducted surveillance of her home. It appears she lives with another woman—who is certainly not Private First Class Ortiz—and her four children.

"We additionally have a mail cover in operation for the residence of Private First Class Ortiz before she enlisted in the army. It is still the home of her grandmother, and another brother, Jimmy Ortiz. The postal inspector who is facilitating the mail cover called early this morning to report something he learned by watching the news. We have since confirmed through law enforcement sources that Jimmy Ortiz was shot and killed Saturday morning by an off-duty sheriff's deputy during the commission of an attempted robbery.

"We've had no indication that Private First Class Ortiz has made any contact with family members over the years, if she is in fact alive and well. Quite frankly, this case has grown cold. Though Morgan and I have kept it open, the case has not been actively worked for all intents and purposes beyond monitoring the mail of Ortiz's grandmother and, as I mentioned, the mail and phone calls of an incarcerated brother. Up until now, we've had nothing of value come from anything we've done. But now, it seems, we might have something to work with.

"Our thought on this is that if Ortiz is indeed alive, and if she has remained in country, she will likely hear of her brother's passing. What she will do is anyone's guess, but we're hoping she makes an appearance. As such, we are going to establish surveillance of Grandma's house around the clock, and I'd like to start ASAP with teams of two taking twelve-hour shifts. I know that will stretch us thin, but—much to my chagrin—we will get no additional bodies assigned to us for the operation.

"Morgan and I plan to be there at twenty-two hundred hours this date and we will establish the nightshift detail and initiate the surveillance operation. We expect to be relieved by you two" —he made eye contact with Warrant Officers Roy Ridley and Mark Montoya— "at ten-hundred tomorrow."

Farley allowed a moment for his team members to finish with their notes. "We go five days. If nothing develops, we call it. And at that point, this file gets laid to rest, as far as I'm concerned."

It was the only thing said that CW2 Morgan didn't agree with. He believed she was alive, and he felt the case should always remain active.

CW3 Farley made eye contact with the only woman in the room. "Lazarevic, you're going to be a floater. You'll make reliefs as necessary, and you'll be responsible for establishing contact with the local law enforcement and act as liaison for us.

"Any questions?"

Morgan looked around the room, making eye contact with each of the other agents, all of whom shook their heads indicating there was no need for any further direction. It was straightforward: surveillance of a single location to see if an AWOL soldier shows up to light a candle for her brother. Simple enough. It wasn't Fallujah. They routinely performed surveillance and they were confident in their skills as a team. Morgan said to nobody in particular, "Don't get comfortable out there. I have a feeling about this."

AFTER STOPPING FOR DINNER AND MARGARITAS AT MY FAVORITE MEXICAN restaurant in Huntington Park, Josie and I returned to the office to find Floyd and Mongo still at their desks. Most of the detectives had gone home by now—or they had gone somewhere—but a few always remained into the wee hours. Tonight, Floyd and Mongo were two among the late crowd.

"Where the hell have you two been?"

"Getting drunk and lying about overtime," Josie blurted out as we neared their desks.

I chuckled. Mongo grinned. Floyd leaned back in his chair and put the end of a pen in his mouth. His eyes always seemed to glimmer when he set them upon attractive women.

Josie smiled confidently as she continued past the two of them and headed down the hallway toward the kitchen and restrooms.

After watching her past the last corner, I turned to see that Floyd had watched her leave as well. Mongo had refocused on his computer.

"She catches on quickly, uh?"

"I guess she does," Floyd said. "Though, being partnered with you, I doubt she's lying about either one."

I chuckled. "You're one to talk. But actually, if you must know, we've been out trying to solve a murder, which is something you should try sometime. It works up a powerful thirst when you do, I'll tell you that. What the hell are you idiots doing here so late?"

"Mongo's writing a Return to Affidavit for our Cedric the Entertainer fiasco. Which, by the way, is almost certainly *not* a murder, and something that should be handled by the station dicks. But no, we have to at least get that evidence out of the walls—"

"And the trunk of Chang's Mercedes."

"—so that we can prove that A) Cedric was telling the truth, and B) these are the same assholes who killed my buddy, Ho. Because Lord knows if I leave it to you and cha-cha, nothing's going to get done around here."

"So you served the warrant?"

"Yeah, tonight. Me and Mongo found a judge in South Gate to sign it, and we just finished up with it about an hour ago. I tried to call you, see if you wanted to come lend a hand. But you no-acked me."

"I was busy."

"Well, we let Cedric tag along so that he could point some things out to us, and the truth is, he was probably more help than you would have been anyway."

I pulled up an empty chair near his and took a seat. "I believe it. Hey, what would you say if I told you that one of our killers is a woman? Would that get you a little more excited about this case?"

He stared for a long moment and seemed to be scrutinizing me. Mongo swiveled around to pay attention too.

I continued: "The smaller of the two carries a little twenty-gauge shotgun, something that doesn't have a lot of kick. So far, she hasn't hit anything, as far as we know. Is she a bad shot, or is she reluctant to kill?"

"Wait a minute here, Dickie. What makes you think it's a woman?"

"One of the prior robbery cases Josie pulled indicated there were two suspects, a man and a woman."

"Didn't you say they were wearing masks? That's why you were originally interested in it, right?"

"Right. But there's a witness who said the smaller one spoke, and she's a woman. We almost wrote the case off as being unrelated until I started thinking about it. Especially after you and I saw that car down there with the pellet holes in the trunk. I'm convinced she purposely fired to miss the kid. Cedric."

Floyd was nodding. "Could be."

"They didn't recover any pellets in Ho's autopsy, either. We should have the autopsy on the old wino from the parking lot in the next day or two. If each of them was killed by multiple two-twenty-three gunshot wounds, and no shotgun pellets, then I think I'm onto something. We know she fired that shotgun inside the store and again outside in the parking lot. Yet she isn't hitting anything other than walls and parked cars. I find that interesting. It makes me think it's a woman who doesn't want to be a killer, she's just going along with her partner."

"I think you're going soft on me, Dickie."

"I think we may have another Patty Hearst in the making. You're going to want to be part of that, aren't you?"

At 2200 hours Monday night, Farley and Morgan of the army's elite CID team parked their cars on opposite sides of the home of Grandma Ortiz in North Long Beach. Each had a radio tuned to a simplex channel that would allow direct communication between them without the use of a repeater. This was preferred when working in close proximity for a number of reasons, primarily the absence of interference or monitoring by others.

Farley settled in and leaned his seat back which allowed him to sit low in the darkness of his sedan. He keyed his mic and sent a test transmission. "How do you copy me, Jimbo?"

CW2 James P. Morgan answered up. "Gotcha loud and clear, Chuckie. Over."

They sounded like teenaged boys playing a game of prowling. It was by design; there wouldn't be any talk on the radio that could allow anyone listening to know they were military personnel on a mission.

"What do you think the odds are she'd approach through the alley?"

"If she shows up, I'd bet she walks right through the front door. Tina's got balls."

Farley nodded slightly in the darkness of his sedan, thinking about his partner's fondness for the fugitive. Morgan had never said as much, but Farley knew it was there. It had always been a big part of Morgan's motivation to keep the file open. To what end, Farley didn't know. Either way, her life was over, as far as Farley could figure. Either she had died in the turbulent waters, or she hadn't. Morgan would either never see or hear from her again, or she would surface and be a prisoner for the rest of her life. Farley hoped his friend and teammate had prepared himself for either scenario. Two soldiers had been killed in the search-and-rescue efforts after their vehicle overturned and was swept away during the floods. The army would judge her and her accomplice harshly if ever they were captured.

Farley took a sip of his coffee and secured the cup in its holder. He picked up his case file and retrieved the two photographs of the absconders. After looking around outside of his car and not seeing any movement or activity, he cupped his hand over the red lens of a small flashlight and illuminated first one and then the other army file photos of Sergeant Hollingsworth and Private First Class Ortiz. He went back and forth and recommitted the images to memory.

With the light turned off and the file set aside, Farley continued sipping hot coffee in the darkness with an army-issued Sig Sauer pistol P228 on his hip and an M4 carbine readied across his lap. Ortiz may be a cutie, but she was in the company of a dangerous and violent man. CW3 Charles Farley did not expect an apprehension of either one to be accomplished without a violent confrontation.

17

The door flew open. Travis Hollingsworth grabbed his pistol from the table in front of him and came up ready to fire.

"Jesus Christ, Carlos, what the hell are you doing coming in like that? You're lucky I didn't drop you."

"Where's my sister?"

Travis shrugged. "I don't know, she's been barricaded all day in her room. Moody little bitch sometimes."

"I seen the kid."

"What kid?"

"The one from that market. The one that kicked you in the nuts and ran out, and Tina tried to shoot but missed."

Travis sat up on the edge of the couch. Fumbling to lift a cigarette out of its pack, he asked, "Where?"

"At the market. I went by there again, figured I'd scout it out some more at night. I was wondering about those armored cars, if they come back at closing, you know? That's when I seen him."

"How do you know it was the same boy? Did ya see his eyes?"

"His eyes?"

"Yeah, he's got green eyes. Little negro with green eyes. There can't be too many of them."

"I wasn't close enough to see his eyes, but he was with a couple of detectives. I'm sure it was him. I had a pretty good look when he ran by the van that day. Same kid, I'm telling you."

Travis fell back into the cushions of his couch, deep in thought. He'd made it clear they needed to find the boy and take him out, and he had hinted that maybe it would be Carlos's job to do so. Carlos needed to get his hands bloody. It would be the kid, or the storeowner. Maybe both. You had to eliminate witnesses, and that'd be a good job for Carlos. *If* he could handle it.

"Was it the same detectives that was there when Tina watched?"

Carlos frowned. "How would I know? I wasn't with Tina when she saw them. But they were detectives, no doubt about that. One was a pretty boy, the other looked like a fucking sumo wrestler, big Hawaiian-looking dude."

"Did the other have a hat?"

He shook his head. "No, nobody had a hat."

"She said one of 'em wore a fedora, like an old-style detective."

Carlos was still shaking his head when his eyes drifted away from Travis and toward the hallway behind him. Travis turned to see Tina leaning against the corner, covering herself with her arms. She wore gray sweat shorts and a scant undershirt with no bra. Travis held his gaze on her as she chimed in on the conversation: "That might have been the one, the pretty boy you describe. But I didn't see no Hawaiians. The other guy was a white boy with a hat, like Trav said. An old-time detective or a Chicago gangster. Mean looking. He wasn't cute like the other one."

Travis frowned at her. "Cute?"

She rolled her eyes at him but didn't respond. Travis turned back to Carlos who had lowered himself onto the other couch. "So, were you smart enough to tail them, see where the kid lives?"

Carlos smiled. "Of course."

TINA GOT A SICK FEELING IN HER STOMACH AS HER BROTHER, THE FOOL, told Travis about following the detectives a few miles north to a home near Firestone Boulevard. He said he could find it again in the daytime easily. Travis told him good, they'd go have a look tomorrow, and if given the chance, they'd eliminate a witness.

She changed the subject. "What about the armored car deal, anything new on that?"

"Nah, nothing tonight. But I can go back out during the day tomorrow and have a look."

"I'll go with you."

Travis eyed her suspiciously. "Maybe we'll all go."

She needed some time with her brother. She had an idea of how to get rid of Travis and save Carlos from becoming a savage killer. She didn't like the idea of Travis having Carlos kill a little boy. She hated the whole idea of a little boy being murdered, and she wouldn't have any part of it. In fact, she'd stop it if she were able.

She nudged her shoulder against the wall to push herself into a standing position, and walked toward the kitchen as she replied. "Your big white ass would blow it. You stay here and watch your damn war movies. Carlos and I will handle the scouting. This isn't Oklahoma."

IT WAS NEARLY MIDNIGHT BY THE TIME JOSIE SANCHEZ DECIDED TO CALL it a night. Her partner had been gone nearly an hour. Floyd and Mongo had left with him, everyone seemingly tired from a long weekend. Only a few hardy souls remained. So it was quiet, and Josie took advantage of the tranquility and put her nose to the books. She had gone over the armed robbery reports again looking for any detail she might have missed before, and then she went through her notebook again and studied each note of all of the activity so far on her first murder case. All of the notes other than those taken at the autopsy; she didn't feel the need to relive that just yet. But now her eyes were tired, and she was hungry, and tomorrow would be another long day. It seemed, so far, that all of the days here were long.

She pushed her chair under the desk and collected her purse and brief-case and started for the door. Just as she turned to push it open with her backside, the door flung open and she fell into the arms of a man who felt thick and solid and smelled like beer.

"Whoa," he said.

She regained balance on her own two feet and stood facing him. It was Davey Lopes, one of the detectives assigned to the Unsolved Homicides unit, and someone whom she had known before coming to the bureau. "Shit, I'm sorry!"

His smile seemed devious to her. "Hey, it's okay. I just happened to be in the mood for a dance myself."

She looked away. It was obvious he had quickly moved to the realm of flirtation; they always did. Josie had been used to it her whole life. On the department, it had been no different. It started during the application process with the creepy background investigator wanting to visit with her over and over to "clarify" a few things with her, and generally wanting to have those meetings at night. Then the academy came along, and two of the six drill instructors were quick to show their interest in her. One of the two had had the audacity to ask her out before they were halfway through the eighteen-week regimen. She resented him for it, knowing if she didn't play it perfectly, he could make her life difficult. Graduation was never guaranteed in the sheriff's academy. When she worked custody, she oftentimes wondered who was worse, the inmates or the deputies. She had never quite decided. Patrol came along, and first her training officer and then the training sergeant both gave her their best shots. Both were married, and as with the other instances, Josie handled them perfectly. Which is to say that all of them had been given clear boundaries and made to believe she meant business. All with a bit of a smile though, to leave them confused enough to not be vindictive. Once all of her training was behind her though, there were few smiles offered at the pigs who made their moves. Especially the married ones. She might be best known for the male deputy she beat up at an off-training party. The rumors made it much worse than it actually was though. The deputy had been harassing her all evening and finally walked up behind her and rubbed her ass. He was drunk, and Josie had had enough. She had turned and punched him squarely on the jaw and he had dropped. It was the only time in her life that she had punched a person like that outside of sparring at the kick-boxing gym where she trained. That had sent a message county-wide. Maybe Lopes was deaf.

"I don't dance, thank you."

He stepped back and held the door open widely. "No offense, Sanchez. I was only joking. Have a lovely evening."

The door closed behind her as she stepped past him into the parking lot. She stopped, turned back, and opened the door. Lopes was twenty feet away now, his back to her. "Hey!"

He stopped and turned to face her, and nodded his head as if to say, "What's up?"

"You want to get a beer somewhere?"

18

As the sky showed its first signs of light after a long and quiet night in North Long Beach, CW2 James P. Morgan was jolted from his dozing by a sudden pop and crackle followed by his superior's voice.

". . . still awake over there, Jimbo?"

He shook the sleep from his head and cleared his throat. "Yeah, you bet. What's up Chuckie?"

"I'm about ready to peel off. Ridley and Montoya are just a couple minutes out. I just got off the phone with Lazarevic who said there's nothing new cooking on their end. They met for coffee and a quick briefing this morning."

"Sounds good, boss. I'm ready to get some shut-eye."

"Me too. Listen, I'll sit here until they're in place. Go ahead and ease on out, so we aren't leaving at the same time. I won't be far behind."

"Okay, boss. See you tonight."

"Yeah, you bet. I'll give you a call around twenty-one-hundred or so, and if you're up for it, we can meet for a cup or a bite to eat before starting our shift."

Morgan thought about his boss's use of military time over the radio. He thought he'd water it down with his reply. "Okay, that's nine o'clock, right?"

A moment of radio silence lingered. Then a click of the mic, but nothing said. Finally, "Yeah, Jimbo, nine o'clock or so. Ten-four, good buddy, over and out." The accent was thick and might be described as redneck.

Morgan smiled as he set his radio aside and started his car. He moved his M4 off of his lap and placed it on the seat next to him where the grip and trigger were within arm's reach. He pulled away and drove past the house where Private First Class Ortiz had lived before joining the army, and he wondered what secrets the modest home held.

LOPES OPENED HIS EYES AND KEPT HIS HEAD STEADY AS HE SCANNED HIS surroundings. The ache in his head was sharp and his memory dull. For the life of him, he couldn't figure out why he was sleeping outdoors on a chaise lounge, nor did he have a clue about where he was. Slowly he lifted his head to see he was dressed in his slacks and t-shirt. He looked left and right. There was a pool and Jacuzzi to one side and a patio set to the other. His shirt, tie, and suit coat were thrown haphazardly over a patio chair, his shoes were on the concrete beneath it. He saw two beach towels draped over the backs of other chairs, but he had no recollection of swimming. Or anything else, for that matter. Where the hell was he?

As he gathered his clothes, he found his gun and badge partially concealed beneath the dirty socks that sat atop his wingtips.

Where was his phone?

He checked various pockets but couldn't find it. When he sat to slip on his shoes, he found the phone with his left foot inside the corresponding shoe. The first thing he checked was his call log. The last call he had received was at 11:30 p.m. and it had gone unanswered. *Maria L.* showed on the log, rather than the number. She was his new informant.

Well, sort of. Maria Lopez was a former corrections officer who had been involved with the Mexican mafia through family ties. Lopes had met her on one of his many trips to Pelican Bay State Prison where he squeezed certain inmates for information on various cases. They, too, were informants. He didn't know it at the time, but the corrections officer, Maria Lopez, had been providing information to the *carnales*—the *brothers* of La Eme. Davey Lopes, on the other hand, had made a career out of investigating the Mexican mafia, and he had sent many of them to prison for the rest of their lives.

Davey Lopes and Maria Lopez had had a romantic interlude the night they met. Shortly after that, she had come to L.A. to see family. And Lopes. But as he was driving to pick her up from her grandmother's home in Whittier, Maria was shot by two young gangsters as she sat waiting on the front steps. A hit had been put on her for reasons neither she nor Lopes had yet discovered. Maria was nearly killed, and Davey Lopes became her handler. She would give him everything she knew about the mob, and she would testify against her own family members in exchange for immunity and protection. Lopes had taken care of securing Maria and her two young children nearby while her debriefing on the mafia continued. That turned out to be a full-time job. It wasn't easy keeping people alive, safe, and happy, when the mob is trying to kill them.

Meanwhile, Davey Lopes was working hard to keep her at arm's distance, and it was no easy task with the young Latina beauty.

Staring at the phone, Lopes knew he hadn't spoken to Maria Lopez, and so he was comforted knowing he hadn't done something extraordinarily stupid with an informant.

He looked around the backyard which was encircled by tall block walls. The nearby houses had windows with a view of the pool and patio, which made him thankful he was partially clothed. He scanned his phone again, checking text messages and going deeper into his call log. He recalled sending Maria's call to voicemail, intentionally not answering her late-night call, though it had been tempting. As he pondered that for a moment, he recalled running into Sanchez at the office. Literally. He began smiling as memories of drinking with her in a nearby pub returned.

Lopes opened his map app on his phone to see where he was. Downey. A residential neighborhood not far from Imperial Highway. Easy enough. He'd find his car and head for home and pray nothing unforgivable had taken place.

Jesus. *Sanchez?* Lopes shook his head as he went through a side gate and found his car in front of the house. There was another sedan in the driveway, and it was obviously a county car. A department-issued, Homicide Bureau car. No doubt, Sanchez's. Lopes smirked and shook his head again. Someday, maybe he'd learn. Not likely anytime soon though, he conceded to himself.

TINA DROVE, AND HER BROTHER RODE SHOTGUN WITH HIS L.A. BALL CAP sitting low on his head, shading his face against the morning sun. She glanced at him from behind the wheel. "You need to shut up around him."

"What? What did I say?"

"He wants to kill that little boy."

Carlos didn't respond. She looked back and forth from the road to see him sitting in silence, looking straight ahead.

"You want to kill a little kid? That's what you've become?"

"We're outlaws, right?"

She shook her head slightly and drew a deep breath before continuing. "I never should have allowed you in. I don't want to see you spend the rest of your life in prison, like your brothers."

He sat staring out his window, not saying a word.

Tina slapped the back of his head.

"The fuck?"

"I'm talking to you."

"You're talking shit. You want to treat me like a little kid, yet you're out there smokin' motherfuckers."

She wasn't sure what to say. Should she confess to her brother her closely-guarded secret? What would he think of her? Tina thought it would be best to shut up; that's something she was able to do that her brother wasn't. Whatever she said to him would get back to Travis. His hero. The big, bad, war veteran who now gunned down civilians as a way to make a living—and for his kicks. The truth was, the killing was unnecessary, and she didn't like it. But one bad decision had led to another, and now she was stuck.

Tina thought back to the day of the flood when the decision to disappear with him seemed like a great idea. What had she been thinking? Sure, she had grown tired of the military and longed for her civilian life, but did she really think she could live a normal life if she went AWOL from the army? She didn't know what she had thought. Though she knew when

Travis killed the motel clerk that her life would never be the same. She was smart enough to know she'd go down with him if he were caught, and they'd been running ever since.

Again, Tina began thinking about how to stop all the killing. There was only one way, and that was to get rid of Travis. She wasn't sure, though, that she could count on her brother to help her, or even to go along with her plan. She didn't think she could trust him to keep his mouth shut. No, she would be on her own, but she had a plan.

Just as they pulled over across from the market, the armored car turned into its parking lot. Carlos said, "Right on time."

LOPES HAD STOPPED TO EAT AND REPLENISH HIS PRECIOUS BODILY FLUIDS before continuing to the office. When he arrived, he walked through the back door, haggard and in need of even more coffee. He really needed a shower and a shave, but he had a ten-thirty meeting with the district attorney regarding the wire they had going on the mafia. It was the task force that had been assembled after Maria Lopez was nearly killed, and when it was learned that the Mexican mafia had not only called for that hit, but had put a hit on Dickie Jones as well. A hit on a cop got the attention of more than a few detectives and lawyers.

He found Sanchez at her desk. She had beat him to the office, presumably leaving right after him but not stopping along the way. He thought about approaching her to get a feel for the mood. It might help him fill in the gaps as he was unclear about the events of the night, beyond having drinks at the bar. She looked up and he felt overpowered by her stare. Lopes continued past without a word and headed to the kitchen. *Jesus Christ*, he thought, *what the fuck was I thinking?*

BACK AT THE HOUSE TRAVIS, TINA, AND CARLOS TALKED ABOUT HOW IT would go down. Carlos would drive the van. Travis and Tina would ride in the back, ready to come out of the side doors quickly when the guard exited the store with the money bag. Just as the guard reached the truck and the driver popped the door open for him, two things would happen simultaneously: Carlos would take down the guard with the money, and Travis and Tina would enter the truck and take down the driver. Then Carlos would bring the van up beside the armored car, so they could quickly load the bags of money into their van. They should be finished and gone from the scene in less than two minutes, Travis said.

"We need to practice," Tina said.

Carlos and Travis both looked at her. Travis said, "How do you suppose we do that, woman?"

"I mean, we need to have a range day. Let's go up in the mountains and do some shooting. Carlos needs to learn to handle your AR, and it wouldn't be a bad idea for all of us to practice with the pistols. These guys are armed, and they will shoot it out if we give them the chance."

Travis nodded. "Okay, let's go. Carlos, run down to the corner and get us some beer and ice. I'll gather up the hardware. I'm always up for slinging lead downrange."

Carlos stood and checked his pockets for cash. He had a ten and a couple of ones, a handful of change. He looked at Travis, hopeful. Travis pulled a twenty from his wallet and flipped it toward him against the table. Carlos took the cash and crossed the room toward the front door.

Tina waited for her brother to leave, then turned to Travis. "I don't like it. It's dangerous."

He ignored her. "Did he take you to the kid's house?"

"We couldn't find it," she lied.

"That's next. Before the armored car deal, we need to find that kid and kill him. Him and that fucking gook."

———

I WALKED INTO THE BUREAU JUST BEFORE 10 A.M. AFTER STOPPING BY THE crime lab to check on the ballistics evidence from the market murder. Keith in the Firearms section had provided a synopsis of his examination: the bullets recovered from both victims were 69 grain, .22 caliber. The barrel had eight lands and grooves with a right twist. Basically, it was probably a .223, and likely an AR-15. However, there were hundreds of manufacturers of this particular type of gun, added to the fact there were hundreds more ways to customize the barrel configurations. So, our data thus far was nearly useless. That was, unless we recovered a weapon for comparison. He said he'd have a report typed up by the end of the week, sooner if I needed it.

"Good morning."

Josie didn't look up from her desk. "Oh, hi."

I pulled out my chair, set my briefcase on the ground and set my hat on top of a stack of reports at the corner of my desk. "Want a cup?"

"No thanks."

Still no eye contact. *Women.*

On the way to the kitchen I bumped into Lopes coming out of the men's room with his head on a swivel. I chuckled. "You running from someone, Davey?"

He was drying his hands with paper towels. "No, buddy. What's up?"

"I don't know. What's everyone acting strange about this morning?"

"Who's everyone?"

I felt something was going on. "You. My partner. That's about it, so far. Any ideas?"

We had drifted around the corner as we spoke and were just feet from the coffee pots. I turned to get a cup and offered one to Lopes. He tossed the wadded paper towels into the trash and took a Styrofoam cup from me and waited as I filled it. "Well?"

"Thanks," he said. "Nah, man; I've got no idea. I have to get to a meeting on the mafia wire. That's all that's going on with me."

"You look a little haggard," I said. "Looks like you might have forgotten to shave this morning, Davey. Did you have a late night?"

"What are you, my mother?"

With that he turned and headed toward the Unsolved Homicides office. I shook my head and frowned at his back. Something was in the air, I could feel it. I hoped it hadn't been my partner's ankles.

CARLOS WALKED IN WITH A 30-PACK OF BUD AND TWO BAGS OF ICE, AND kicked the door closed behind him. "Where's the ice chest?"

Travis snapped the lid closed on an ammo container that sat among three others on the living room floor. "You walked past it on your way in, dumbass. It's right outside the door."

Carlos retreated with his beer and ice, leaving the front door open behind him. Travis grabbed two of the ammo cans and followed. He said over his shoulder on the way out the door, "Leave those cans; I'll be back for 'em."

Tina watched him continue toward the van, and then she went to work. She unzipped his "war bag" and pulled his Colt .45 auto from its holster. She dropped the magazine, racked the slide to eject the live round, and then released the slide forward on an empty chamber. She put the fully-loaded magazine back in the gun, left the hammer back in the cocked position, and thumbed the safety on. It would appear "cocked and locked," the manner in which he normally carried it, but if he needed it to go "bang," he'd be in for a surprise. This was the gun he would no doubt wear on his belt while they were in the mountains shooting. Travis loved his Colt .45.

19

There were places you could go shooting in the San Gabriel mountains north of Azusa, and there were places you could get lost or get killed or disappear without a trace. Angelenos flocked to the Angeles National Forest via Highway 39 for a variety of reasons. If you were dumping a body, the key was finding a remote area where a hiker or biker wouldn't stumble upon the evidence. You'd look for a similar place to go shooting if you were a fugitive, and especially if you had murder on your mind.

Tina hadn't been in these mountains since she was a kid. During the drive north, she was surprised by the number of cars and trucks and motorcycles traveling in both directions. Cyclists clad in neon-accented tights and sunglasses beneath their helmets crowded the edges of the winding roadway, taking their chances with the motorized outdoor enthusiasts. She knew they would need to get far off of the highway, with people seemingly everywhere.

She glanced back at her brother who sat with his legs outstretched on the carpeted floor of the van, leaning against a duffle bag. "*Hermanito*, where did we used to come shoot up here when we were kids?"

Travis, behind the wheel, glanced toward Carlos. "Yeah, Carlos, where did you and your asshole brothers go *chooting* when you were just a little *vato?"* He looked at Tina after he said it, and chuckled.

"How the hell do I know?" Carlos answered. "You gotta get off the main road somewhere and drive on dirt for a while. There's all kinds of places."

Travis smashed the heel of his hand against the horn and yelled across Tina as they passed a pair of bicyclists. "Get the fuck out of the middle of the road!"

Tina watched one of the two flip them the bird as they dropped behind the van. She glanced over and was glad to see Travis had apparently not noticed. He was looking in his sideview mirror now, smiling as if he were pleased with himself. The wind rushing through the open window lifted his hair from his shoulders and wrapped his beard around his face and neck. She wondered if he ever planned to cut his hair or shave again and thought it wouldn't matter if today went the way she had planned. She pictured him on his knees, begging for his life. She'd call him a *vato* and say "Adios, motherfucker" before putting a cap in his forehead. She was startled by his sudden glance. Though his eyes were concealed by mirrored sunglasses, they seemed to penetrate her. Could he read her mind? Sometimes she wondered.

"What are you over there thinking about, woman? You aren't up to something, are you? You and taco back there?"

She frowned at him and shook her head. "Shut-up, Travis. You're so stupid sometimes."

He laughed and veered toward another cyclist, again slamming his palm against the horn.

When I got back to my desk, Josie was gone. Our team lieutenant, Joe Black, looked up from his reading and offered a smile and went back to the stack of reports. Brenda Clay, two desks down, had her arm propped on an otherwise uncluttered desk, supporting her head with one hand while holding a phone to her ear in the other. She seemed to be arguing with someone on the other end about something that had been said on Facebook. Troy Walker sat on the other side of her, mesmerized by his computer screen. It appeared he was looking at his department email, but who really knew? The rest of the bureau seemed quiet for a Tuesday afternoon, as if everyone was low on energy or was otherwise occupied. Everyone other than Floyd, who came through the back door with his shades covering his eyes, smiling, a cell phone propped to his ear.

"I don't give a shit, call Ghostbusters if it makes you feel better."

He was saying goodbye as he veered toward my desk. He slid his phone into his suit coat pocket and pushed his glasses up into his hair. "What's up, Dickie?"

"The hell was that all about?"

"What?"

"Ghostbusters?"

He pulled up a chair, so I took my seat and set a cup of coffee on my desk.

"Margie's back and it's driving Cindy nuts."

I frowned. "*Margie?*"

"Yeah, my grandma."

I cocked my head to the side. I'd never heard about Margie before, and we'd been friends and partners for the better part of a quarter-century now. "Oh. You've never mentioned her."

"There's not much to talk about, until she comes around. Then, everybody seems to be out of sorts."

"Why's that?"

"Because that's the only time anyone seems to give a shit about her. Otherwise, she's gone and forgotten and almost never mentioned. Sometimes—holiday dinners and such—she'll come up in a story about my mom's family in Texas, or growing up poor, or Grandpa getting thrown in jail for cracking some asshole over the head with his cane—"

"That explains a few things right there."

"—but otherwise, nobody mentions her."

I conjured an image in my head of a small but strong Texas woman who wore dresses rather than jeans and had her hair up in a bun. I pictured a log home where clothes hung from a taut rope that had been strung from the porch to a tree over yonder. Chickens scurried about over the dirt and Grandpa rocked in a porch chair with his cane—his weapon—across his lap, a pipe protruding from his gray beard. Maybe a jug by his dirty boots.

"Do you ever go see her?"

"No, but she visits us sometimes."

"When? And why haven't I met her?"

"Whenever the hell she feels like it. We never know when she's going to show up, Dickie. Or how long she'll stay or how she'll behave while she's here. It drives Cindy fucking crazy, and then Cindy gets all pissed off at me about it, like I have any control over how Margie behaves."

"Well, if it's causing problems with your family, you could ask her to either change her behavior or leave. Family or not, you have that right in your own home."

"I never see her."

"Well, take some time off, spend a little more time with your family. That's what I would do if I were you with a cute wife and nice kids. And a grandma visiting."

"No, Dickie, you don't understand what I'm trying to tell you. It's not that I'm never home, that's not why I don't see her. I don't see her because she's been dead for twenty-three years."

I watched his eyes, looking for something to tell me he was kidding. He wasn't.

"But she visits you."

"Uh-huh."

"Oh."

"I don't know what the hell to do about it. She comes and goes, does what she wants, and it spooks the hell out of Cindy. Me and the kids think it's funny."

"How do you know when she's there?" I indulged.

"Well for one, you can smell her."

I held my gaze, waiting for more.

"She smokes, and you can smell it all over the house when she's there. Plus, she'll turn on the TV in the middle of the night or go through the cabinets and leave shit open. What drives me crazy is she'll turn on lights and not bother turning them off. You wake up in the middle of the night and the kitchen light is on. I'm like, 'Jesus Christ, Marg, turn the lights out and go to bed, for fuck's sake.' "

I still didn't speak. I didn't know what to say.

Floyd looked around. "It's quiet in here today. Where's your partner?"

"I don't know," I said, and quickly scanned the squad room myself. "She was here earlier, and now—I don't know man—she's just gone. Everyone's being weird today. I've got you and your dead grandma, my new crazy partner and her moods . . . Jesus, even Lopes is up to something, and I suspect it might have something to do with my partner."

Floyd laughed. "Well yeah, dipshit. Of course it has something to do with your partner. I'm sure he's trying to bang her, or he already has."

I frowned. "Why do you say that?"

"They were out drinking last night, down at Fiesta. You do the math."

For some reason the comment felt like a slap in the face. "Wait, how do you know that?"

Floyd stood and lowered his sunglasses over his eyes. It must have seemed bright in the office. "Dickie, you know that I know everything that happens around this place. Especially if it involves *punani*. You need to pay better attention to the office dynamics, buddy, now that you've got a smoking hot partner."

He walked away and I glared down the row of desks at Lieutenant Black whose nose remained buried in paperwork. I *really* didn't need this.

TRAVIS AND TINA FINALLY AGREED ON A SPOT A COUPLE OF MILES FROM the main highway down a dirt road. There was a flat, open area with a hillside for a backstop that many others before them had used as an illegal shooting range. There were metal plates, appliances, boards, and miscellaneous junk used as makeshift targets. Broken glass and perforated tin cans littered the clearing near the hillside, and bullet casings and expended shotgun shells were scattered about. They got out and gathered near the side of the van.

"Carlos, just leave the ammo cans inside. We'll leave the slider open and reload from there, keep shit from getting dirty."

Tina pictured shooting Travis as he stood at the van, reloading and barking orders at Carlos. But to do so would create a crime scene within the vehicle she and Carlos would need to get them home. She'd have to wait until he was away from the van, but she'd also wait until he needed to reload. She wouldn't take a chance of having this turn into a gunfight. She wanted it to be quick and clean.

Tina had an image of Carlos in her head, shocked at what he would see happening. She'd have to get control of him fast and get the two of them out of there. She'd drive home; she wouldn't trust Carlos to keep his cool after seeing Travis killed. She would tell her brother about the abuse she suffered at the big man's hands, and she'd explain that this was the only way to make it stop without drawing attention to herself. She'd overplay the abuse part.

Hopefully the army had stopped looking for them by now, but if Travis were discovered murdered, the hunt would be on again. And she would be the prime suspect. They'd have to drag his body out into the forest, away from the clearing. Carlos wouldn't be happy about it, but she'd retake her control of him once Travis was dead. She used to have her little brother under her thumb, but he'd changed since Travis came into the picture. That could be fixed.

Travis was strapping his holstered pistol onto his belt at the side of the van. Carlos was loading magazines for the AR-15s. Travis told him to load them full for practice, and for when they went on a job, but to never leave them stored that way. Load the magazines a couple of rounds shy of capacity so that you didn't store them with full tension on the springs. Travis was disciplined when it came to the handling and maintenance of his weapons, though he was a slob in every other aspect of his life.

Tina watched the two men speaking civilly to one another, sharing this one interest. Carlos had taken to Travis and likely saw him as a father figure. Travis seemed to like Carlos, though he constantly talked down to him and made disparaging remarks about Hispanics. Yet when they worked together or spoke of working together, it was all business and a cohesive union. She hoped Carlos wouldn't lose his mind when she did what she had to do.

And she had to do it.

CHIEF WARRANT OFFICERS 2 JAMES P. MORGAN AND PAULINA Lazarevic were asked to have a seat in the lobby of the Homicide Bureau headquarters in the City of Commerce. They took the only two chairs for visitors and watched as a steady stream of detectives in suits and skirts passed by. It seemed to Morgan to be the hub of the wheel, the intersection of all traffic within the warehouse-sized office building that sat discreetly among identical buildings housing workers of various private industries.

Paulina whispered, "Have you noticed their guns?"

"Well yeah, of course. How could you not?"

"But, I mean, they are all different. I would have expected law enforcement to be more like the military, where everyone trains with and carries the same weapons. Look, the guy by the fax machine has a Glock. The lady that just walked through had a Smith on her belt. When we were talking to the black guy at the front desk, I was surprised to see he had a Beretta 92F sitting on the desk without a holster. It's weird."

"They're detectives. It's probably different than that for the street cops. Besides, they'll probably wonder why we're not wearing uniforms."

She smiled. "Well, we're detectives."

Morgan thought about that and wondered how many of the detectives in this building would recognize army investigators as actual detectives. He had mostly had good rapport with civilian law enforcement, but occasionally he would get the feeling that many of the local law enforcement officers were unimpressed with anything federal. Especially the FBI. They —the local cops—hated the FBI, or so it seemed.

A man with a hat popped around the corner, eyeballed Morgan and his partner, and then turned to the black detective at the desk. Morgan overheard him say, "Them?"

RICH FARRIS HAD CALLED ME ON MY CELL AND SAID SOMEONE WAS IN THE lobby to meet with me. When I asked who it was, he said, "army investigators." What the hell would they want? Farris didn't know.

I had just come back from lunch and had seen a slick car with government plates pulling into the lot. It must have been them. When I rounded the corner to the front desk lobby area, I nodded to Farris and asked if it were the two sitting in the chairs in civilian attire. They didn't appear to be soldiers. Farris affirmed it was them, and I crossed the lobby to meet them.

The man stood, and the woman followed his lead. "Hello, sir. I'm Chief Warrant Officer James Morgan, and this is Chief Warrant Officer Paulina Lazarevic. We're with Army CID."

I shook his hand, and then removed my hat and shook the firm hand of the woman called Lazarevic. "I thought you guys were feds, when I saw you pulling into the lot."

Morgan smiled. "No, sir. Not technically. Army CID."

I nodded, though I wasn't entirely sure what that meant. "How can I help you?"

"We understand you were the detective who made notification of death with the grandmother of Jimmy Ortiz, a man killed by an off-duty deputy sheriff."

"That's right, me and my partner, Detective Sanchez."

"We'd like to talk to you about that, if you have a few minutes."

"Sure," I said. "Why don't we go into the kitchen and grab a cup of coffee. We can talk there, or if you need more privacy, we can go into a conference room."

Morgan said, "Coffee sounds good."

The three of us started for the kitchen. Lazarevic said, "Is your partner available?"

I stopped. "That's an excellent question. I haven't seen her in a while." I turned back toward the desk. "Farris, would you mind paging Sanchez and asking if she would meet us in the kitchen, please?"

"You got it, Dickie."

"Dickie?" Lazarevic questioned as the three started again, heading through the hallway toward the kitchen.

"It's a nickname my old partner stuck me with. If you're lucky, you'll get out of here without meeting him."

"Why is that?" she asked.

"Well, for one, he's insane. Also, since you're an attractive woman with dark hair, he'll put more moves on you than an all-state wrestler."

She narrowed her eyes at me.

Her partner said, "Lazarevic had no problem handling the Taliban; I'm pretty sure she can handle your old partner."

"You haven't met Floyd."

20

When Sanchez arrived, Morgan had just finished explaining all of the structural nuances of the United States Army, its Cavalry unit, its Criminal Investigations unit—which is called CID because it used to be Criminal Investigations Division. He had just started to explain why he and the light-skinned woman with ink-black hair and a name I couldn't remember nor pronounce, were here at the bureau to speak with my partner and me.

Josie Sanchez came to the table, and I introduced her but allowed Morgan to introduce himself and his partner, to save me the embarrassment of having forgotten her name. She sat abruptly, and she seemed frazzled. Her normally cool eyes revealed worry or stress. She avoided eye contact with me and seemed relieved when Morgan began: "Nearly three years ago there were floods in Texas and we lost some soldiers from the First Cav—"

Being the newly christened army know-it-all, I told Josie, "That's the legendary First Cavalry Division. Did you see *Apocalypse Now?*"

She shook her head.

Morgan continued: "The soldiers were sent out on a Class One mission —dropping food and water to a unit in the field—and were crossing a creek in an LMTV—"

"Light Medium Tactical Vehicle." I had learned that during a previous investigation and wanted the colonel or whatever he was to know I knew what it meant. A suspect in the prior case had purchased one at an army surplus and used it as his daily commuter.

"—when a flash flood washed them down the river and turned the truck onto its side, killing at least four of the seven soldiers. Three were never found, including Sergeant Travis Hollingsworth and Private Christina Ortiz."

Ortiz. I was starting to see where this was going. "She's related to our dead robber, Jimmy."

"Exactly," Morgan confirmed.

"I know her," Josie said.

I turned my eyes to her. "That's right, you said you knew the whole family."

Josie looked at Lazarevic and then Morgan. "I worked in North Long Beach where her family lives. I knew the brothers more than her, but I did know her. The brothers were all in trouble, so we knew them well. All but one, the youngest one. And then I remember hearing that she had gone into the army, and I figured she would do good there. She seemed to be on the right track growing up."

Morgan made some notes.

"So, she's dead?"

Lazarevic answered her. "We don't know. There's reason to believe that she and the sergeant went AWOL."

"Absent without leave," I added.

"Really?" Josie said, her brows crowding her eyes. She seemed to be deep in thought, or maybe just surprised to hear it.

"What is it? What's bothering you?" I asked.

"I don't know. It's just not what I expected to hear. I guess you always hope there's one or two that make it out okay—out of these neighborhoods."

Morgan looked up. "She was doing well in the army, so I have no idea. I knew her too. We were at Fort Hood together for a while."

"It doesn't make sense," Josie continued.

"Is that a bad neighborhood, down there where the grandma lives?"

Josie smiled. "Well it's gang- and drug-infested, and we're usually good for a couple of murders a month down there. Why do you ask?"

"Because we have a surveillance going at the grandma's house. That's how we found out about you guys. Chief Lazarevic contacted the patrol station down there to let them know what we had going on, and they told us we'd better check with Homicide. She called here, and someone said you two had been to the home and met with the family for the death notification, so we thought it would be good to speak with you."

Josie looked at me when she said, "There's not much to tell you. We just talked to the grandma, and she said she wasn't surprised that Jimmy was killed. We didn't talk about much else."

"She didn't mention her granddaughter, Tina?" Lazarevic asked.

Josie shook her head as she answered. "No, she didn't. But wait, she did mention one of the brothers was in prison, if that helps. But that's about it. I have no idea what happened with the others."

Morgan cleared his throat. "The reason we're watching the house is we think that if Ortiz—that's the private, Christina Ortiz—is still alive, and if she has heard about her brother being killed, that she might make an appearance."

I agreed. "Seems reasonable."

Josie added, "You'll have trouble sitting down there. They'll make you for feds in no time."

"We figured that out the first day," Morgan said. "We did okay through the first night, but in the daylight hours, the boys drew too much attention and had to back out. That next night, in the wee hours, we had a pole cam installed across the street. We'll be watching the location on a monitor from here on out, at least during the day. It's hard to see at night, so we will probably continue with live surveillance during the night. We'll at least be doing some random spot-checks."

I smiled. "Hope your camera doesn't get shot out. The fellas down there like to shoot out the street lights, and if they see a camera, it'll be game on with those fools."

Lazarevic finished writing something on a piece of paper. She tore the page out of her notebook and handed it to Josie. "If you need anything from us, we're staged at this hotel. It's about two blocks from the target loc."

"Jesus, you're staying at that dump?"

"No, it's where we're staged. Monitoring the pole cam and radios. It's our command post. The army has us up in the Best Western, down in Long Beach."

"I have a question, before we wrap this up. Why would they go AWOL, this private and the sergeant?"

"That's an excellent question, Detective, one that we have been asking ourselves for nearly three years. I knew them both. At the time of the accident, I was also assigned to the First Cav, and although they didn't work directly under me, our paths often crossed. I was a lieutenant at the time. Hollingsworth was a bit of a hothead, a guy who'd been in more than a decade but never made it past the rank of sergeant due to disciplinary actions. Early in his career he had qualified for Ranger school, but washed out. Later, he was sent overseas on a deployment with the First Infantry Division, but when he returned, he reclassified as a fueler after failing multiple PT tests. The army gave him the option to go support, which he jumped on. He's strong as an ox, but apparently he never worked on his cardio. It was one of the reasons he failed in Ranger school as well. That and he didn't fit in.

"Since that time, he has made a career of trying to mentor young soldiers, being the hotshot. He'd invite them over to his house to drink, go out on the town with them on weekends, et cetera. Mostly because none of the other non-commissioned officers would hang out with him. But also because the kids were easily impressed with his tales of having been *down range,* and they'd eat up the war stories which just fueled his ego. In reality, he had never left the FOB, that's Forward Operating Base, for more than a few missions. His unit never received contact when they were out, not during his deployment. Not according to the records.

"Anyway, I say all that, to say this: Ortiz, a young female soldier who was a Private First Class, had somehow fallen under this guy's spell. The two were dating, or whatever you want to call it, and at the time of their disappearance, there had been a couple of investigations opened up on them. It seems he—Hollingsworth—had got into a few scrapes with civilians in town, and on at least one occasion, she was a participant in a bad beating and had stomped on a man's head once he was down."

Josie said, "Damn, girl."

"To look at her, she's as sweet as can be. Pretty, smart . . . I thought rather highly of her right up until the end when some of these allegations were surfacing. I tried to warn her about him, tried to tell her that he was no damn good, but—"

"Did they know they were under investigation?" I asked.

"Right before the flood and their disappearance, they did. In fact, there was an investigation under way and each had been advised of forthcoming interviews which they would be required to participate in, with or without representation.

"Normally, they may have been grounded pending the outcomes of those inquiries. The floods changed all of that. No soldier was spared from assisting in rescue, reconstruction, water diversion, and aid to local rescue and law enforcement. We were very involved in all aspects of the emergency response, as the army often is with natural disasters.

"At the time, Private Ortiz was a truck driver—eighty-eight mike was her M.O.S."

"M.O.S.?"

"Sorry, Military Occupational Specialty. The crew she was driving out on the Class One was led by Sergeant Hollingsworth. He was the truck commander.

"So, to answer your question, Detective, we think she was under the influence of a bad man who had a history of making bad choices. She was young and impressionable, and who knows, maybe in love. We think if the two survived, it would have been a spontaneous idea to go AWOL. One of the two—likely Hollingsworth—may have reasoned that they would be presumed dead and nobody would ever look for them.

"Which may have been the case, had a motel clerk not been murdered and his vehicle stolen, a short distance from the base. Though they haven't been positively linked to that murder, a witness reported a man and woman who match the general description of Hollingsworth and Ortiz, and who were undoubtedly army personnel, having been at the motel in the day or two prior to the murder."

Now it made sense to me. "That would be enough to keep them underground, I guess."

He nodded. "That's life in Leavenworth."

Josie said, "I guess they were all pieces of shit, the whole family."

The four of us sat in silence for a moment. I drained the last of my coffee which was now cold and bitter. The thought rattling around in my head seemed to be quite a leap, but I couldn't make it go away.

"Can we get photographs of these two, and physical descriptions?"

Morgan looked over at Lazarevic who shrugged. His eyes settled on Josie as he said, "I don't see why not. What are you thinking?"

Josie said, "We have a man and woman team out robbing and killing folks."

Lazarevic began thumbing through a case file. "Do you have a scanner handy?"

After copying the photos of Hollingsworth and Ortiz, Josie found me at my desk. I shook her off when she began to hand me the pictures. "Put them in the file."

"What's wrong with you?"

I looked her in the eyes. "Where have you been today?"

She puffed at a strand of hair that hung in her face, and sat down. "I had some personal business to take care of."

Biting at the end of a pen: "Okay, I have no problem with that. But you should let your partner know. Right?"

She nodded and looked away. Slowly, she turned to the work on her desk.

MOBY SERVED A COLD BEER AND ASKED WHERE THE LADY WAS TONIGHT. Out of town, I'd told him. He faded away to the unmistakable sounds of U2 starting on the jukebox. I sipped my beer and once again admired the paintings of pirates and their wenches that adorned the walls of my new favorite bar. Chinatown had too much baggage now. Yee Mee Loo's, my former watering hole, now conjured images of muzzle flashes and the smell of burning gunpowder. No amount of gin could drown those memories, I had discovered.

I took a long drink of the cold beer, and it felt good. Fixated on the frosted mug before me, I found myself dwelling on our newest case. I thought about the killers, and wondered who they were and what really motivated them. My mind drifted to the witnesses: Latisha Carver, who feared for the lives of her hungry babies. Cedric Staley, the little boy with green eyes and a zest for life, unaware of the shitty cards he had been dealt. And the victims: Ho and Frazier. *Especially* the victims. Because the dead never leave. Their spirits take refuge in the minds and souls of those who have both the honor and the burden of seeking justice for them. Their presence evokes a range of emotions: frustration, heartbreak, anger, resolve. Of these, it is the resolve that matters.

For some reason, the wino, Frazier, who died violently and needlessly in the parking lot of Ho's, had stuck with me more than others. It had been yet another senseless death of the weak and vulnerable. An undeserving, underprivileged man who already lived a hard life, had been gunned down like a rabid dog and left as discarded refuse by a pair of vicious sociopaths. Savages. It was these acts of violence that drove me, now, to solve the cases and send bad men to prison. When I was younger, that was all the motivation I needed to put on the gun and badge each night and put myself in harm's way. Most cops I knew were the same. We lived—and sometimes died—to find brutal men and step between them and the weak, the innocent, the vulnerable. Look them in their eyes: *Say when.*

I drained the cold mug and placed it in the well before me, a signal that I would need another. My God, how I would need another. My pulse thumped against the walls of my neck as I glared at the wall in front of me but saw a liquor store and its parking lot and two dead men who never had a chance. At times, I believed I was capable of murder myself, in the name of vengeance. Or so I told myself.

I checked my phone. No messages. Katherine was also on my mind, thanks to Moby. Or maybe I was searching for something else to think about. Who was I kidding, she had been on my mind anyway, and likely would continue to be whenever I had time to think. The idea of calling her didn't sit well with me, though I couldn't understand why. Stubbornness? Fear? Fear of what? Relationships, a shrink might suggest. I chuckled at the irony. Moby had his eyes on me as he fished a frozen mug from the cooler. He probably questioned my sanity. He and some others: Floyd, Katherine, Captain Stover . . .

Another beer arrived and the U2 song faded, only to be replaced by Bon Jovi rocking "Wanted Dead or Alive." Which took me back to the liquor store in Compton and a pair of ruthless killers. I silently vowed to see justice done. Resolved.

21

Tina and her little brother, Carlos, sat at the dining room table. McDonald's breakfast sandwiches sat before them on opened wrappers, and each had a Coke to wash it down. Tina was nibbling at her sandwich and sipping her Coke, though her stomach was tied in knots. Carlos seemed to have lost his appetite also.

"What's the matter, *manito*?"

He started to pick up the sandwich, but retreated. "I don't know. Nothing. Everything. Where do I start?"

"Yesterday."

"Okay, yesterday. Then what?"

"Carlos, I know you look up to Travis. I understand that, and I know you are upset about yesterday. But we have to move past it. There's so much I need to tell you when the time is right. The time isn't right yet, because, well, because yesterday didn't go as I had planned."

She saw the anger as she looked into his eyes. It seemed to grow as the two held their silent gazes. Tina remembered *her* anger, yesterday, last night, and again this morning as she saw her left eye black and purple and swollen shut.

Finally, he spoke, "I should've killed him."

"Carlos . . ."

"No, don't . . . just—"

"You're just a kid. You did the best you could."

But Carlos had been knocked out by one punch. It was something she had seen Travis do to others, on more than a couple of occasions. His fists were hard and fast. She was lucky to not have been hurt worse than she was. She hadn't thought about Travis checking his weapon, but she should have known that he would. It had been her mistake, and it could have been a deadly one. Fortunately, Travis was too stupid to know why the round had been removed from the chamber of his gun. He assumed Carlos had been messing with it, and he had gotten in Carlos's face about it. When Tina intervened, he backhanded her and knocked her down. She didn't see what happened, but she looked in time to see Carlos on the ground, out cold. When Carlos came to, Travis made it clear to them both that nobody had better ever touch his guns again, without his permission.

The door flung open and there he stood. Carlos glanced over and then looked away. Tina watched him closely, and when she realized her jaw was tight and she was holding a breath, she let it out slowly and turned back to her meal.

"What's everyone so down about around here?"

Neither answered.

Tina heard the door close. Moments later, she felt his presence. Still, she didn't look up.

"When you two crybabies get over your damn selves, let me know. We have plans to make. I want to do that job tomorrow. We're flat broke and the rent's coming due. And we still need to find the boy, and finish with the gook."

Tina heard his footsteps carry him down the hall, and she heard him using the restroom without closing the door. She pictured him standing at the toilet, peeing all over it, and walking away without flushing. She reached over and tapped her brother's arm, and whispered, "Just be cool. It's alright. Everything is going to be fine. I have something in mind for his big dumb ass. You wait and see."

AT THE WEEKLY OFFICE MEETING, JOSIE BRIEFED HER FIRST HOMICIDE CASE to a gathering of about fifty detectives and professional staff. Sixty percent of the bureau seemed about average as far as attendance of the *mandatory* Wednesday meetings. We were not an overly regimented lot. When finished, she fielded a few questions, ignored a few jeers, and walked back to her desk to the subtle applause that always followed briefings of murdered civilians.

As she settled into her seat next to mine, another detective began briefing a case involving *Florencia Trese,* a Hispanic street gang in South Los Angeles with hundreds of cliques and an allegiance to the Mexican mafia. Hence the *trese,* which represents the thirteenth letter of the alphabet, M. Or, *Eme.* Apparently, "Florence" was at war with 38th Street—again—and the bodies were stacking up.

I whispered to my partner, "Good job."

She widened her eyes and drew a deep breath. "That's scary up there."

"It's a tough crowd for sure."

She nodded and turned back to face the front of the office where the detective who had briefed the gang war walked away to the sound of subdued applause.

The captain stepped up the microphone for his final lecture of the meeting. "You guys are killing me on the overtime," he began.

I tapped Josie on the shoulder and nodded for her to follow me as I stood up and started for the back door. Outside, I put my shades on and lowered the brim of my hat against the late morning sun. Josie joined me but neither of us spoke as a train passed behind the office, the ground vibrating beneath our feet.

Once I could hear myself think, I said, "I did some thinking about this case last night, and about that Ortiz woman and the sergeant she went AWOL with."

"You think they might be our suspects?"

"It's a long shot, but worth consideration. My question though—one I haven't been able to answer—is *why*? Why the killing? As I sat at my new watering hole last night, alone in my well-lubricated thoughts, I pondered that. This place has paintings of pirates with their loot and their wenches, and you know what? All of that makes sense to me. The reason for the pursuit, is the broads and the loot. How's that for poetry? Oh, and the booze."

A slight grin on her face, Josie rolled her eyes.

"To me, this seems like the robbery isn't the driving factor of these cases. Like, they're not in it for the money. Know what I mean?"

Josie's head cocked slightly, a dark mass of hair flowing over her shoulder. "But they did take the money."

"But why the grape outside? Why did they kill the wino? That was a thrill-kill, plain and simple. That old man wasn't ever going to be a witness. Plus, Floyd's case, the one with the little kid—"

She smiled. "Cedric."

"—that one is so strange, the victims won't even admit it happened. You know, like maybe it was a hit or something."

"So, you don't think they're doing this for kicks, necessarily, but that maybe there's even more to it than that? Contract murder?"

"That army guy yesterday, Chief Morgan, said the sergeant, whatever his name was—"

"Hollingsworth."

"—played up his deployments like a war hero to the younger soldiers. That tells me something about the guy. Morgan also said they believe he did a murder right after the two of them went AWOL, killing a motel clerk for his car, presumably. Maybe the money in the till, too. But a guy like that, someone who boasts about valor, yet hasn't seen action, might have a glitch in his psyche. Like a bully who only hits people who won't fight back."

"Yeah, maybe."

"I'm just saying, it's something to think about. And I don't know about the contract thing. That takes us way off in the weeds, but I guess it's something we should keep in mind."

"Okay, so where are we going?"

I didn't know what she meant. "I give up."

"I thought that's why we left the meeting, that we had somewhere to be."

I grinned. "I just get tired of listening to the captain. If we both walk out, they figure we have something important to do."

"But we don't?"

I glanced at my watch. "Not until lunchtime."

ROLAND YOUNGBLOOD HAD THREE YEARS TO GO BEFORE RETIREMENT from his second career as an armored transport officer. He had retired after twenty-eight years of service as a police officer for the city of Inglewood, where he had spent his entire career on the streets. He had always worn a uniform and was comfortable doing so. When not in uniform, he wore shorts and some type of loose-fitting, button-up short-sleeved shirt, the louder the better. And sandals. It fit his laid-back personality, a character-istic that had allowed him to survive nearly three decades as a cop in a high-crime community, the same city where he had grown up and also raised his family.

Three years to go, he would tell people, speaking of ending the second career and spending his time fishing. Three more years because that's when his youngest would be finished with college. She was currently enrolled in El Camino Community College, but she had hopes and plans to get into the nursing program at the University of California, Los Angeles. Roland feared it would break him, and he often joked that it was the reason he had decided to drive an armored car for a living. "Where else am I gonna get the kind of money it takes to get these young'uns through school?" Also, three more years because he had seven years with the company currently, and at ten he would earn a second retirement. Roland had done the math, and the two retirements meant he and his wife of thirty-eight years would be financially able to take vacations and enjoy their golden years.

He'd started his shift at seven o'clock this morning, as usual, to make the route he'd been driving for the past four years. It was a loop that took him south from the headquarters in downtown Los Angeles through Maywood, Bell, Cudahy, Lynwood, and Compton, before taking him north with stops in Willowbrook, South Los Angeles, and Vermont. Finally, he would pull back into the fortified headquarters of L.A. Armored. It was eleven a.m. when his courier went into a market in Compton—they were running ahead of schedule today—so Roland opened his lunchbox. The engine purred and the air-conditioning blew cold air at him as he waited behind the wheel. His partner's name was Darnell, and as always, Roland had warned him to "Watch out for them niggas." Both were black and had grown up in gang-infested neighborhoods, so although they were cautious, neither was frightened of the youngsters in their baggy pants and bandanas or sideways ball caps. It was an ongoing joke and both would laugh each time Roland said it.

After a few minutes, and just as Roland finished the last of his peanut-butter and banana sandwich, he looked up to see Darnell strolling out through the glass door with a money bag in his left hand, keeping his gun hand free. He had a big smile across his face. Roland chuckled, knowing Darnell had been messing with the little Korean woman inside. It seemed there was someone on every stop that Darnell would make friends with, and usually they were female. His stories would often take Roland back to his days of youth and he'd wonder where the years had gone.

Darnell's free arm swung back and forth passing the pistol on his hip, and his head was on a swivel. Roland looked past his skinny partner as he neared their truck, watching Darnell's back. Roland also checked all sides of their vehicle through the various mirrors, watching carefully for an ambush. After all of these years, Roland knew to never relax when the money was in play, his partner heading back to the truck. That's when it was most likely to go down. They could laugh and joke all day inside the rig with the radio going and the air blowing, but when the money man made his way back to the truck, it was all business, all the time. This is when junkies and gangsters would watch closely and lick their lips while staring at the bag of money, no doubt wondering if they could pull off taking it from them.

Roland suddenly stopped chewing and moved quickly from the driver's seat in a near panic. Twenty-eight years on the streets as a cop, another seven working in the security industry, and a lifetime spent surviving the streets of South Los Angeles, had honed Roland's instincts. The man coming up in Darnell's blind spot was an immediate threat.

I BUMPED INTO LOPES AS I WAS COMING OUT OF THE MEN'S ROOM. "What's up, Davey?"

He averted his eyes and continued past me with a nod and a "Hey, man," as if that was all there was to say. It was out of character, and I still felt something was going on with him.

I turned and followed him into the restroom. "So, what's going on, man?"

"Nothing."

He was all business at the urinal.

"Dude, what's going on with you?"

"Whaddya mean?"

"Come on, man, you know what I mean. You've been weird around me all day, and coincidentally, Josie's been acting strange too."

He glanced over his shoulder and frowned. "What'd she say?"

"She told me what happened."

He looked back to his business at hand, zipped up, and brushed past me on his way out the door. "You're so full of shit, Dickie. Nice try, though."

I caught the door. "You didn't wash your hands."

22

The greatest weakness of armored transport services is that a courier must exit and enter the bank-on-wheels several dozen times each day in order to move the money from one place to another. The second vulnerability is the integrity of the men and women who are entrusted with large sums of cash. Most company owners worried most about the second.

L.A. Armored carefully screened each applicant. Several former law enforcement officers worked for the retired LAPD officer who started the company. Many of his employees had worked LAPD, others came from other departments throughout the southland and beyond. He paid them better than his competition paid their guards, and he had a unique offer that stood in spite of the controversy it had stirred: any of his officers who shot and killed a would-be robber would receive a fifty-thousand-dollar bonus. The boss was serious about his company not being robbed. In twenty-one years, he'd only paid it once, but he did so gladly.

Word of the bounty spread on the streets. Had that made a difference? It was hard to say. There had never been an attempted robbery of any of the L.A. Armored's fleet, though in the seven years Roland had been driving, other companies had been robbed. One such occurrence had resulted in two guards being killed.

The policy for many companies was that in the event of a robbery attempt, the driver was to flee with the truck and money, leaving the guard outside to fend for himself. L.A. Armored didn't operate that way. The owner, the former LAPD officer, had stated: "We don't run, we gun. If someone tries to take our money, there's going to be bloodshed." Unlike other transports, L.A. Armored not only equipped their officers with sidearms, they also supplied each truck with a shotgun, and they trained and qualified their officers with both.

Roland had often thought the fifty-G would be a nice way to retire. He could hang up the gun belt for good and see the last of his kids through college. Sometimes he would sit in the truck and watch Darnell wade through the onlookers and say to himself, "Come on, motherfucker, try it," while caressing the grip of his Colt .45 that sat on his hip. Sometimes, when Darnell would return, Roland would joke with him. "You gots to quit scaring them niggas outta trying you. That one was looking at your money bag like a fat kid looks at cake. I was fittin' to collect my fifty-G." They'd both laugh and motor off to the next stop.

Roland eased his pistol back into its holster and fastened the thumb snap as he retreated to his seat behind the wheel.

Darnell locked the door and dropped his money bag on the floor of the truck and wiped at the beads of sweat on his forehead, turning the light-blue long-sleeved uniform shirt dark across the forearm. "Now, that was weird. I thought you was gonna finally get that bounty today, boss."

Roland was checking his mirrors and merging into traffic. You didn't want to be stationary any longer than necessary. He glanced over his shoulder. "What'd that asshole say?"

"Motherfucker axed me what time it was. I was like, 'Get the fuck away from me, motherfucker, or the nigga in the truck gonna smoke us both.' " Darnell chuckled as he settled into his seat in the cargo area of the truck, sweat beading on his forehead. "He must've known we wasn't playin' around."

"What do you think, was he gonna try you?"

"I don't know," Darnell said, "maybe. He might've just been stupid, too. Goddamn Mexicans."

"Maybe," Roland conceded. But in his mind, there was more to it. "Could have been a dry run. A test. We'd better pay close attention for a few days, closer than usual. Especially at this stop. Them Mexicans can be sneaky little shits, actin' like they *no habla* till they have the drop on you."

"Don't I know. I grew up 'round 'em, had to go to school with them cholos. Motherfuckers be stabbin' niggas in they backs."

Roland drew a deep breath and let it out slowly, steering his rig through the afternoon traffic and thinking about his woman at home. That had been as close as he had come to dropping the hammer on anyone since he left law enforcement. He replayed the scene in his mind, seeing the man walk quickly and directly at Darnell from an angle that would be considered a man's blind spot. Roland had moved to the rear, drawn his pistol, and even thumbed the safety off as he stuck the barrel through one of the gun ports near the back door. He had taken a bead on the would-be bad guy and had started putting pressure on the trigger when the man suddenly retreated. Roland replayed it slowly in his mind, and he saw Darnell's expression change. His face twisted from its usual smile to intensity and anger. Roland remembered Darnell's right hand going for his pistol as he stepped back and yelled at the man who was near him, stopping the man in his tracks. As Darnell backed toward the door, Roland had opened it and grabbed his partner's collar, guiding him back inside the truck. The Mexican had disappeared by then, but it was as close as either of them had ever been to being robbed, at least while in the course of their employment.

He was too old for this shit, he thought, his heart still pounding, the palms of his big hands damp with perspiration as he gripped the wheel tighter than usual. The air blowing from the vents did little to cool his temperature. Fifty grand or not, he didn't need this shit. Maybe he had pushed his luck too long. Maybe it was time to call it quits. He'd talk to the wife about it over dinner. Tomorrow. Today was his long shift. When they finished their normal route, he and Darnell would make the big run downtown. They would load up all of the day's proceeds from all of the routes and take the money downtown for a big deposit, usually in the ballpark of a hundred grand. They'd each get double-time plus a hundred-dollar bonus for their efforts.

In the van, Travis said, "You trying to get yourself shot?"

"I just wanted to see how alert the dude is."

"Right, but we didn't want to put these guys on edge, either. This was just to see how they react when someone gets close. You damn near got shot."

Carlos chuckled. Tina sat with her lips pursed, drawing deep breaths through her nose and trying to calm herself. She had seen the guard go for his gun and had panicked during the brief moments that followed. Travis was right, Carlos pushed it a lot harder than he should have. His job was to get a close look and give Tina and Travis the opportunity to see how they responded to a man approaching the guard outside of his truck. They had definitely been given a good look at how the guards might respond. The guard outside was alert and had gone for his gun, and the one inside remained steadfast. He didn't drive away, as they had heard was the protocol for these drivers. He had remained, though they couldn't see what he did in response to Carlos's approach. Maybe he had been asleep, for all they knew.

Carlos said, "That dude's pretty alert, aware of his surroundings. He isn't going to be easy to creep up on."

"Probably a veteran," Travis said. "Civilians don't act that way. Vets, and cops. Some crooks. Not many of these two-bit guards. Look, we're going to watch them all day and see their whole routine. There might be a better time and place to make this happen."

"Just follow them around?" Tina asked, touching her swollen eye around the edges.

"Why not wait until the truck is full? Hell," Travis said, "this could be our last job, if we do it right. One big hit and head for Mexico. Spend the rest of my life surrounded by beautiful Latinas."

He glanced back at Tina, but she didn't smile. To her, it sounded like a great idea. Get the money and head south. She could pay a Tijuana whore to cut the fat fucker's throat for a hundred bucks, and keep her hands clean of it. Though maybe she'd at least watch.

After lunch, I took Josie into the conference room where it was quiet and out of view of the rest of the detectives in the bureau so that we could dictate our reports to date. Homicide Bureau was the only place in the department where working cops dictated reports and secretaries typed them for us. Everywhere else, you typed your own reports. Of course, there was no other assignment where typewritten reports routinely exceeded fifty pages. Some case reports would exceed a hundred pages, and occasionally there would be reports of several hundred pages. A murder book—the completed investigative file, which consisted of all of the investigators' reports plus the reports of all others: crime lab, coroner, et cetera—would routinely consist of several hundred pages. Some cases would require several volumes of books to contain thousands of pages of documentation. Good secretaries were imperative in the murder business.

The act of dictation was a learned skill, one that always seemed awkward when first attempted. Soon, you could dictate with people watching. You could dictate while riding down the road with your partner, or even while driving in L.A. stop-and-go traffic. You could dictate anywhere: at home, on a plane, in the court hallway or jury assembly room while waiting for your case to be called. You could stay at home and dictate naked, for all anyone cared. You could go outside and dictate naked. I wouldn't put anything past homicide detectives. Especially Floyd.

We left our clothes on and passed the digital recorder back and forth to keep a chronological order of events. Dictating together would make correcting the rough draft and finalizing the report a simpler process when it came back from the secretaries.

When we finished, I tried again. "Is something going on, I should know about?"

Silence hung in the room for a moment as she looked deep into my eyes. The longer she waited, the more uncomfortable I became.

"Never mind," I said, "it's probably something personal, and I don't need to know. You both are single, anyway, so it's none of my business what you're doing."

"Who's single?" she snapped. "Who's 'you both.' "

"You and Lopes."

She grinned. For a minute, I thought she was going to start laughing. But she didn't. She just stood and walked to the door.

"I guess that answers that."

She turned from the door. "Look, my personal life is just that—personal. But, so that you can put it to rest, there is nothing going on between me and Lopes."

"Didn't you guys go out for drinks?"

"Don't you and Floyd? You guys aren't gay, are you?"

"Jesus Christ, Josie."

She hit me in the chest with the back of her hand. It was a surprisingly strong blow, though clearly meant to be playful, given the smile on her face. "I'm just fucking with you. I know Floyd's not gay."

She walked out and the door closed behind her. I was stuck in my tracks. "Jesus," I said again. I opened the door. "Wait, what's that supposed to mean?" She didn't look back.

I followed her to our desks where the usual bustle and typical banter of our colleagues prevented any further discussion. It was probably for the best. I may have bitten off more than I could chew with this woman.

I had left my cell phone in the top drawer with my car keys, and I gathered both with the thought of heading for the bar. But my phone showed three missed calls and two text messages, all of them from Katherine. I pulled my chair from my desk and sat to read the texts while Josie sat within arms reach, acting as if nothing had happened.

Hey there, tried calling but no answer. There's some things we need to talk about, a lot is changing back here and not for the better. I'll be home this weekend. I hope we can talk then. Will you be off?

I started to return the text but didn't know what to say. Staring at my phone, thumbs at the ready, I stalled and my mind went blank.

"That your lady you're texting?"

I looked up and Josie was smiling. Then she winked. She fucking winked at me!

Floyd appeared over my shoulder. "Did you figure out who the ninjas are yet?"

"The ninjas?" Jesus, had everyone around me gone crazy?

"Those assholes in black everything who killed Ho and the wino. That could be a group: *Ho and the Winos*. A real ho-down for the homies. What the hell are you doing, Dickie?"

A beat went by before I answered. "What the hell am I doing?" I glanced at my partner. "I'm trying to figure out women."

"Good luck with that. You'd be better off trying to solve the Zodiac killings. No offense, Detective Sanchez."

Josie turned in her chair and smiled widely at him, her eyes almost sparkling. "None taken, Floyd."

He grinned back. "Well check you out."

"Jesus."

"What's wrong, Dickie?" Floyd asked, now smiling and glancing from me to Josie.

"Oh, nothing. Other than the fact I'm the only sane person in this goddamn place."

Josie answered a call. Floyd helped himself to an empty chair and put a shoe on my desk. "Anything new on the case?"

"No. What about yours?"

"Cedric the Entertainer left me a message, said he needs to talk to me about something."

Floyd pushed his sleeves up. "He's probably just lonely, wants to go for another ride-along. Mongo's in court today. Do you want to take a ride with me?"

I looked over to see Josie had finished her call and now sat grinning at the work in front of her. I was pretty sure she was still enjoying her comment about us being gay. I also knew that Floyd was going to die when I told him the story. More than anything, I needed some time *away* from her, and with my old partner. We had a lot to discuss. The subject matter was right up his alley. I'd lay it all on him and see what Doctor Floyd would come up with. "Let me hit the head and grab a soda for the drive."

When I returned to my desk Floyd was nowhere to be found. I pictured him outside waiting by my car to suggest that I could drive, *if I didn't mind*. Josie had earphones on and a sheaf of papers in front of her. At a glance, it appeared to be some type of court transcription. I tapped her on the shoulder to get her attention. She removed one earbud and nodded.

"Listen, I didn't mean—"

She held up a hand to stop me. "No need to say anything. We're good. I hope I wasn't out of line."

"No, no, not at all," I stammered.

We sat looking at one another for a long moment.

"What are you proofing?" I finally asked.

"Transcripts."

"Oh." I waited, but it didn't seem she was going to offer any further details. But we were partners, and this was obviously business. Even though I knew it wouldn't be anything from our case at this point, it seemed appropriate for me to know what she was working on. I was her training officer. "Transcripts from what?"

She hesitated, looked back at the sheaf of papers, and sighed. After a long moment, she swiveled her chair around to face me squarely. "I'm being sued, and we're going to trial next month. These are transcripts from the criminal case, my testimony and my partner's. I'm going through it when I have time, a little here and a little there, to prepare myself. It's all county business."

I pulled my chair back out and plopped down, took my hat off and set it crown down on my desktop. "I know, I didn't mean to imply that it wasn't. So, what's it about, anyway? What are you being sued for?"

"This one's a force beef. We caught a man in the act of raping a woman in a public restroom. The suspect spent some time in the hospital, the result of our arrest. It's not the first time I've been sued, but it's the first time the county didn't pay it off to avoid trial."

I nodded.

"Have you been sued?"

"Yeah, a few times," I said. "I've only stood trial once, and it was a bitch. I don't envy you."

Her brows were low, showing concern in her soft brown eyes. "It's not going to be easy. I know that. I've been dreading it for a long time as it kept being continued. Now, of course—now that I am here and really don't have time for this shit—it's set for trial." She shook her head as she finished saying it.

I was back in the driver's seat. She had put me on the ropes in the conference room, and showed me her strength. Showed me to be careful with her. But now we were back to business and that is where I held the high ground and where I found strength, courage, and confidence. I nodded as I thought about her situation. "How's the case against you look?"

"In today's climate? The jury will hang us out. The only saving grace might be that the victim is black, and we expect her to testify favorably. The suspect—oh, I'm sorry, the *plaintiff*—is also black. I don't know if that matters, but the attorney has of course played the race card since the cops aren't black."

"Who was your partner?"

Her gaze fell to the floor. "Lopes."

23

"*L opes?*"

Josie closed her eyes and gave a slight nod to affirm it. Her eyes remained down and she picked at lint on her black slacks.

"How long ago was this? He hasn't worked patrol for fifteen, twenty years."

She quietly responded. "About four, five years ago. He was here at Homicide at the time; I was working gangs. Both of us were carped out one day and that's when it happened."

CARP, *Cadre of Administrative Resource Personnel* was the department's ingenious way to cut overtime costs by reassigning detectives to various other assignments one day each month. There was no doubt some house-fairy had promoted behind the creation of it. Everyone else hated it. At least the real cops did. It wasn't as if detectives had extra time to go play bailiff or jailer somewhere. But to my knowledge, nobody from Homicide had ever been carped out to work a patrol assignment.

"In patrol?"

"No," she said, now looking up at me with soft eyes. "We were each assigned to work court security on a high-profile case at the Criminal Courts Building. That was the first time I had ever worked with Lopes, but

I knew of him and had seen him around more than a few times over the years."

"Everyone knows Lopes."

"At lunch, we decided to go to Stops down in Lynwood. He actually decided, and I agreed to go with him. We were doing a speed run and picking up lunch for the entire crew that was working the detail. There were six or seven of us, and one of the guys there had worked with Lopes at Firestone, back in the old days I guess. They were reminiscing about the good old days and eating spots had become central to the conversation. They started talking about hot-links at Stops, and everyone sounded interested. So, Lopes and I took a black and white and headed south. Crazy man was driving, and as we're headed down Central, we get flagged down."

I chuckled. "Crazy man, huh?"

"Well, he is a bit wild, I'd say. I can only imagine what he was like in his twenties."

"Was this in LAPD's area?"

"No, it was in Firestone. Will Rogers Park."

"No shit huh?"

"It was a lady, and you could tell she was really upset about something. Lopes asked what was wrong. She said a man followed a woman and her little boy into the women's restroom, and she pointed out a building across the park.

"Lopes jumped the curb and drove across the park like a bat out of hell. Mexicans were grabbing their soccer balls and diving for cover. Some were yelling at us. He didn't hit the siren, and thinking back, picturing the intensity on his face, he wanted to catch this guy in the act."

"Oh, I'm sure of it. Who wouldn't?"

"We tore up twenty feet of sod skidding to a stop by the restrooms, and then the two of us hurried inside."

As she told the story, I could see the park in my mind, and I reflected on chasing gangsters through it back in the eighties. They would congregate at the far sides where the advantage would be theirs in seeing the cops before we saw them. Occasionally, we would coordinate swoops on them, and some of us would go in on foot from the back side while patrol cars would come at them, driving across the park. Inevitably, there would be runners—those with guns or dope who knew the hammer was coming down. It would be chaos for a few minutes, like an out-of-control rugby match with cops running and tackling gang members and cop cars skidding across the grass as they came to the aid of their colleagues. Patrol had by far been the most exciting days of my career.

Josie's eyes were fixed off in the distance as she recounted the afternoon that had been seared into her memory, and now she was being forced to bring it to the surface.

"Well, the lady had it right. There was a man in there, and he hadn't been invited by the woman. He had a knife to her throat. Her pants and panties were down around her ankles, as were his. The woman's top had been removed and placed over the boy's head to cover his eyes. The little boy was standing next to them in the stall."

"Jesus."

"Yeah, it was the real deal. Right in front of us. The dude had a hold of himself and was just about to penetrate her when Lopes screwed his gun into the asshole's ear. *Surprise.* The guy dropped the knife immediately. We pulled him out of the stall to get him clear of the woman and child so we can hook him up. This asshole makes the mistake of resisting arrest. He actually tried to run past us to escape through the door with his pants around his ankles. Lopes hit him across the head with his pistol, cracked him open like a ripe melon. The guy went down, hard. But he still had plenty of fight in him, so the two of us basically beat him into submission. It wasn't pretty."

"Sounds clean, though."

"It was, but since when does that matter? He's got the scars and the medical reports to show we beat his ass."

"He deserved it."

"Sure, in our eyes. In normal peoples' eyes. What about attorneys, jurors?"

"This is different though. You have a victim—a woman being raped! I can't imagine they'll find you guys liable. Jesus, the asshole's lucky Lopes didn't shoot him in the face."

"We talked about it later, and both of us wished we could have. But with the woman and kid there—"

"Did they file it federal?"

She nodded. "Civil rights violations."

I shook my head. "Ridiculous . . . Well, still, I bet you guys will be okay. As long as your case doesn't get assigned to Smetts's court. That's one federal judge who hates cops and will do everything he can to help the plaintiff's case."

"I'm hoping for a woman judge."

"That'd be perfect," I said. "Hopefully, a black woman."

Josie turned back to the papers on her desk, having finished telling the story that would stay in her mind for the rest of her life. I pictured her shooting the man in the market, a story I had only recently heard, and I knew if she had been able to, she wouldn't have hesitated to shoot the armed rapist. There was no doubt in my mind that the fighting preceding the rapist's arrest had been vicious, and not just on the part of Lopes. I had seen him in action, but I could imagine my partner right alongside him.

I had a new perspective about her and Lopes. They had been through the shit together. Floyd would assume—and he had—that Lopes and the hot new detective, Josefina Sanchez, had hooked up and had a fling going or at least in the works. But now I knew what Floyd didn't: that Lopes and Josie had a history. And now they had a situation to deal with together, a federal civil rights trial. It made sense to me, someone who had been through it. It even provided an explanation for the late-night drinks; they had things to discuss before trial begins.

Floyd's voice bellowed from behind me. I turned to see him standing at the back door, his shades in place. "Are you coming, Dickie? Jesus."

I glanced at my watch. "We'll be back in a couple of hours, if you're still around. Otherwise, I'll see you tomorrow."

She smiled curtly. "Goodnight, partner."

Before walking away, I said, "Hey, partner . . ."

"Yeah?"

"Sorry."

She smiled and we parted ways.

"WHAT DO YOU SUPPOSE THEY DO WITH THE MONEY?" CARLOS ASKED.

The three of them sat in their van across from a windowless structure protected by block walls topped with razor wire. The building appeared as a prison but with various bay doors on at least two sides, from what they could see. The armored truck they were following had pulled up to one such door that lifted automatically and closed after the armored transport had pulled inside.

"I guess they store it there," Tina said. She was kneeling on the floor between the two front seats, watching through large sunglasses with her one good eye; the other still half closed. Travis was to her left, behind the wheel, and her brother, Carlos, sat riding shotgun.

"I wonder how much money's in there," Carlos muttered.

Tina noticed Travis browsing the landscape, taking it all in. He appeared to be deep in thought. Planning. It was quiet inside the van, a steady humming of the air-conditioner and the soft rumble of a motor the only sounds. Occasionally a car or truck would pass them on the road, and the gust of wind would shake their van. Tina was deep in thought as well, first wondering how much money was behind those solid doors, and then thinking about getting all of it and heading south. Which made her again think about how easy it would be to have Travis disappear in Mexico without a trace. She and Carlos would live happily ever after in Mexico, and like royalty. They would have to surround themselves with body-guards, maybe build a fortress to keep the peasants and killers at bay.

A few minutes later, another armored truck arrived, its brakes squealing as it powered down and turned into the driveway directly across from where the trio sat watching. The exterior gate opened and closed automatically, and the truck motored over to a bay door adjacent to the door where *their* armored car had driven into.

Carlos said, "How could we get inside? That's the key. Better than robbing one truck on the street."

Travis lit a cigarette and took a long drag before lowering his hand. After exhaling a plume of smoke that filled the cab, he glanced at Tina and then to Carlos. "This ain't a bank. The money has to leave here and go to a bank somewhere. *That's* the key. Figure out when all of the money is hauled out in one load, and take *that* truck down. That's how you retire from the business."

The three of them watched in silence for two more hours and counted a total of six trucks arriving and entering the building through the bay doors. Civilian vehicles trickled out, and the pattern seemed to show two employees at a time leaving shortly after another truck arrived and disappeared into the building. Nobody seemed to notice their van. The area was industrial, and little traffic remained other than the activity at the warehouse. Plenty of other cargo vans traveled through the area and were parked along the streets and in the parking lots of businesses. They were somewhere near downtown Los Angeles, though Tina wasn't sure exactly where.

Just before dark, one of the bay doors opened and a truck pulled out, its headlights on against a dusky sky. The gate closed behind it, and the armored transport rumbled away, its tail lights shrinking in the distance.

Travis started the van and pulled away, following the route the truck had traveled. "That's the same truck we followed up here. Everyone else has gone home for the day. Where do you suppose this truck is headed?"

"To the bank?"

Travis looked over at Carlos in the passenger's seat and smiled at him. "Fuckin' A, to the bank, *amigo*. Get your guns ready to rock and roll. There's probably a million bucks in that rig being driven by twenty-dollar-an-hour assholes. What do you want to bet they ain't willing to die for *the man* and *his* money?"

IT WAS NEARLY NINE BY THE TIME FLOYD AND I RETURNED TO THE OFFICE. We had decided to get a bite to eat after visiting with Cedric the Entertainer at his foster home in Watts. During dinner, I told Floyd all about the lawsuit involving Lopes and my partner, Josie. I told him that she and I had talked, and I didn't think there was anything going on, or anything more to them having gone out for drinks.

He said, "That's bullshit."

"What's the difference? You and I go out for drinks."

Floyd scoffed at the idea of it being the same thing. He said, "Plus, now you know the two of them have a history together. You didn't know that before. It makes perfect sense now, Dickie. If they were in the shit together, you know that means they had a drink together after the asshole was booked at the hospital ward that night and the paperwork was finished. Like you and me going to Chinatown after we shoot someone, only they probably didn't go their separate ways when the drinking was finished. That's the way it is, Dickie. I've tried to tell you that, but you don't listen. Men and women can't work together in this kind of an environment without shit happening. And by shit, I mean unadulterated sex."

"You don't think they could have got together just to talk about the trial?"

"No."

"No possibility."

"Negative. She's too hot. Those two are banging like a wood screen door in a Texas tornado."

The conversation and cold beer had kept us at the restaurant past dinner and into the evening hours. When we pulled into the Homicide bureau's lot, we were surprised to see more than a few cars still remained.

The television at the front desk was tuned to a news station, as it generally is, only it was not muted as usual and an audience had gathered. There were four detectives huddled beneath where it hung on the wall, one of whom had a remote in his hand. He kept fiddling with the volume as the screen showed the type of action that generally preceded our phone lines getting busy: flashing red and blue lights, cop cars, firetrucks, ambulances, the lights from helicopters panning the scene.

"What's going on?"

Rich Farris was one of the detectives glued to the action. He glanced back. "Armored car robbery, two dead."

"Is it ours?"

"No, thank God. It's in the city. LAPD gets this one."

With that I found my way to the kitchen where coagulated coffee beckoned me. There was too much of our own action to think about to be worrying about what our brothers in blue had going on.

Floyd joined me. "Make a fresh pot, Dickie, for Christ's sake."

"You staying around?"

"I'll be here for a few, anyway. It looks like they have something cooking downtown."

"Yeah, but it's LAPD."

"You know how it goes, Dickie, they always come in threes. Something like an armored car job is a perfect primer for the whole county to fall apart. You just make us some coffee and hold onto your hat."

24

Floyd and I lingered near the front desk talking to Rich Farris while half-watching the news coverage of the armored car robbery in downtown Los Angeles. Rich was lamenting about his ex taking him back to court, trying to get a larger cut of his pie. He didn't know if he'd ever be able to retire at this rate. Floyd asked if he had a new woman in his life, and the two lady-killers spun off into an all-consuming conversation about Farris's complicated sex life.

My attention drifted back to the television where the latest update said three men had been shot. Two guards, and one of the three suspects. The reporter confirmed that all three were now pronounced dead. The two dead guards were said to be employed by L.A. Armored, a local armored transport company owned by a former Los Angeles Police Officer. A woman with bright red lipstick smiled into the camera as she told what she knew about the robbery and deaths, while first responders worked frantically in the background. Those men and women behind her would leave parts of themselves there at the scene with the spirits of the departed, and they'd take other parts home and harbor them for the rest of their lives. The reporter wouldn't give anything other than her hair and wardrobe a second thought.

I turned from the TV, noticing that Floyd and Farris were no longer talking girls, and an increased level of activity suddenly buzzed around me. Phones were ringing and the two detectives manning them were juggling calls, speaking to some of the callers and placing others on hold. Farris had gone behind the desk and grabbed an empty chair and a ringing line to lend a hand. There were only three phones at the desk, so Floyd and I stood at the counter watching and listening.

Farris put a call on hold and looked up with dark, tired eyes. "It looks like we've got a dead cop in Compton. Can you guys roll?"

FOR THE NIGHT WATCH ON THE ORTIZ HOME IN NORTH LONG BEACH, IT had been decided that Farley and Morgan would continue live surveillance after midnight when most of the activity on the street had slowed. The pole camera they had installed did not have night vision capability, so monitoring from afar did not provide sufficient visual coverage.

CW2 James P. Morgan arrived just after eleven and took a position half a block from the target home. He avoided the overhead streetlight by parking beneath a tree. He felt comfortable in the shadows with his carbine resting on his lap. He leaned back and adjusted the squelch and volume of his handheld, knowing it would be much closer to midnight before he was joined by his supervisor, CW3 Charles Farley. Morgan harbored a restlessness that caused him to arrive early and stay longer on nearly every assignment. The same anxiety caused Morgan to never stop thinking about his cases, even during his off time.

Alone in the darkness he thought about their target. PFC Christina Ortiz. AWOL. Or was she dead? Morgan wasn't a religious man, but he did have a sense of spirituality which he attributed to his Native American heritage. Though only one-eighth Cherokee, he was proud of his ancestors who had lived in the isolated hills and valleys of the highest portions of the Southern Appalachians, until driven south. Eventually, his people were forced to give up their lands east of the Mississippi River and migrate to Indian Territory, presently known as Oklahoma. It was Morgan's ancestors whose journey west would be known as the Trail of Tears. At times, he could hear his forefathers whisper offerings of wisdom and guidance, especially when it involved his warrior spirit. Other times, he could feel their tears of defeat. But all of the time, he felt a spiritual existence that hadn't come from inside the walls of a church nor from the teachings of man. It was an inner voice that mostly spoke to him when he was alone, hiking and camping in the Great Smoky Mountains, or riding across the coastal plains on any of his several trusted steeds. Occasionally, he could connect with these spirits while confined to the civilized world by gazing across the horizon or settling into quiet darkness, alone in his thoughts. Morgan had always been driven by a desire to see, hear, and touch that which remained unmolested by man.

As the leaves above his government-issued sedan stirred gently in the darkness, the spirits of his forefathers whispered warnings to him. There were never voices, only feelings that Morgan could never describe to others. He never would try. If he did try, he had often thought, he would liken this phenomenon to the feel of a horse. A horse seems to hear your thoughts, to both the success and detriment of horsemen everywhere. Those who know to listen closely to the subtle hints of those magnificent creatures—a nearly imperceivable lift of a head, the softening of an eye, the flick or pinning of his ears—find their interactions with them less volatile. The spoken word is the simplest form of communication, and as such, it is also the most unreliable. As to the feel of a horse, one is better suited to close his eyes and listen to the inner voices. On this night, the winds whispered that trouble awaited him, that violence was unavoidable. Morgan saw the painted faces of his forefathers and silently thanked them as the flow of cool air hastened through his open windows.

TRAVIS GRABBED HER WITH BOTH HANDS AND SHOOK HER VIOLENTLY. "Get ahold of yourself! Let's go, damnit!"

He was at the sliding door of the van, parked in the darkness of an alley of crumbled asphalt and weeds. The narrow passage was littered with trash, the walls covered by graffiti. The smell of urine, vomit, and feces had Travis looking in the nearby shadows and crevasses for bums or remnants thereof.

He released his grip of her, and she curled into a ball on the floor of the van among assorted firearms and ammunition and the cases and containers of both. All of which had been scattered throughout the rear of the van during the intense getaway from the botched armored car robbery. She was bawling as she had been for the five minutes it took Travis to drive them several miles from the crime scene, changing directions numerous times and employing counter-surveillance tactics as they traveled most of the way without lights. He had run over someone in an alley, which had forced him to drive several more blocks before deciding to abandon their vehicle.

"We have to go!"

"Nooooooo," she whaled, "nooooooo."

He pulled her back to a seated position and ripped her blood-soaked shirt from her and tossed it further into the back of the van. He leaned past her and pulled a duffle bag over to him. He retrieved a black button-up tactical shirt that was twice her size, and told her to put it on while forcing it over her arms. Tina's face, purple around one eye, was streaked with tears and smeared red from her bloody hands. It was Carlos's blood, and it covered her. Travis had violently pulled her away from her brother's dead body and forced her into the van when the shooting had stopped. Now they needed to move out and never look back, or neither would ever see another day of freedom.

With a clean shirt wrapped around her body, but not buttoned, Travis pulled her from the van. He released his grip on her long enough to stuff two pistols into his waistband and sling his AR-15 over his shoulder. "Come on," he said, as he grabbed her again and tugged her away from the van and further down the desolate passage.

Floyd and I arrived at the scene of the murdered cop. It wasn't the first time for either of us. We wouldn't be assigned the case, as neither of us, nor our teams, were up for murders. This would be a Team 4 handle, though dead cops were an all-hands-on-deck situation. There would be time to sort out who was doing what, later. For now, we needed to stabilize the situation.

When a cop is killed, to say emotions run high would be a gross understatement. Unfortunately, we were accustomed to the chaos that ensued when a colleague has fallen, as we had stood in many such crime scenes both as patrol deputies and detectives. We had felt the soul-crushing, gut-wrenching reality of our vulnerability as a colleague lay bloody and life-less, dressed in the same uniform as our own. *Because* of the same uniform as our own, and for no other good goddamn reason.

Mistakes are made when emotions run high. I recalled a night when a colleague had been killed and the gang member who murdered him was on the run. Floyd and I and scores of other deputies who knew and loved the fallen colleague scoured the streets, the alleys, the motels, bars, and homes of all known gang members, and we leaned heavily on each and every one in order to get information about the whereabouts of the wanted killer. Though arguably ineffective, it was a tactic that came as a natural response for me and for all of my grieving brethren. The public might not accept, understand, or even tolerate all of our conduct, but at the time, the public was furthest from our minds. Because, quite frankly, it was that same public and the gutless politicians who allowed the scourge of these gang-sters and their lawlessness to be considered mainstream, if not acceptable. We knew gangs offered society little more than the destruction of life, peace, and prosperity. Those of us who battled them on the front lines understood that the public had no stomach for a real war on gangs. Because a *real* war on gangs would eliminate them from our society.

As investigators, it was our job to rein in these emotions. To play by the rules—as absurd as they might be—as to not jeopardize the eventual prosecution of the sonofabitch who took the lawman's life.

Such a scene would be chaotic until someone took command. That someone would generally be dressed in a suit and wearing a name tag that identified their assignment as Homicide. It is the one assignment that commanded respect from the troops as they instinctively knew you were there to see justice prevail. All of the other suits that converge on the scenes of fallen officers are often regarded as being there to scrutinize the actions of the cops—those who were involved and even those who have fallen. This was true, to a degree. The men and women from Internal Affairs and Force Review, the district attorney's office, even our department executives, all of them were there to provide the oversight that had become necessary to preserve order in modern-day law enforcement. It was part of a larger picture that would often be overlooked or disregarded by the troops, but an important one nonetheless. Homicide detectives, however, were unmistakably the working cop's investigators. Real cops who most often hailed from the same haunts and had suffered the same grievances that the street cops now endured.

Floyd cleared the area, taking command of the scene and getting any unnecessary personnel away from evidence. The victim had been transported, as was almost always the case. Every effort to save a cop was always made. In the case of a murdered cop, the body would never be left at the crime scene while the investigation proceeded, the way another hopeless victim might. In this case, the deputy's body had been transported, but evidence of his death remained, marking the exact site of where he had fallen. Soon, the bloodstains would be washed away. Flowers and candles would adorn the site and soon thereafter disappear. No permanent memorial would ever be resurrected here, but this exact location would be remembered with great reverence by his brothers and sisters, even those not yet born. For the passage of these tragedies from one generation to another is imperative to those who patrol these streets, so that the sacrifice of their colleagues is never forgotten.

With the radio cars and rescue personnel cleared from the immediate area, the scene was cordoned off by yellow tape and road flares were strewn across the street to reinforce a boundary. An eerie silence fell upon the night as floods of investigators, supervisors, administrators, and support personnel gathered at one end of the crime scene. From this point forward, nobody would cross into the restricted area without absolute necessity, and each person who entered would be documented on crime scene logs. Those who had come and gone before the scene had been established would be accounted for as well, and every minute detail would be memorialized in excruciating detail.

Floyd and I had done our jobs. We had arrived quickly and had taken control of the chaotic setting while other detectives from our bureau were still being notified of the tragic event. Now we were gathered with the administrators and support personnel at the edge of the scene. Bloodstained clothing of a deputy sheriff and paramedic debris marked the nowsacred ground behind us. An abandoned radio car, its doors standing open, sat alone in the darkness like a ghost ship anchored in a deadly cove. We waited in heavy silence as members of Team 4 gathered and assumed the lead role of this investigation.

Captain Stover stood with the lieutenant and his investigators when Balding and Quintana, the two who were assigned as the primary handling detectives on the case, began designating tasks for all who were there to assist. Four investigators would work the scene along with crime lab personnel. Two investigators would go to the hospital and detail all of the activity and action from the rescue personnel to hospital staff. There would be a total of six investigators dispatched to the station where approximately ten deputies were waiting to be interviewed. Most of them were witnesses only to the aftermath, but their statements were equally important. The surviving partner of the murdered deputy sheriff, who had discharged his firearm during the incident, would be the most important witness in the case. The handling team would interview him at length.

Once the assignments were made, there was a pause in the action. An unplanned moment of reverence maybe. Then two investigators turned and broke away from the group, and others began dispersing as well.

When only Captain Stover and the lieutenant remained, Floyd asked, "Is there anything else we can do?"

Stover studied us each for a moment and it seemed he was puzzled by our presence. He was likely so accustomed to Floyd and me being part-nered at scenes, that he hadn't thought anything of it until just this moment. "What are you two doing here, anyway?"

I elected to stay silent, for a change.

"We were both at the office when it came in, boss," Floyd said. "Farris asked us to roll and get a handle on it until the team could arrive. It was chaotic out here when we first rolled up."

Stover nodded. He looked at me, and then back to Floyd. "I want you two to get the details on the deputy and make the next of kin notification. Find out what you can and let me know. The commander and I will follow up with whoever it ends up being, tomorrow. Wife, mother, whomever."

The next of kin notification might be an important part of the case; you never knew. We didn't chance that it wouldn't be in these situations. A pair of homicide detectives would make the first notification, not the brass. And the notification would be documented in the murder book with the same attention to detail as every interview, every examination, and every piece of potential evidence of the crime. These were capital cases of the utmost importance.

I nodded and stepped away. Floyd said, "Yes sir," and followed me through the maze of sedans that littered the roadway.

We drove away in silence and proceeded slowly through the empty streets of Compton until we reached the station. It was as if the community knew, and everyone had gone into hibernation. It wasn't a good night to find yourself on the wrong side of the law. When I shut the ignition off, I looked over at Floyd whose face appeared chiseled from stone. "You all right, partner?"

"Just brings back too many memories, I guess."

"Yeah, it does. Let's get this kid's name and his next of kin, and get it over with. There's nothing I hate worse than this part."

25

Tina waited in the shadows while Travis checked the doors of parked cars until he found one unlocked. He ducked into the car and closed the door. She looked up and down the street again; all was quiet around them. Moments later she heard the car start, and she ran toward it.

She climbed inside and adjusted the AR-15 that was on the passenger's seat as Travis pulled away from the curb. Tina didn't know Travis knew how to steal a car. She looked at the steering column. It had been stripped, showing bare metal and wires and all of the internal workings that are usually covered by plastic. A large screwdriver protruded from his seat, tucked partially between his thigh and the cushion. After shifting gears and accelerating up an onramp, he reached over and pulled the AR-15 away from her and tucked it between his leg and the seat. She could see the intensity in his eyes and the perspiration seeping from his pores.

The scene continued to play in her mind as she stared out the window in silence. The city lights stretched across the horizon, glowing against a black sky. It all seemed surreal to her, yet she knew it had happened. Everything had gone wrong with the armored car job, and now her little brother was dead.

The drive to downtown had taken more than an hour. The trip was short as far as distance went, but every driver in Los Angeles knows that distance means nothing on the city's congested streets. The armored truck had led them to a commercial bank building. Travis had gotten excited when they spotted the ramp to the parking area beneath the building. The driver of the truck had turned on its flashers and waited. But for what? Tension had built in the van and Travis and Carlos argued about how to do it. Travis had said, "We do it another night, now that we know the pattern. We have to somehow set up a diversion, something that would get one of the guards out of the truck."

"But what would that take?" Carlos had asked. "They have to be trained to not fall for anything like an accident, or something else that could be staged."

The two vehicles had sat in the middle of the street for what seemed like hours, but was only minutes. Flashers blinked monotonously on the money truck as the three of them sat patiently behind it in their van. Travis seemed deep in thought. Tina didn't like the idea of anything happening there; it was too congested, too many witnesses, too much traffic to allow an escape.

Travis had said, "We'll wait a week," at just about the time an armed guard emerged from the parking structure carrying a large bag in his left hand. His right hand rested on the butt of a holstered pistol as he walked toward the armored truck that sat waiting.

Carlos had said, "It's on!"

And as the back door of the armored truck began to open, Carlos had bailed from the rear sliding door and was on the street, approaching the truck. The guard they had seen earlier stepped out of the truck to meet the approaching guard with the bag.

Travis had yelled, "Shit," and jumped from the driver's door of the van. Tina had followed Carlos out the slider.

Gunfire erupted, momentarily drowning out the clattering of trucks laboring through traffic as motorists honked their horns and jockeyed for positions during the end-of-the-day mass exodus. But all of the sounds had disappeared when Tina saw her brother falling backward in slow-motion. She tried to get to him but couldn't move quickly. It had been as if she were stuck in time, as if she were captured in a dream. She saw the guard falling at the same time, the guns of both men continuing to erupt in flames as gravity pulled the two combatants further apart and to the ground. Then everything froze. Tina had stood over her brother and saw his eyes searching hers for answers, or for help. As she reached down to grab him, another man in uniform appeared from the rear door of the truck. His eyes were on her, and his gun pointed toward her, but only for an instant. The guard swung the barrel of his gun in another direction just as a barrage of gunfire rang out. The guard fell, and as Tina stooped over her brother's lifeless body, Travis had grabbed her and pulled her into the van.

"Carlos!" she had screamed, over and over. But he was left lying on the street as she and Travis made their escape.

Now they were headed south on the Long Beach Freeway in a gold colored Toyota Corolla with a stripped steering column, but otherwise blending in with the hundreds of other cars crawling through traffic.

"It was his own goddamn fault," Travis said. His tone was quiet and soft, melancholy.

She wouldn't look over. She couldn't. Not yet. If she looked at Travis now she might pick up the rifle and shoot him in the face.

No, it hadn't been his fault; it was hers. She was the reason Carlos was dead. She had allowed him into the dark world that she and Travis had created, and all along she had known something like this could happen. She had even predicted that it would, that if anyone among them were to be killed, it would be Carlos. But still. She now hated Travis more than ever before. It was time to end their relationship, but she knew he wouldn't allow it. She needed to get south of the border and have him taken care of by a cartel, by people who would make sure his body would never surface. She could change her appearance and live a normal life, but only if Travis were dead and this madness came to a stop. She was done with it. Tired of the killing. It had gone too far and now her brother was dead.

"I have to see my *nana*," she said, still looking out across the darkness.

"The hell?"

"I have to tell her about Carlos, and then we can go. South. We'll cross the border and start a new life. It's the only way now, Travis. It's our only hope. But first, I have to say I'm sorry, and tell my *nana* goodbye."

26

Dead cops were bad enough. Partners, friends, and colleagues—even those you had just briefly encountered in the course of your duties —were nearly unbearable. And it never got any easier.

Floyd finished the business in the captain's office at Compton Station, getting the address for the fallen deputy's next of kin. He stepped out and stood next to me where I leaned against a row of file cabinets, staring off across the administrative offices. Normally, at this time of the night on a weekday, this area would be dark and quiet. Now, the lights were on and desks were filled with visitors from other stations and units who were using any available space as a temporary base from which to make phone calls or to log into department computers. The entire county would know by now that a deputy sheriff had been killed in Compton, and it would affect every single person affiliated with our department, from top to bottom, the top brass to the newest deputy, the professional staff to the hundreds of volunteers. Regardless of race, religion, or politics, every man and woman associated with the Los Angeles County Sheriff's Department would, on this night and in the days to follow, harbor a hollow, sick feeling in their guts. Every eye would fill with tears from sorrow, sooner or later. It would be later for those who were involved in the investigation or in the pursuit of the suspect, and who had not yet allowed the emotion to rise to the surface. For some, it would come when seclusion allowed the honesty of weeping. Others would cry with their partners, friends, and significant others. But for all, the time to mourn would come.

"I guess you knew him."

I nodded. "Not well, but I liked him. He was the type of deputy who made me proud to be part of this department. Hard-charging, energetic, a real command presence about him. Smart and polite, respectful of old farts like us."

Floyd didn't say anything. I didn't blame him; there was nothing you could ever say at times like this.

"He and his partner had the handle on the double murder at Ho's Liquor. He had said he knew me from other cases, but you know how that goes, I didn't remember him. He was a training officer. He's the one," I said, still gazing across the room buzzing with activity, "that I told you about his trainee, Nelson. The black kid with a big smile on his face all the time."

"Yeah, well, I don't imagine it's still there."

"No," I said, "I guess you're right about that. This will be the beginning of its erosion. We see the kid a decade from now, we won't recognize him. Permanent frown, bad back, shitty attitude, limping in for briefing with a broken liver. I wonder what happened out there. I wonder if the kid —Nelson—was there."

There were men I had looked up to, legends in the department when I was a youngster. Now, I would sometimes no longer recognize them because they were broken down. There were investigators at Homicide who'd been hauled out on stretchers due to heart attacks, strokes, mental breakdowns. Some had drunk themselves to death, others had chosen a quick exit by sending a department-issued projectile through the roofs of their mouths. That was what we referred to as eating your gun, and it had happened enough that it took time to recall each one.

I shook my head at the thoughts. "We have no idea what this job is doing to us."

"Yes, we do," Floyd whispered.

WE ARRIVED AT THE HOME OF THOMAS AND MELISSA JOHNSON, A MODERN American Craftsman tucked in the center of an expansive tract of similarly designed homes. There were few cars parked on the streets and fewer yet left in driveways. I assumed there were homeowner's association rules that required residents to park their expensive cars inside their three- and four-car garages. Lawns were perfectly manicured, and block and brick were accented by roses and shrubbery. It amazed me what deputies were able to afford nowadays, though I knew too many of them counted on dual incomes to do so. Or, they accepted insurmountable debt as a lifestyle, all to keep up with the Joneses.

"Is the wife a deputy?"

Floyd scrunched his brows. "I don't know. Why do you ask?"

"Lot of money here."

He grunted and popped his door open. I followed suit, in no hurry. This was the worst part of the job, hands down. All notifications were difficult, but were a necessary process in homicide investigation. Nothing came close to knocking on the door of a cop's newly-widowed wife. Floyd turned and waited.

"I'm coming."

"You want me to handle this?"

I was beside him now. "Sure, why not. I'll keep the notes."

We stood at the threshold of a residence that would never feel like a home again, the glow of a streetlight casting our shadows against the doors. The occupants inside had no idea that the reaper had come to visit, that we were there to inform them. My feet felt cemented to the walkway. Floyd appeared absent, just a shell of his larger-than-life persona, there to carry on through the darkness that encircled us both. We were silent, still, paused to delay the task if only for a moment.

"Come on," he finally said, "it isn't going to get any easier."

Floyd knocked lightly. I stared at the illuminated button for the door-bell but elected not to push it. Not yet. Maybe nobody was home. That thought brought hope for an instant until I heard shuffling and faint voices inside. A woman. Children. My throat tightened, and I blinked at the moisture collecting behind my eyes. I tried to swallow, but there was nothing to send down. My mouth was dry as cotton as the door opened slowly and the knowing eyes of a young woman met mine. She was a cop's wife. She knew. They always knew.

"Mrs. Johnson?" Floyd inquired.

She nodded slightly, her eyes shifting from Floyd to me and back.

He pulled back his suit coat to reveal the gold star clipped to his belt. "We're detectives with the sheriff's department. May we come in?"

She clung to the door, appearing suddenly weakened, the life in her drained in the brief moments that seemed as hours. I smelled the fresh fragrance of soap or shampoo, and for the first time noticed that her short, dark hair was wet. She wore denim shorts and a pink t-shirt with its sleeves turned up. Her skin was tanned, her legs and arms toned. She wore no makeup but was beautiful. A young, beautiful mother whose life had been shattered by a gunshot few had heard, and only a handful would remember as the years passed by. Her eyes would dull and her skin would wrinkle and sag, while fatherless children grew to accept but never understand why daddy didn't come home. A child of no more than six appeared at her side, and then another just a year or two older. The younger was a boy with her dark hair and complexion, the other a girl with sun-bleached blonde hair and bright blue eyes. They were silent, question and apprehension showing in their eyes. Slowly, the mother stepped backward while directing her children to do the same. She gestured for us to enter and instructed the children to go to their rooms. The two bounded up the stairs while we drifted toward a sitting area adjacent to the entryway.

"Close the door," she said softly but firmly, without looking in the direction the children had gone.

We waited for the click of a door, and then Floyd broke the silence with the beginning of a statement that would ring in the widow's head for the rest of her days. "Ma'am, we are very sorry to have to inform you . . ."

Her eyes welled with tears as she whispered, "Dear God," and Floyd continued with dampening eyes and brows that rested heavily over them. I looked away from them both, and began making a note of the date, time, and location in my notebook. I wrote her last name but couldn't remember the first name, even though I had read it again as we pulled up in front. All I could picture were the curious faces of her children as they were sent to their rooms, and the cheerful face of Deputy Thomas Johnson from my last interaction with him. My jaw clenched, I continued to fight back the emotion brimming inside me.

Floyd continued, ". . . he was killed by gunfire—"

She wailed, and Floyd stopped. I could feel his eyes on me, but I wouldn't look at him. Mrs. Johnson cried out hysterically, and I looked up to see the children peering through the banister, their delicate little fingers wrapped around the balusters the way prisoners clutch the bars of their cells. Back in my notebook, I made a pointless note of the two children being present, upstairs. It was something to do, something to think of other than the shattered family around me. The thought passed through my mind that I could come and mow their lawn on my days off, or maybe take the boy to his ballgames. I saw Floyd walking the girl down the aisle some-day, and realized that although it wouldn't be us, someone—his partners, brothers, friends—would be there for her. The way we had been there for the families of our fallen colleagues, this generation would be there for theirs.

As she settled, slowly, Floyd powered on. "We have to ask you some questions about Tom, questions that might seem off-putting to you, but you have to trust us. There will come a day when every detail will matter in a court of law, and we have to get this right. We're very sorry for your loss, and we will be as brief as possible. There will be others coming, likely not far behind us, who will help you in other ways. But ma'am, we're from Homicide, and we need to memorialize some details about your husband, and this day."

Their marriage was good, normal; his relationship with the children strong. They had been married for twelve years. Not that it would ever be a factor in this case, but you never knew, and you left nothing to the imag-ination of sleazy attorneys. His day begun as most others: after breakfast, he had taken his daughter to school. He had come home and the two of them exercised in the garage and then went for a run with their son in a jogging stroller. They had taken turns guiding it. When they returned from their run, Tom had played with his son in the swimming pool. After lunch, he had showered, and watched the news as he began getting ready for work. He had left an hour and a half before briefing which allowed him enough time—even if traffic was heavy—to take his time at work, dressing in his uniform and preparing for his shift. He took pride in his job as a deputy sheriff and enjoyed being a training officer and working at a fast station. He had not spoken of any recent events with colleagues, supervisors, or the public, that had bothered or concerned him. Everything seemed to be perfect. Until.

Melissa was a firefighter. She worked for the Pasadena City Fire Department and had been so employed for six years. When they both worked, Tom's mother took care of the children.

Floyd and I exchanged glances. He seemed as surprised as I had been that Melissa was a firefighter. I again appraised her toned body and realized she was more than just toned, more than just fit from working out and jogging; she had the body of an athlete, strong and agile and likely fast. For some reason, it made me feel a little bit better about the situation. As if she was one of us, a first responder, accustomed to death and trauma. And although she would be devastated for years to come, she would overcome this and carry on with the strength we all seemed to find during these darkest hours. She would be okay, eventually. She would carry on.

27

Tina directed Travis toward her grandmother's neighborhood in North Long Beach, guiding him through the tangled interchange of the southbound Long Beach Freeway to the eastbound Artesia and then a quick exit on Atlantic Avenue and south. Traffic was light, which allowed a relatively easy process in an otherwise complex interchange. She told him to continue south to South Street, but he pulled into a liquor store instead.

"I need a drink."

Tina looked around the lot and noticed homeless people, a gangster on a bicycle, and several cars carrying undesirables of all races, men, women and children alike. "Hurry up. Did you notice this isn't a great place to hang out? Do you see all the druggies, the gangster?"

He chuckled. "Right. These fucking criminals give me the creeps. I'm a-scared for my safety now."

"The cops, Trav. These lowlifes draw the cops to this place like flies to shit. Hurry up."

Travis took his .45 pistol that was tucked between his leg and the seat and stuffed it into his pants. He covered it with his untucked shirt and popped the door open. "Do you want anything, or not?"

"Yeah, get me a bottle of tequila. Any kind. And hurry up."

As he walked away, Tina looked over her right shoulder to see the gangster on the bike had been watching them. He was, most likely, a *pee wee* gangster, a clique of youngsters who were members of the North Side Longo gang. This was their turf, and he seemed comfortable hanging out on his lowrider peddle bike with a sparkling banana seat, chrome fenders, and high handle bars with chrome mirrors. Tina knew many of the older members of the gang—the O.G.s—as her brothers had been part of the gang when she was a kid. She had grown up around many of these boys. But this kid might have been in kindergarten when she left for the army, and wouldn't know who she was, nor would he care. The youngest were the most foolish, always out to prove themselves. He was at the age that many of them began selling dope or jacking people for cash to make money for the gang, for the *big homies*.

Tina pictured a gun beneath the oversized flannel shirt he wore and wondered what the odds were that he was thinking about using it. She figured fifty/fifty if he was in fact packing, and then she thought now would be the time he'd make his move, if he was planning it. It would happen now, while Travis was away, and as she sat alone waiting in the car. She turned her eyes from him, not wanting to challenge him. Staring at a gang member is considered *mad-dogging* and is a form of disrespect. She didn't want him reacting to that. If he wasn't going to try to rob her or sell her dope, he'd leave her alone if she didn't stare at him.

Out of the corner of her eye she saw that he was peddling away. Tina glanced in the mirror and realized he had continued watching her as he did. He made a big circle behind their car and came up in what he would believe would be her blind spot, but she was aware of his presence. His feet left the pedals and found purchase against the pavement as he stepped from the bike and reached toward her door. As he opened it, his right hand disappeared beneath his oversized shirt, and then he froze, and his eyes widened.

Tina didn't raise her sawed-off shotgun above the top of the door; rather, she kept it low and out of view of others nearby. The two barrels were directed upward, and from the look on Pee Wee's face, the dual .20-gauge holes were nicely aligned with his eyes. She smiled. "Not tonight, *vato*. Not this baby girl."

His hands came away from his shirt. "Where're you from, eh?"

"I'm from right fucking here, *ese*, before you were born. North Side. Now get the fuck out of my face before I cut you in half."

The gangster paused for a moment, seeming to ponder his options.

"Go on," she said. "I don't have time to play games with a peewee. *Vámanos!*"

He slowly got back on his bike and drifted away. Tina closed her door as the tiny gangster distanced himself from her car. The driver's door was opened behind her. She kept her eye on the cholo and heard Travis ask, "Everything okay?"

The kid disappeared from the parking lot. Tina turned in her seat.

Travis noticed the shotgun. "Whoa, did we have a problem?"

"Nothing I couldn't handle."

"I guess." He handed her a brown bag and backed out of the space. "Where to, killer?"

MORGAN WAS RESTLESS.

He stepped out of the government-issued, unmarked sedan and walked over to the curb. The roots of the tree he had parked under had, over the years, broken through both the curb and the sidewalk next to it. Morgan stood on the uneven surface and looked up and down the street, and up and down the sidewalk. Being quiet in all directions, his attention was drawn to the roots of the old tree. Morgan saw the tree as an ally who, like himself, had been meant to live without societal encroachments, but was instead smothered by concrete and buildings and the civilization that had created both. He needed to find a remote post to serve out his twenty, or he was going to go crazy.

In the darkness, he thought about PFC Christina Ortiz. Tina. He knew she was alive; he could feel it more now than ever before. But he always knew. Now, she was close. He could feel her presence. It could be because he sat just houses away from where she had grown up, but he didn't think so. He felt she was actually nearby, but he also felt that something bad was going to happen. These feelings had haunted him all night and had him unnerved. He glanced at the glowing watch face on his wrist; it was nearly midnight. The witching hour. It had been unusually quiet all night, and now it was just eerily so. Like the calm before a storm.

Morgan pictured the young private in her early days at Fort Hood. Small but mighty, green yet confident, serious but with playful, if not mischievous, eyes. Drawn toward excitement, thrills, and danger, seduced by bad boys. He thought of the night they'd spent together. He had never experienced anything like it before, and never would again. She was in a different league than he was, sexually, uninhibited and adventurous. But she also had been unattached emotionally. Like a sailor in a port of whores, she felt nothing beyond the physical act of sex alone and had left Morgan feeling used. His feelings for her now embarrassed him, and he'd never admit to anyone how he had fallen in love after a night of wanton sex on her part—passionate love making on his. He remembered seeing her with Hollingsworth the next day, the cocky sergeant who preyed on young soldiers who hadn't yet had the chance to see that he was a fraud. Morgan had wanted to warn Ortiz, tell her the sergeant was no good for her. But he knew then it would be in vain. She was out for adventure and, like a testosterone-driven teenage boy, she wouldn't be otherwise persuaded. He thought he had gotten over her, but as he sat with what he believed to be her spirit present, he admitted to himself that he hadn't. Morgan wondered what would happen to her when she was captured. He allowed himself to see them together someday, she, a repentant desperado, and he, a rescuer of the downtrodden. But he knew deep down inside that it would never be, and he told himself to come to terms with it now and move on. Maybe he could, with some sort of closure to her disappearance. But maybe he couldn't.

CW2 Morgan plopped back into his car, confused and unsettled. He caught himself before closing the door and forced himself back into the game, mentally. Physically. Get the woman off his mind. He quietly clicked the door shut behind him. He adjusted the volume of his handheld radio to the lowest setting and turned the knob less than an eighth of a turn. He keyed it once to check the volume level against its squelch and was satisfied that it wasn't too loud. He keyed it again and called the command post and provided his status. "All is still quiet out here."

A moment later, the soothing voice of their one female operator,

Lazarevic, responded. "Quiet here too, Morg. But by the news, it appears the rest of the city is falling apart."

"Oh? Do tell."

"LAPD has a robbery murder downtown, armored car deal. Sheriffs had a deputy killed in Compton. There's a pursuit somewhere they're calling the west side, and if that isn't enough, the Dodgers have fallen three games back and it might rain Saturday."

"This is why I don't watch the news."

"Roger that."

A moment of silence passed as he considered the information he had received before keying his mic again. "I've had a bad feeling all night. Hopefully it will stay quiet here."

"Be safe, Morg, and let us know if you need anything."

"Roger that. Out."

"WHERE TO?"

"Might as well head back to Compton, see what else we can help with, I guess."

That made as much sense as anything else, other than driving right past Chinatown where Floyd and I used to enjoy a cocktail at times like this. Gin was one of the only two cures for these nights. The other was to hit the streets with a partner you loved and trusted and do the work God intended for you to do. Not that I wasn't fond of Josie by now, and not that I didn't trust her—I did—but being back with Floyd at a time like this seemed natural and appropriate.

We agreed to go straight to the command post which had been set up a couple of blocks from the scene in the parking lot of a church. The key to establishing a C.P. was to be far enough from the scene as to not disrupt its investigation with the tremendous flow of traffic that would come and go throughout the days and nights. A dead cop's case would likely run both day and night, maybe for several of each. Schools might be an attractive option for a case that would be wrapped up before the morning buses ran, but a church wouldn't be used until Sunday. The church offered room for the mobile command post, an eighteen-wheeled tractor-trailer, and plenty of space left over for all of the radio cars of SWAT teams, investigators, and administrators who would come and go in the hours and days ahead.

Once checked in, we would notify the handling team and their lieutenant of our next of kin notification, and let them know we were available for anything they needed from an investigative standpoint. There were never too many investigators when it came to murdered cops.

I thought about Katherine and remembered she was coming to town this weekend. It occurred to me that I harbored mixed emotions about it. Were those my feelings toward her, or my concern about her feelings toward me? For some reason, our stars no longer seemed to be aligned. It was the story of my life.

As we descended into the southland, Floyd and I rode in silence.

28

The peewee gangster rode around the corner to his house and dropped his bike on the front lawn. Two *veteranos* watched from the porch.

"Some old *chola* just put a gat in my face at the market. She's with a white dude."

He was speaking to his big brother, Juan Medina, who everyone called Oso. *Bear*. He was a big, round-shouldered man who wore a blanket of hair everywhere other than his head, which he now shaved bald. He'd adapted the style during his last incarceration, a six-year stint in the California Department of Corrections for robbery-murder. The murder had been dropped to a manslaughter and he had received twelve years for both. The great thing about California is they negotiate your crime and then slash your time and you could kill people and only do a couple of years in the joint. Doing time for gangsters meant time to see old homies and get a break from the drama on the streets and your old ladies for a while. Put another teardrop under your eye and come out with more respect from your homies and the *cholitas*. Doing time was just part of the life.

Oso set his beer on the ground next to a folding chair where he sat on the porch with an old friend. He rose and glanced at his homie sitting next to him, and then at his little brother who the family called Junior but whom the homies on the street were now calling Little Oso. But Big Oso didn't call him that; he still called him Junior. He knew that Junior hadn't yet made his bones with the gang and was itching to do so. Oso wasn't so sure he wanted him to follow in his footsteps.

"She just pulled a gat on you, for no reason?"

"I was going to ask her for a smoke. I don't know what homegirl's problem is."

"So, what did you do?"

"I left, eh. What am I going to do when a bitch sticks a shotgun in my face?"

"A shotgun?"

"Yeah, *mano*, a sawed-off heater. Pointed it right at my face, ese."

Oso thought about it for a minute. "What'd this homegirl look like?"

He curled his lip. "Ugly bitch with a fucked up eye, like someone else had already fucked her up. She prolly was talkin' shit."

"Okay, Junior. So what do you want to do about it?"

"Take me over there, I'll fuck her up. Shit, *mano*, this is *our* mother-fucking neighborhood, eh, not some old hood rat's."

Oso stood silent for a moment.

His homie, Bandit, had stood and was now walking down the steps ahead of him. "Come on, homie. Let's take Little Oso back over there and let him put in some work. He needs to represent, eh. Plus, we can't have bitches over here chumping out our little homies. That shit ain't right, man."

But Oso hesitated at the thought of his little brother putting in work. The older he got, and the more time he spent locked down, the more Oso saw how pointless his life had become. He slurped the saliva in his mouth. "I don't know, ese. Where did she say she was from, anyway?"

Junior lied. "She said she was from nowhere. I should have blasted that bitch right then."

Bandit was getting in his car, a '79 Oldsmobile that sat low on skinny tires and chrome rims. "Come on, Junior, let's go see what it's all about."

Oso followed Junior to the car, not wanting to be seen as a punk. When the three were inside, and Bandit was backing out of the driveway, Oso said, "Don't be jumpin' off, ese, 'less I say so. Let's see what's going on, first. See what this bitch is all about. Plus, she's probably gone now anyway."

Bandit glanced over but didn't respond. Junior was silent in the back seat. Oso glanced back to see if his little brother was even paying attention, and he saw the revolver in the boy's small hands.

"Where'd you get the gat, eh?"

"From a big homie."

"Who?"

"I ain't no rat, eh."

Bandit chuckled and took a swig of his beer. "Attaboy, Lil' Oso. Let's go fuck some bitches up." He looked over and smiled at Big Oso, but received nothing in return. "The fuck's your problem, homie? You didn't find God in prison, did you?"

"Fuck you," Oso said to his homie. "Shut the fuck up and let's ride, ese."

————

AT THE COMMAND POST, JOSIE SANCHEZ FOUND ME AND FLOYD HUDDLED with half a dozen other homicide detectives. We were discussing the direction of the case with one of the two handling investigators, Tim Crane, and waiting for an assignment. Tim looked over at Josie, who stood quietly behind me. "Are you here to help out?" When I turned I was surprised to see it was Josie he was speaking to.

"Sure. What do you need me to do?"

"You speak Spanish, right?"

Josie nodded.

Tim said, "Don't go anywhere; I will definitely be putting you to work."

She nodded, and Tim turned to his lieutenant and began speaking in a low voice. I nodded to my partner. "What brings you out? Did they call you?"

"No," she said, "I just figured they might need help here. I also expected you and Floyd to be here too."

"She has your number," Floyd said.

"I went up to that armored car robbery in downtown."

"Oh?"

Josie pulled a notebook from a pocket of her suit jacket, swiped the tip of her thumb across her tongue and began leafing through it. "I have a friend who works Robbery-Homicide with LAPD, and I saw him on the news. I was having dinner in Hollywood and thought, what the hell, I'd stop by and see what they had. I hadn't seen him for a long time anyway, and when they mentioned that the robbers wore ski masks, I was just a little bit curious if these might be our same shooters."

Floyd and I exchanged glances. "What'd you find out?" I asked.

She looked down at the notes. "Three suspects, two male and one female. One of the males was killed at the scene by a guard. The other two escaped."

"How did they identify one as a female?"

"She went crazy when the one was killed. Ran to him and cradled him and was talking and crying. It was a woman."

I nodded. "Interesting."

"But three?" Floyd asked.

"We think the third was the driver in our Compton murder, never seen by anyone."

"Oh, gotcha. Interesting."

Josie closed her notebook. "He said when they I.D. the dead guy, he'll let me know."

"Who's your friend?"

"Bobby Gillette. Do you know him?"

I smiled and looked to see Floyd smiling too. "Yeah, we know him."

"Yeah, I know, he's a dog. But I don't know him like that. We met working gangs and I've never dated him."

I threw my hands up. "I didn't say anything."

"I know what you both are thinking though. You're all pigs. Every last one of you." She pushed past me and Floyd and approached Tim. "Where do you need me?"

Floyd grinned at me. "You've got yourself a real pistol with that one, partner."

TRAVIS HAD STARTED TO BACK OUT, AND STOPPED. HE PULLED FORWARD IN the parking stall and looked at Tina. "I forgot to get smokes."

"Hurry up."

"You'll be fine, killer."

"And stop calling me that."

She watched the glass front door close behind him. Tina turned and looked behind her, and then scanned the parking lot and adjacent areas. She kept watch for the bicycle while absently thumbing the shotgun that lay across her lap. She felt nervous about being here and was anxious to get out of town. Travis was smiling as he shouldered through the door while tapping a pack of cigarettes against the palm of his hand. He acted as if nothing in the world was going on. They hadn't just botched an armored car robbery. Her brother hadn't just been killed. They weren't AWOL from the army. She hadn't just threatened to kill a little gangster. Tina knew you didn't put the blinders on after something like that. The gangster had been on a bicycle, which meant he was close to home—and homies. They would be back for her. Yet the big dummy Mr. First Cav and I've Seen the Shit was having a ball, enjoying life with a pack of fucking Marlboros.

When he closed the door she said, "Hurry up, goddamnit. Let's go!"

He started the car and began backing out when a low-rider pulled in behind them. "Get the fuck out of my way," he said to the image in his mirror.

Tina turned her head to look. "Fuck, it's them!"

CHIEF WARRANT OFFICER 3 CHARLES FARLEY SAID TO LAZAREVIC, "Why don't we go sit out there a while, give Morgan a break."

They were in the command post a couple of blocks from where Morgan sat at the home of the AWOL soldier's grandmother. After Lazarevic spoke with him on the radio, she had been unsettled and had mentioned it to their team leader. "Charlie, Morg's got that Indian shit going on again. He's listening to the spirits of his forefathers who your people slaughtered for their land. They're apparently sending him bad juju."

"You believe all that spiritual wagon-burner bullshit?" Farley had asked.

"If you remember, he had the same thing going on right before we were nearly captured in Kandahar. He also mentioned his 'bad feelings' right before the shootout in Fallujah. Morgan has something the rest of us don't, and you can call it whatever you want. But I've learned to trust his gut, and right now his gut's telling him something isn't right."

It had been quiet for a moment after they discussed it. The news played on the television across from where they sat, at a round table with fast food containers and empty coffee cups piling up. Farley had sat fiddling with his mustache while looking at the TV, which still showed the news. But Lazarevic could tell his mind was elsewhere. She could see in his eyes that he was contemplating what she had said. He was a smart man, and she respected him for his leadership abilities. He would take time to analyze a situation, to contemplate, and avoid overreacting. He wasn't the type to put much stock in feelings or hunches. He had a responsibility to all of the team members, and to the United States Army, to follow solid leads and be able to justify the actions of his team subsequently. "Feelings" would not be part of any debriefing.

She knew when he suggested going out to relieve Morgan, that he had considered how all actions would be reported. Now it was his idea. They would go "relieve" Morgan for a while. And while they were there, well, maybe they'd just hang out for a while.

As they prepared to leave the command post, Farley said, "Give Montoya or Ridley a heads up that we'll be out in the field, just in case they were to stop by the C.P."

"Yes sir," Lazarevic replied, sharply.

"YOU'RE NOT GOING TO BELIEVE THIS."

Floyd and I turned to see Josie coming toward us. She had her phone held out in front of her, the display illuminated, and she glanced up from it only after nearly bumping into me. I could smell a lavender scent as she leaned in to show me a message on her phone. "The dead guy is Carlos Ortiz."

"What dead guy?" Floyd asked.

I was searching my mind for the name. It seemed familiar, but I couldn't recall where I had heard it.

"The armored car guy."

"Wait," I said, "the guard, or the robber? There were one of each killed in that deal, right?"

"There were two guards killed, and one suspect. The dead suspect is Carlos Ortiz."

"Okay, Josie, I'm not tracking here. Who is Carlos Ortiz?"

"Well, there may be more than a few of them, but I know of one for sure. The little brother of Jimmy and Christina Ortiz was named Carlos. Jimmy's the one that was killed by the off-duty deputy last weekend in Long Beach. Christina is the sister who is AWOL from the army, or that's what those army investigators believe. Remember? I couldn't remember his name before, but I'm pretty sure it was Carlos, now that I've heard it. In fact, I'm sure of it."

I was nodding as it all came back to me and began lining up in my head. "And the girl who went AWOL did so with a big white boy, as I recall. Is that right?"

"Yes, and that makes three. Two men and a woman. I think this is them. I think this is who we're looking for."

"Weren't the CID guys watching grandma's house?"

She nodded. "Last we heard."

"We need to get ahold of them. Do you have their contact information?"

"Not with me," she said, meeting my increased energy.

I began walking toward my car. Floyd followed, and Josie, having paused for a moment, jogged to catch up. "It's at the office, in the file. I'm sorry, I didn't plan on working tonight."

"None of us did. Don't worry about it."

"Should we run up and get it?"

I stopped at my door and looked at her. "No. We'll go straight to grandma's house. You remember how to get there, right?"

"Pfft. Those are my stomping grounds, dude."

Floyd chuckled. "You heard her, dude. Let's go!"

I snaked through the conglomeration of emergency vehicles and media strewn about the parking lot. Once clear, I put my foot into the gas and headed toward the freeway. "Are you texting your boyfriend, Bobby?"

"He's not my boyfriend. But yes."

"Let him know we're on our way to grandma's house, and tell him that CID might be out there Code Five. There's going to be too many cooks in the kitchen if something goes down."

Floyd said, "Wait, they have a surveillance going?"

"The army does. They were thinking after the one brother was killed last weekend, that maybe the AWOL chick would come by grandma's. Now she's got two dead brothers, if Josie's right about this."

"Too much to be a coincidence," she said from the back seat.

"You think she's headed there now?" Floyd asked.

"I don't know. You wouldn't think so, but maybe if she's going to head for the border, she'd stop and pay her respects. But then again, how do you face grandma if your actions got her grandson killed? I don't know, partner, what to think."

"Um, actually, I'm your partner now, Dickie."

Floyd and I both glanced behind us, and grinned.

29

Tina had turned in her seat, her shotgun leveled just above the window and her eyes locked on the occupants of the car. The boy in the backseat had his head and shoulders out the window, and he was bringing his arm up toward them. She saw the gun in his hand. "He's got a gun!"

Travis yelled, "Hang on!" and floored it in reverse.

"Fuck!" she yelled as the shotgun went off—*BLAM!* The stolen Toyota smashed into the side of the Oldsmobile, and Tina's shotgun flew out the window. Travis pulled forward, and then floored it in reverse again, crashing into the Oldsmobile. He pulled forward again, and Tina heard tires squealing behind them. He raced backward once more but the other car was no longer blocking him in. He pulled the shifter down to Drive and cranked the wheels as more gunshots rang out. There were five or six shots, and several projectiles hit the windshield, spraying fragments of glass throughout the car. Tina covered her head and tucked it between her legs. Travis held a hand up to shield himself from the debris, and hit the gas. He made a sharp left, and they drove over a parking block and off the curb. Once in the street, he accelerated and they headed south. He yelled over the revved engine and sounds of air whistling through open windows and bullet holes, "Get another gun out of my bag. Back seat."

Tina reached back and unzipped the bag. "What do you want?"

"I've got what I want. Get something for you. One of the pistols, probably."

She took a Glock and fished around until she found two of the extended magazines. While doing so, she saw the Oldsmobile coming up behind them. "They're following us."

Travis glanced in one mirror and then the other. A smile crept onto his face. "Perfect. Let's take them somewhere special and see what they've got. Now that I think of it, get me the short AR out of my bag, and a couple of thirty-round mags for it. This is going to be fun. Fucking wetbacks."

"Take the Atlantic Avenue south up here," Josie said, from the back seat. "I should have told Crane or the lieutenant we were leaving."

"There's plenty of people they can get to *habla* for them. We need to let the little green army men know what's going on. This could get interesting."

Floyd chuckled. " 'Little green army men.' " He turned his head toward the back seat. "So, you grew up down here, or you worked the area?"

"Both," she answered, before continuing with directions. "Go straight now."

After a moment, he said, "I guess you know the area then, huh?"

"I know the streets, and I know a lot of the players."

Floyd seemed to be thinking of what else to talk about. "So, what's the deal with you and Lopes?"

"Jesus, dude. Really?"

He looked at me. "What?"

I shook my head.

Josie said, "There's a liquor store about a mile south of here where the *Longos* hang out. Turn left on the first street after it."

"Actually," Floyd said, "stop at the liquor store real quick so I can pick up a can of Copenhagen. It might be a long night, Dickie."

"Perfect. We can kick it with the Longos."

From the back seat: "Fuck that."

I turned into the lot. There were people gathered outside of the store, milling about, looking around. All of them watched our arrival with great interest. Something had happened here, I could feel it. A man in his fifties headed toward our vehicle with urgency in both his gait and expression. Josie said, "That's Abram, the owner. Something's wrong here."

Floyd rolled down his window and the man called Abram began pointing south. "They went that way. Both of them."

Josie jumped out of the back seat. "Who, pops? Who went that way? What happened here?"

He went to her, his hands extended toward her. "Sanchez, thank you for coming."

She took his hands in hers. "Pops, you need to tell me what happened."

"I told you on the phone, the nine-one-one. They were shooting."

"Who, pops? The gangsters?"

"Everyone. The gangsters. The girls. The big man in his army coat. He crashed his car into that cholo, a dozen times. Then they went that way." He pulled one of his hands from Josie and again pointed south.

Floyd and I had exited the car and were standing near Josie and Abram. Neither of us was looking at them, though. I was scanning south, and then north, and also taking in the crowd of onlookers to see if any of them met my eyes. Sometimes a witness would let you know they had information, but not now, not here. You had to watch for it and then figure out a way to slip them a business card without singling them out. Other times, you'd see the face of someone you knew had information, but they had no intention of ever telling anyone. Like one of the homeboys, or homegirls. You'd deal with them directly, which would often lead to a semi-consensual ride to the station—*You don't mind coming with us, right?*—where a private conversation might be more beneficial.

Josie was writing down what the owner told her about the cars. "A foreign job, and a low-rider," he said. "It's a white one with the shiny rims. You see it around here all the time."

Floyd had looked at me and shrugged. "Gang shit?"

"The dude in the army jacket though. What's up with that? White boy."

He nodded. "Robbery maybe?"

"Maybe."

Josie turned from the storeowner. "Sounds like a robbery in the parking lot. The victim would be the white guy who rammed his car into the cholos trying to get away. There was a female in the car too. She may have been the intended victim. The cholos chased them both away. That way," she said, pointing south.

I looked past Josie and grabbed at my gun as a wino stepped from the shadows with a sawed-off shotgun in his hand. He held it up and called out, "They left it here," just as I cleared leather and shoved Josie out of the path between him and me.

I realized immediately the man was no threat. I approached the wino and retrieved the shotgun from him before lowering my pistol back into its holster. "Where did you find this?"

He rubbed the gray stubble on his face and then pointed toward the ground close to where I stood. "It was right there. The lady dropped it. When they left, I picked it up. I figure it's worth twenty bucks, anyway."

I reached into my pocket and thumbed through my money clip, peeled off a ten and gave it to him. He was thirsty, but twenty bucks might kill him. Floyd took the shotgun from my hand. He broke it open and cleared the chamber, removing an expended shell and a live shell, and headed toward the trunk of our car. Josie opened a notebook and asked the man for his identification. He didn't have any, he said, so she asked for his name and date of birth and wrote it in her notebook. When she asked where he lived, he pointed toward an alley behind the store. "Mostly back there."

The wino headed into the store and the three of us stood silent for a moment. Abram lingered, watching us with great interest. I said to my partners, "What do you suppose she was doing with that?"

Floyd shook his head. Josie said, "I have some ideas, but let's talk about it in the car."

It was her way of politely finishing our business with the nosy storeowner. Josie seemed to know he shouldn't be trusted to keep to himself any of our discussion he might hear. She was right. We needed to conclude what we had here and, as soon as a radio car arrived to take the report, continue on with our quest to warn the army investigators about the recent developments.

After a moment, Josie asked, "Do you guys have any other questions for pops?"

Floyd said, "Do they carry Copenhagen?"

CURIOUSLY, THE CHOLOS FOLLOWED TRAVIS AND TINA WITHOUT PUTTING pressure on them. When Travis stopped at a red light, their pursuers stopped far behind, and waited. Were they holding back, waiting for the right time and place? Travis didn't know, but *he* was definitely looking for just the right spot. His training had taught him to think tactically, and to consider the many possibilities before engaging an enemy, when possible. In this case, he knew there were three in the car. Was each of them armed? He didn't know. The cadence of the gunfire indicated to him that a revolver had been used when they came under fire. That told him that he and Tina had the superior firepower. He had to assume that he also had far more ammunition than a couple of cholos rolling around in their low rider. Travis was confident that once he opened up with the AR, the cholos would lose their desire to fight. He guessed they would rapidly retreat, if able. He hoped they wouldn't be able. The Mexicans had fired on him and he planned to make them pay for it.

Travis turned onto a side street that led them into a quiet neighborhood, and he drove slowly as he watched for a park, a playground, the parking lot of a church. Someplace he could bring them in, off of the street, so that their flight would not be so easy once the shooting started.

The Oldsmobile followed at a distance.

"I wonder if they're waiting for backup."

Tina watched the headlights in the mirror on her door. "Calling up some homies?"

"Could be."

"What are we going to do?"

"Find a spot and get to it. We need to get the hell out of this town. Plus, I don't need two more carloads of gangsters coming to their aid with more firepower."

"We still need to go by the house and pick up the rest of our stuff."

Travis shook his head. "No way. Too risky now. They'll have Carlos identified by now and his picture will be all over the news. Some goddamn do-gooder neighbor will call it in, tell the cops where he lived and then describe us too. No, we're fucked now, Tina. We need to kill these wetbacks behind us and get the hell out of here. I don't think we can even take the chance of going by your grandma's now."

"We're stopping by Nana's, if only for a second. I have to tell her about my brother, and I have to say my goodbyes. I know we're never coming back."

WE PULLED OUT OF THE LIQUOR STORE PARKING LOT AND HEADED SOUTH on Atlantic. I glanced at my rearview mirror to see Josie in the backseat. Floyd sat next to me. We were each scanning the streets for a gold compact car and a white Oldsmobile with chrome rims. A gangster ride. "Honestly, the last thing we need is to spot those two cars right now, with all we have going on. Hopefully a black and white will spot them first, or at least be close by if we run into them."

"Do you guys realize we're less than a mile from the Ortiz family's home?"

I saw her in the mirror again. "No, I guess I hadn't realized that."

Floyd shrugged.

"If her brother was killed in the armored car robbery, and there were three—"

"I see where you're going with this," Floyd said.

"—a larger man and what we now know was a woman, who happened to use a sawed-off shotgun—"

"Twenty-gauge," I added. "Same as the one we just received."

"What do you think the odds are that the Ortiz girl and her boyfriend are our killers?"

I looked in the mirror again and saw her waiting for a reply. "I think the odds are pretty good."

"Then I say head straight to grandma's house. Turn left up here at the light."

I settled into the left-hand turn lane and waited for the light, only because there was a car in front of me impeding my travel and single-handily enforcing the traffic laws, unknowingly. The ticking of the blinker was the only sound in the car. Floyd and I each had our windows down, which was a custom from our days in patrol. We always kept the windows down so that we could hear what we might not see and have no obstruction if we needed to shoot.

The silence was broken by the sounds of gunfire nearby.

"Did that sound like it came from over there?" I asked, nodding the direction we had planned to turn, which was the direction of the Ortiz home. Sometimes it was hard to tell the direction of gunfire when heard from inside a car.

Floyd said, "Yeah, go!"

I had left room between our car and the one stopped ahead of us, another practice learned early in a cop's career. If you needed to get out in a hurry, you didn't want to have to rely on others to move out of the way. The law-abiding motorist in front of us continued to wait for a green light while gunfire erupted around us. I yanked the wheel and veered into the on-coming lane of traffic to go around him. He honked and flipped us off as we did, disgusted by our disregard for traffic laws and public safety.

Floyd returned the gesture.

30

Chief Warrant Officer 3 Charles Farley and the lone woman in his squad, Chief Warrant Officer 2, Paulina Lazarevic, had blacked out —shut their lights down—as they turned onto the street where James P. Morgan sat alone in a dark sedan. They eased up behind him and killed the motor. When they got out of their car, they closed their doors carefully so that only two slight clicks were heard. Morgan did the same, and the three of them met on the dark, uneven sidewalk adjacent to their cars.

Morgan's restrained demeanor matched the concerns he had voiced to Lazarevic over the radio earlier. Farley, on the other hand, knew the odds were that this was all for naught. Ninety-some percent of all operations lacked action. Especially stateside. He had often complained that being an investigator was the most boring job he'd ever had, and he joked with his team that he was trying to finagle them back to the sandbox. Tonight, he tried to lighten Morgan's mood by good-natured ribbing. "What are the spirits telling you now, Morg? Because honestly, I asked Siri and she didn't know anything about bad juju coming our way."

But Morgan was all business. "I don't know, boss. There's just something that doesn't feel right to me. And I'm more confident now than ever that she's alive. I feel her."

"Ortiz."

Morgan nodded.

Farley allowed that to marinate for a moment as the three stood in silence. The night was so still that Farley could hear the buzz of electricity snaking through overhead wires. He looked up and saw nothing beyond the yellow glow of a nearby street light—not a star or a hint of the moon anywhere—though he knew it was a cloudless sky above them. Morgan stood soberly in the shadows, his eyes dark and troubled. Farley had just begun to feel anxious himself when gunshots cracked the silence.

"That's close by," Lazarevic said, excitedly. "A block or two over."

Morgan went to the nearby passenger door and reached in to get his M4 carbine that sat on the seat. Farley walked quickly to the vehicle he and Lazarevic had driven, and retrieved a shotgun and a carbine identical to Morgan's from the trunk. He came back and offered both to Lazarevic; she took the carbine. They each remained in the shadows but moved closer to the trunk of the old tree that offered cover and concealment on the other side of their cars. And they waited.

WE TURNED INTO THE NEIGHBORHOOD AND DROVE IN THE DIRECTION OF the gunfire. It wasn't the first time, and it wouldn't be the last. And it never really crossed our minds that the act of doing so was counterintuitive for most of mankind. The streets appeared empty, so I blacked out and accelerated from one intersection to the next, where we would quickly scan the cross streets before moving on. At the third intersection, Floyd said, "On the right!"

I looked and saw movement toward the end of the block. "What is it?"

"Blacked out car just pulled onto the street. Let's get it."

I floored it. "Who has a radio?"

Over the roaring motor, Josie said, "I'll call it in on my cell."

"Where did it go?"

"I think it turned left up ahead," Floyd said.

As we passed the area where the car had first appeared, Floyd yelled, "Wait!"

I hit the brakes and looked to my right, following Floyd's gaze. There in a dark parking lot sat the Oldsmobile with its small tires and chrome wheels. The doors stood open and an interior light glowed against the darkness. There appeared to be a body on the pavement outside of the driver's door. "Shit!"

I looked forward and then back at the Oldsmobile. "Damnit!"

"Quick check, come on," Floyd instructed.

He was right, but as I jammed the car in reverse and then wheeled into the parking lot, I envisioned the killers getting away while we checked on the victims. A quick glance and we'd report it to the desk, ask for radio car assistance and an ambulance and be back in the chase. Those were my thoughts until we stopped and saw a young teenaged boy in the back seat holding his hand to his neck, trying to slow the spurting blood.

Floyd pulled the kid from the back seat and squatted next to him. He removed his silk tie and used it to compress the boy's neck wound. Sanchez stood next to him, speaking urgently into her cell phone, updating the report of "shots fired" to request paramedics and additional units to respond to a shooting scene with multiple victims.

The driver was dead on the ground just outside of the car, a bloody pistol near his hand. His gaze was fixed only on the darkness that had befallen him, and his lifeblood slowly oozed across the pavement below him. His passenger was slumped across the front seat. Blood was smeared over his bald head and caked to his heavy mustache, and his eyes were partly open. Slowly, he blinked. He tried to speak but a throaty gurgle was all I heard. There were no guns in the vicinity of the passenger, so I encouraged him to remain where he was seated and told him to hang on, paramedics were on their way.

A bloody revolver lay on the back seat near where the kid had been before Floyd pulled him out. It changed my feeling about his age, and his plight. The hole in his neck was just the way it turned out. A lesser opponent, and it might have been he who did the killing.

The white Oldsmobile had been perforated by gunfire. The strikes to the hood and windshield were evidence that they had rolled into an ambush, head first. The shooter, or shooters, had been efficient, deadly, and committed. These were no amateurs. I looked around the dark parking lot, and for the first time noticed it was an elementary school. The killers had somehow lured their victims into the lot where they would only be able to get out of the kill zone by backing up. Trained shooters and hunters alike know that tracking a target going away from you is simple, compared to shooting at something fleeing across your field of view or coming at you. It is instinctive to flee, and all untrained people would do just that in this situation. The counterintuitive but appropriate response would have been to floor it and drive directly at their attackers. Put the pressure on them and only allow them an instant to fire before the fight is upon them. I noticed the car was in park. It made sense with the driver being outside. He had decided to stay and fight. He had better instinct than most who would try to back out, but he lacked professional training and didn't know to advance on his enemy. He had been outgunned and had died at the hands of a more committed and prepared opponent. This had military written all over it. The dots had connected to reveal a solid line from Fort Hood to Los Angeles.

Using the small light of my cell phone, I walked forward, careful not to step on evidence. Expended shell casings were scattered on the ground twenty-five feet forward of the victims. I estimated twenty or so and pictured a thirty-round magazine for an AR-15. The casings were small, and I assumed they were .223 caliber. It was likely that one of the shooters was armed with an AR-15 style rifle, as had been the killer at Ho's Liquor. The bigger of the two. His smaller companion had used a 20-gauge shotgun. I panned across the lot, imagining the width of a car that no longer stood where the killers had stopped. After several moments of searching, I saw additional shell casings on the ground. These were small, probably 9mm handgun casings, and few. I spotted only four. If the passenger stood outside of the door, shooting toward the victims directly behind them, the spent casings would have ejected toward the car. Many more rounds had probably been fired, and the casings were likely inside or on the suspect's car, gathered in the cavity beneath the windshield. Having lost the shotgun in the parking lot, the passenger had apparently armed himself—or, more than likely, herself—with a pistol.

Satisfied, I drifted back to the Oldsmobile as sirens drew near. Floyd continued to compress the boy's neck, and encouraged him to hang on. Josie finished her phone call and stood silently taking in the scene. Our eyes met. "This is the work of our killers," I said.

Two sheriff's radio cars skidded to a stop on the street adjacent to our location, abruptly turned, and came toward us, tires barking against the pavement. Paramedics were close behind, wheeling into the lot with their red lights flashing. I pointed out the obvious scene area and beyond it where the casings were found, to give the deputies an idea of where evidence lay. Floyd stood after being relieved of his life-saving efforts by two paramedics, one male and one female. A helicopter flooded the area with brilliant light as it orbited in a tight circle above us, its blades chopping violently through the heavy night air. But as the bird faded to the far side of its orbit, and the sounds of its propellers were but a far-off whooshing in the dark, similar chopping sounds came from another direction. I looked up and across the horizon, but I didn't see any other birds. I looked over to see Floyd meet my gaze with a frown.

He said, "Gunshots?"

31

A compact sedan came around the corner and slowed as it approached where the three CID investigators stood in the shadows, their firearms readied.

Morgan saw her in the passenger's seat. "Tina," he breathed.

Her eyes met his and he saw panic on her face. Quickly, she averted her eyes, and the vehicle sped off. Morgan ran to his car. Lazarevic and Farley scrambled to theirs. Morgan peeled away from the curb with tires squealing and his motor revved high. The compact car was turning ahead of him. He glanced in his mirror and saw his partners were on his tail.

The car ahead of him shot through the residential district, blacked out. Morgan saw the car race around another corner, this time to the left. He followed, and checked again to see that his partners were with him. They too were blacked out, driving by the streetlights, careful not to silhouette Morgan.

He could still see Tina's face as the car had passed by and their eyes had met, and they had recognized each other. What had she thought? What had she turned and said to the driver? Morgan didn't get a look at the driver but saw enough to know it was a large-framed man. Hollingsworth, no doubt. Morgan's romantic ideas were now all but erased as the lady soldier who had stolen his heart fled. She was, as he had suspected, alive and well. Fleeing from the army, from justice, from civility. What had she become? They screeched around another corner.

Morgan's thoughts moved from those of romance to his earlier premonitions of her presence, and the feeling that something bad was about to happen. Hollingsworth was unhinged; Morgan had always known that. Now it was quite evident he was a killer as well. They had heard the gunfire, and Morgan had recognized it as semi-automatic small arms. Probably a .223 caliber. He knew the two wanted soldiers would be heavily armed, and he feared this two year pursuit of them would end violently.

The fugitives made an abrupt turn into an alley, vanishing behind a wall of dust. Morgan followed, but his bright lights reflected back as if he were in a thick fog. Suddenly, he could see the vehicle ahead of him had come to a stop. Ambush!

Morgan slammed on his brakes and shoved the shifter into park. He grabbed his M4 carbine while stepping out of the car. Rapid popping sounds, flashes in the darkness, and the sounds of bullets whizzing past him confirmed he had been set up by his adversary. He aimed his weapon at the peppering flames and pulled his trigger, first toward one side of the suspect's car, and then the other. There were two shooters. Both were shooting at him. *She* was shooting at him, he realized.

Morgan squatted in the door opening for cover. As he focused on the shooters downrange, his vehicle was suddenly struck from behind. The jolt knocked him to the ground and away from the cover of his car. More gunfire erupted. It came from both directions now, his partners behind him and the fugitives ahead of him. Morgan was stuck in the middle. He tried to stand and realized he had lost feeling in his legs. Looking down, he saw that his pants were soaked in blood. Using his hands and elbows, Morgan pulled himself away from his car and propped himself against a fence that ran the length of the alley. He heard a door slam, an engine cranked, and the fugitives sped away down the alley. Morgan emptied his gun toward the sounds of a racing motor fading into the darkness.

"He's hit," Lazarevic cried as she ran to Morgan. She set her weapon on the ground and wedged her body behind his, picking his torso up slightly to cradle him. She called out on her radio for assistance.

Morgan writhed in pain. His intestines felt as if they were on fire. Heat permeated his body. He turned his head and vomited violently.

Lazarevic held him tightly, telling him it would be okay. "Hang in there, Morg," she said, her voice crackling. Morgan felt comforted by her presence, and wished he had the strength to tell her not to worry. He wasn't going to die. The spirits had already come to him and assured him of it. With this knowledge he found himself at peace, and he began to breathe more easily. Lazarevic stroked his head, wiping the sweat away with her sleeve.

Morgan, his eyes now closed, heard Farley's distant voice confirm what the spirits had already told him about PFC Christina Ortiz. "She's dead."

STANDING NEAR THE LOWRIDER IN THE SCHOOL LOT, JOSEFINA SANCHEZ faced a uniformed patrol deputy. She was pointing toward the direction of recent gunfire and yelling over the sounds of the orbiting bird. "Get the airship on your radio, tell them to go north two blocks and look for a light-colored compact car, gold or tan. Let them know there are army investigators Code Five in the area in plain clothes and unmarked cars, and that we've now got shots fired from that direction."

Floyd jogged to my car, yelling, "Let's go!"

I had already climbed in behind the wheel and was ready to take off. Josie hurried behind Floyd. At the sounds of two slammed doors, I took off.

The Crown Vic bounced and jerked as it grabbed the pavement when we sailed off of the curb from the parking lot onto the street. I was practiced at this type of maneuver and knew that speed and the proper diagonal angle were the keys to a smooth landing and to maintaining control of the vehicle. Through our open windows I could hear the helicopter peel away, and I saw the beam of its spotlight traveling north across the school grounds, across the street, and through the houses and trees. We followed the pavement while watching the bright streak across the sky for direction.

Floyd, sitting up front, fiddled with the dial of a sheriff's radio and yelled against the wind rushing through open windows. "What frequency are they on here?"

Josie shouted from the back seat: "Compton's on twenty-two, but go over to L-tac for the bird. If they're not there, try A-tac."

I turned left on the next street to head north. I could see the bird ahead and west of my location. I went two more blocks and turned left.

Josie shouted, "Grandma's street." Seconds later: "That was her house we just passed."

"Nobody around."

"No."

Floyd was on the radio: "Airship above North Compton, can you copy? This is David-Five-Adam-Six, Homicide."

"Go ahead, David-Five, this is Air Twenty-two," the handheld radio squelched.

"We're in a gray Crown Vic, just south of you, coming your way."

A ray of brilliant light washed over our car, then disappeared as quickly as it had come. "Roger that, I've got you coming north, David Five."

"Be advised, there are a couple of unmarked cars in the area that belong to Army CID. Our suspects are in a tan compact, and we believe they're armed with rifles."

Josie, now leaning across the back of my seat, pointed toward the sky. "The bird's circling now, up ahead. Looks like another block or two north, a couple of blocks west."

The radio crackled: "David Five unit, this is Air Twenty-two, we have a gunfight in the alley!"

"Fuck! Where are they?" Floyd said, craning his neck to follow the bird.

Air Twenty-two: "Shots fired, numerous shooters. Stand by! . . . Okay, looks like the suspect is fleeing now. You have two unmarked cars in the alley, but the suspect is fleeing. You might have officers down, guys."

I pushed the Crown Vic hard around a corner. The rear fishtailed while the tires squealed against the pavement. I glanced toward the sky and accelerated, heading north.

The airship came back on the radio: "Okay, guys, you have a suspect on foot, a male white who just bailed out of a tan compact at the end of this alley. Suspect is wearing all black. We need some units up here to set up a containment."

I glanced at Floyd. "Why'd he bail?"

Floyd shrugged and keyed the mic. "Air Twenty-two, any idea why he bailed?"

"Possibly a disabled vehicle. Not really sure, to be honest."

"Is he armed?"

The radio crackled back: "Nothing we could see."

Floyd and I exchanged glances. "Would you have seen a rifle?"

"He definitely wasn't carrying a rifle," the airship reported.

"Interesting," I said in the car.

Floyd nodded in agreement.

"We need to check that car," Josie said.

We reached the alley where two unmarked sedans sat with lights on and engines running. I skidded to a stop, dust and debris sailing past us. We were exiting when a man with a protective vest worn over his shirt rushed toward us, a badge displayed in his hand. "Army CID, we have an officer down."

Floyd announced on the tactical frequency that we had an army investigator down at the mouth of the alley and requested that paramedics be dispatched to our location immediately.

I went to the man who was down and recognized him as one of the two we had met with in the station. Morgan. The woman cradling him was Lazarevic. Morgan moaned softly, his blood-soaked hands and arms clutching his stomach. A tactical vest was in the dirt at his side. Lazarevic saw me looking at it. "Must have hit him right beneath it," she said. "I took it off of him."

I nodded. Finding no words, I looked to the other CID man, the one who had flagged us down. He and Floyd were crouched near a body that lay twenty feet away. It was a woman, crumpled on the filthy pavement. I left Morgan and his partner and walked over to them. The CID man glanced up, and I introduced myself. He stood up to meet me and shook my hand. Floyd remained on his haunches, studying the dead woman. All of us were silently appraising her for a long moment before anyone spoke again.

"Charles Farley," the army man said softly. As an afterthought, he mentioned that he was in charge of the team. CW3, he said. I knew that meant his rank, *Chief Warrant Officer 3,* and I recalled that Morgan and Lazarevic had said they were each a CW2.

The dead woman lay in a fetal position. She was dressed in black tactical pants that were soaked in blood and covered with dirt. Her dark hair was matted with blood, and her eyes were open, staring off into the distance. Dead eyes can offer glimpses into the final moments of life: fear, surprise, regret, sorrow. Hers said knowing. Expecting. Death had been at her doorstep and had knocked—maybe more than once. But tonight, she opened the door. Expecting.

"Is that her? The AWOL woman you guys were searching for?"

His nod was nearly imperceptible. "I'm sure it is, but we'll have to get a positive ID through prints."

"So, the man we're hunting now, he's the other one." It was a statement, not a question.

"Yes sir," Farley said. "Travis Hollingsworth. The sonofabitch who no doubt caused all of this, and who downed my best man." He glanced back at Morgan resting against his partner, Lazarevic. She watched us but showed no emotion. After a moment, she lowered her eyes back to her partner.

"We'll get him, chief," I quietly assured him. "I promise you we'll get him."

Floyd was standing with a group of deputies who had gathered at the mouth of the alley. I walked up and listened as one of them set up a containment of the area, using his radio to direct assisting units to specific locations that would seal off two city blocks. The containment would be held until a search for the suspect concluded. SWAT and Canine had been requested.

The airship checked in over the radio with the newly positioned deputies and confirmed that the containment looked good from above. It seemed almost certain that the suspect would be somewhere within it. There were deputies positioned on every corner and others mid-block. Each would vigilantly watch for anyone trying to slip out between their posts. Air Twenty-two provided another description of the suspect as last seen, as well as his last known location and direction of travel. The Tactical Flight Deputy, or "observer" as he is sometimes called, is the one on the airship who operates the cameras, the radios, the stabilized binoculars, and the 50-million candle-watt searchlight. He is the voice from above, and it was his that now crackled that they were going to lift higher. They would continue searching dark crevasses utilizing their night vision camera, but they would do so blacked out and from a higher altitude.

The sounds of the bird faded but you could still hear its blades thumping through the darkness. More sirens drew near, and soon a team of paramedics were working on Morgan. Now it was time to wait for a SWAT team, which could be a while; there was still an intense search for the killer of a deputy sheriff just a few miles west of us.

A sergeant and lieutenant showed up together and gravitated toward the three of us—me, Floyd, and Josie. We had drifted from the group of patrol deputies and gathered in a semi-circle at the back of my Crown Vic.

"You guys are from Homicide?" the lieutenant inquired.

"We are," I replied.

Introductions were quick, and he got right to it. "What the hell do we have out here?"

"A real clusterfuck, LT, if you want me to be honest about it. The suspect in this containment is responsible for shooting that army investigator over there," I turned and nodded toward the action involving paramedics, "and he's good for a murder a couple of blocks from here in a school parking lot. He will likely be made on a murder and armored car robbery in downtown L.A. from earlier this evening, and we think he's good for a double murder at a liquor store in Compton last Friday. And that's just the beginning of it."

The lieutenant stood gazing around the scene as he listened. He had a flashlight tucked under his arm, and he rocked gently in highly-polished uniform shoes. He wore a long-sleeved uniform shirt and tie, as did his sergeant. The two looked like they had come from a funeral, or an interview for another promotion. After a moment, he asked, "Just one suspect?"

"He had two accomplices: the dead female further up the alley, and a dead male—her brother—who was killed in the armored car robbery."

Josie said, "And the dead woman, Christina Ortiz, had another brother who was killed by an off-duty deputy last weekend in Long Beach."

The lieutenant was stone-faced. The sergeant gently shook his head in disgust or disbelief. "Okay, what do you guys need from us?" The lieutenant asked.

Floyd said, "Has the department gone tactical yet?"

"I don't think so. Why?"

"We're going to be here all night, boss. Units are scattered all over the place on this caper and also on the murdered deputy case over in Compton. It's none of my business, but if I were in charge of this area, I'd be asking for reinforcements from all over the county. You've got to be out of patrol deputies by now. I know when we called and asked for two teams of investigators from Homicide, the desk about shit. They said we're about out of personnel, but they'd make some calls. And truthfully, we could use more radio cars on this containment."

He nodded. "The commander is with the sheriff over at the command post in Compton. I'll suggest it, if nobody else already has. I think your captain is over there too, if I'm not mistaken. Stover's still in charge up there?"

Floyd nodded. "Yeah, he thinks he is, anyway."

The lieutenant smiled for the first time in our meeting. "Okay, I'll see what I can do to get more help out here. Be safe."

I chimed in: "I'm not so sure the city's ready to go to sleep yet, L.T. That's what has me worried."

32

A couple of hours passed, and the airship pulled out, citing they were low on fuel. It was now Thursday morning, the end of a long Wednesday behind us.

The containment was tight, and there had been no activity reported. The suspect had either gone to ground, or he had escaped before the containment had been established. Nobody talked about that possibility though each of us likely considered it, if only for a moment. Morgan had been transported to the hospital, and his team members, Farley and Lazarevic, had gone with him. Two other investigators were sent to monitor and assist as needed. These two soldier investigators segregated themselves near their vehicle and watched. Both had declined offers to join our circle.

Josie, Floyd, and I hovered over the trunk of my Crown Vic with containers of coffee and bags of donuts that had been dropped off in two separate deliveries in the last hour. The coffee was needed and welcomed, but the donuts were scarcely picked through. Bored and stiffening from the cool air that had settled during the night, I collected the donuts and two cups of coffee and walked them over to the army investigators. They thanked me and soon were devouring them as if they hadn't eaten in days. It occurred to me that the pair—perhaps the whole unit—

were combat veterans, and as such they knew to eat, sleep, and hydrate whenever the opportunity presented itself. Soldiers never knew when they would go without any or all of the aforementioned needs for days or more at a time.

"If you guys need anything—"

I left them with their sustenance and returned to silent stares from my two partners.

It was one of those nights that seemed surreal. I had experienced others like it during the course of my career, though I had never become accustomed to the feeling. Floyd had too, and I was certain Josie had as well. A cop had been murdered a few hours earlier, yet life went on all around the otherwise all-consuming event. I wondered if combat was a similar experience where there was no time to mourn for the fallen as the battle raged on. I pondered if that might be part of the psychological damage that often resulted in PTSD, the trauma that drives soldiers and cops alike into dark holes too deep to climb out of. We had been forced to continue on as if a colleague murdered on the streets was merely a new file number, another investigation, just one of the thousands of coroner's cases logged throughout the year. There would be a day in the near future where the city would hopefully calm for a few short hours while brothers and sisters and those who support us would pay our respects and mourn the loss of our fallen comrade. Then we would each carry on, vaguely aware of the additional weight we bore. It would be off to the next crime scene, the next family disturbance, another neglected child or the over-dosed junkie to be cleared from an alley, each of us slightly more mindful of our mortality.

I was jolted from my thoughts by the sounds of an approaching airship. I looked across the horizon to see a bird coming in, and then banking sharply just as it seemed to have passed us. "Aero Bureau is back."

Josie and Floyd were looking up as well. Floyd clicked the mic on his handheld radio to hear the short series of varying tones from a repeater that sits high on a mountain in East Los Angeles. It was a way to check the volume and to assure that the battery had not died. A moment later, the friendly voice of Air Twenty-two returned. "David Five and units in North Long Beach, this is Air Twenty-two coming back around."

Floyd said, "Welcome back, boys. It's all quiet here. We're locked down and waiting."

"Okay guys. We just pulled off of a search in Compton where they thought they had cornered a suspect in that deputy-involved one-eighty-seven. SWAT's still clearing several houses there, so I don't know how much longer you'll be waiting. Could be a while, guys. The good news is, we have a full tank and we're not going anywhere anytime soon. As long as the fog doesn't roll in."

Josie drew an exaggerated breath and let it out slowly. I sighed, disappointed at the news about the wait, but glad we had a bird above the containment again.

Floyd said, "We should go get this bastard ourselves. I'm tired of waiting. Are you with me, Dickie?"

Josie and Floyd seemed to watch closely as I considered it.

"How bad do you think it will be if it goes hot and we have to kill this guy? Or if one of us gets killed in the process? I'm not sure it's worth it, though I'm not entirely against the idea either."

"We have a dog," Floyd said. "Perry from Canine is around the corner just waiting for orders. I still have a gun and a badge; what about you?"

Floyd grinned after he said it, his eyes practically challenging me. He was ready to go. One thing we both hated about working Homicide is that at times, some of our colleagues and much of the brass acted like we had forgotten how to be cops, or had lost our police powers. *Wait for SWAT. Call for a radio car to back you up.* In truth, many of us were still very capable and eager to do the heavy lifting, in spite of our suits and ties and dress shoes.

I pictured the contents of my trunk. There was one flak vest, a short-barreled shotgun, and extra ammunition for it and for my pistol. But that was it, as far as weaponry. Floyd and Josie rode with me, so none of their extra equipment was available. We could probably scrounge some extra vests from the patrol deputies, but that was the least of my worries. The fallout could be enormous if the situation went hot. Career-ending enormous. This was a high-risk operation and there were new policies in place that dictated exactly how these situations were to be handled, and by whom. The department had changed over the couple of decades since we were young cops on the job, and we were expected to play by the rules.

Though Floyd and I often stretched, skirted, and at times completely ignored the new policies, this was a volatile situation. Our asses would be in hot water if we didn't follow the book. Especially if it didn't turn out well.

But as Floyd would say, sometimes, you had to reach down between your legs . . . and ease the seat back.

Floyd, still waiting: "Well, Dickie?"

KATHERINE KEPT CHECKING HER PHONE. SHE'D CALLED TWICE AND ALSO sent a text message while at Dallas-Fort Worth on a layover. Now, as she waited for luggage in the baggage claim at LAX, a cold and eerie place this time of night, she tried calling again. Still, there was no answer. Was he ignoring her? She pictured him at a bar enjoying a cocktail, looking at his phone and deciding not to answer it. She knew he would do that. He had told her that he had done that with his wife, Valerie, at times, and he had even ignored his partner at times when he wanted to be alone.

That was the part she had missed, though it had been there the entire time, plain as day for her to see. Richard was a loner. He might enjoy the company of a woman, but he was just as happy by himself. Just him and his gin. Had she actually missed it? Or had she disregarded all signs of danger that hovered around their arrangement?

Anger settled over her as she silently questioned how she had allowed herself to get involved with a cop in the first place. As his psychiatrist, she knew his darkest secrets, his challenges, and his flaws. But she had been drawn to him nonetheless, and she had followed her emotions rather than her head. Now look at her.

Disgusted with herself, she opened the Uber app and summoned a ride from the airport. She would deal with Richard tomorrow. If at all.

FLOYD SAID, "WHO ARE YOU IGNORING, DICKIE? IS THAT KATHERINE?"

Josie watched me, waiting to hear the reply.

"It's the vet's office."

"Really? Interesting, since you don't have any pets."

"I have fish."

"Oh, and one of them is at the vet?"

"Cosmo."

"Cosmo," Floyd repeated.

"Yeah, Cosmo, the wang-tang. It's the purple little bastard with fins."

"The Purple Tang."

"Yes, that's correct. A *Red Sea* Purple Tang, if you're going to be precise about it."

"And he's at the vet."

I nodded. "Minor surgery."

"Well, I'm glad you've gotten into the fish, Dickie. It's good for you to have companionship, living beings that won't eventually take half of your retirement. Now, just out of curiosity, what is it exactly that ails your fish? Cosmo."

"He had a cold."

"So, you took him to the vet, and they did surgery. And now the vet's office is calling you at two in the morning with a report of his condition."

I locked eyes with him as I would an opposing attorney in a jury trial. "Yes, that's correct."

He grinned. "You're doing that thing you do."

"What? What thing?" I insisted.

Josie watched as if it were a tennis match. Enthralled. The helicopter circled above, and a dead woman lay on the ground fifty feet from where we stood, rapidly cooling in the damp night air.

Floyd leaned against the sedan with his arms crossed, the grin now gone. "You're pushing Katherine away. I've been watching, and I've seen you do it. You got scared again, like always. You started to let someone move into your life and then you panicked. Work makes more sense to you, so that's what you do. You work. You can't lie to me, Dickie. Telling fish stories, for fuck's sake."

I didn't respond.

He looked at Josie. "Don't ever get attached to this asshole."

She smiled. "Hey, that's my partner you're talking about."

"Yeah, well . . ." Then Floyd said to me: "Well, what'd you decide about this cluster? Are we going to sit here until dawn discussing your Purple Poon-Tang, or are we going to go kill this asshole ourselves?"

My brain swirled with the possibilities: wait for SWAT to arrive and then wait for hours more as they conducted their search. Or, do it ourselves, now, with the aid of a few patrol deputies and a canine unit. Call Katherine back and tell her what I had going on and explain why I couldn't answer the phone. Send her a text. Deal with it all tomorrow and explain it then. Or just end it, which is where I was headed, and had been for some time now. Jesus. Floyd was right about me. The dead woman hadn't moved. I wondered where it all went wrong for her, and for a moment questioned if it all was luck, or was it destiny. What was the difference? I didn't know.

All I knew for sure is it was time to make some decisions. Somehow, Floyd had managed to put it all on me. How was this my decision? How was it even my circus? We were all equally involved, and we would all have to deal with the consequences. In the old days, I would have said yes to the search a long time before now. There wouldn't have been much discussion or consideration. But now, times had changed. My gut said to wait for SWAT. They were the pros at taking on heavily armed, tactical thugs like the one we now hunted. At least he didn't have his AR-15; we had recovered it from the car. Why hadn't he taken it with him though? This guy was bad news and he would likely be waiting for our next move.

We needed to wait. But Floyd wasn't with me on it; I could tell. I was about to state my position and argue my point when two gunshots rang out a short distance from where we stood.

The three of us looked at each other. Floyd held up the radio and we all stared at it, waiting for some type of news to be relayed from somewhere in the containment. Finally, after what seemed like minutes but was only seconds, a female voice excitedly announced on the frequency, "Suspect just ran into a garage on the north side of the containment, shots fired."

"Who fired?" Floyd said into his handheld.

"I did," she puffed, the transmission crackling. "He's armed. He tried to break containment and when I hit him with the spotlight, he darted toward a garage. He had a gun, and I fired two rounds at him."

"Shit," Floyd said. He keyed the mic. "What type of gun did he have?"

"How would I know?"

The three of us exchanged glances. Floyd grinned. "Was it a handgun, or a rifle?"

"Oh, sorry. It was a handgun. He carried it in his hand while running."

"He definitely did not have a rifle, right?"

"No sir."

Floyd nodded. "That's two now who confirm he doesn't have a rifle. It changes everything. I say we go get him."

"Let's go over to her location and get some more details, see how it looks. Maybe come up with a plan."

"Let's do it," Floyd said. As we were getting into my car, he added, "I don't want to miss out on the chance to shoot that sonofabitch."

As we drove off, Floyd glanced in the back seat. "Here we go, Josie. Tighten your bra straps."

33

The garage stood apart from a two-story residence that remained dark and quiet in spite of the gunshots and now a flood of lights focused on it. The occupants were probably rehearsed at locking up and staying low during times like this. People in safer neighborhoods would often make the mistake of coming outside and insisting that the cops explain what was going on. A man in a bathrobe would appear at the edge of the yellow tape, or the outskirts of a containment, the wife peeking out the door, encouraging him. Not in this neighborhood. Nobody stirred.

We were a hundred feet away with an unrestricted view. Our headlights pointed at the garage and we huddled low in the door openings of my Crown Vic. There were two black and white radio cars positioned closer, though not directly in front of the property.

"First things first," I said. "We need to consider evacuating the immediate neighbors. The two next door, those across the street, and we should consider the next street as well, those houses right on the other side of the alley."

Floyd said, "Let's see about getting some AR-15s out here."

Josie said, "I'll work on that. I know the watch commander." With that, she turned and hustled to a radio car that sat idling nearby. There were two deputies sitting inside, their doors open, the front of the car pointed down the block with headlights and spotlights flooding the street.

"Good, thanks," I called out to her back.

After a few minutes of reflection in the ensuing silence, I looked at Floyd. "I'm not pushing her away. She left to be with her parents. They're old and sick. It's just the way it worked out."

He grinned. "Sure, Dickie."

TWO HOURS HAD PASSED SINCE THE FEMALE PATROL DEPUTY HAD SPOTTED our suspect trying to break containment and had rightfully fired a couple of rounds at him for his trouble. Josie and I spoke with her briefly at the scene, explaining that at some point, another team of homicide detectives would be asking her for a statement. We assured her that she did the right thing and she assured us that she had no problem with her actions. Though she hoped she had hit him, she didn't think she had. We would find out soon enough. There had been no additional sightings of the suspect.

Floyd had ducked his head and jogged from our position in order to get AR-15s from the command post when we learned they had arrived. A short time later, he informed us by radio that SWAT was now at the command post, and that they were going to be systematically replacing the patrol deputies that were near the home with SWAT deputies. I told Josie that we were staying put, and she agreed. I wished Floyd had been able to get back with the rifles, and hoped he still would.

Methodically, men clad in olive drab-colored jumpsuits with blacked out patches and tactical gear and firearms prowled through yards, following the shadows as they took positions of cover in various positions in our vicinity. Once the location was secured by SWAT, a command was made for the patrol units to retreat. A few minutes later, the streets were dark. The patrol cars had retreated, and the airship now orbited higher and wider. They would no doubt continue to watch the garage and its vicinity through their night vision cameras. Soon, an inquiry was made by one of the SWAT members asking for the identity of the unmarked unit that remained inside the containment. I replied that we were Homicide, that it was our case, and we were remaining where we were. There was no response, which told me the inquiring SWAT cop didn't like my position on the matter but thought it best not to argue about it either. This was not the time nor place for a pissing contest. Josie smiled widely at the comment.

Another fifteen minutes clicked off slowly in the quiet early morning hours. In the stillness, a military-style armored vehicle rounded the corner and drove toward the location. Men stood on platforms that line the sides and back of the vehicle, holding onto the handrails along the top. As the vehicle came to a stop, the men leaped from the vehicle and moved to various positions of cover in pairs. Once in position, the announcements commenced. For the next thirty minutes there were pleas for the suspect to surrender peacefully, and warnings that gas would soon be deployed. There was no response.

Soon, canisters of gas streaked through the night crashing through a window in the door to the garage, and another through a window on the side of the garage. SWAT was doing what they do best. What they train hard for, what they prepare for, what each and every one of them live for: action.

We waited. After a few moments, more canisters were fired, and more explosions followed. For the next pregnant moment, I wondered if the deputy had gotten it right, that the suspect had in fact run into the garage, the structure that now had smoke leaking from its pores.

I looked around at the adjacent homes and buildings and wondered if the suspect were somewhere else, and I began to worry that we had blown it. The whole operation, the entire night. A killer still on the run, not contained as we had thought for the past several anxiety-filled hours.

It happened more often than we cared to admit. Containments thought to be airtight could net no results after a thorough search, and this would leave many cops scratching their heads and doubting the results. But it was part of the game, a game we didn't always win.

Smoke billowed out of the garage, through its broken windows, beneath the doorways, from vents on the roof. SWAT cops stood by patiently, gas masks in place beneath their helmets, rifles and shotguns at the ready. Another loud pop accommodated a teargas canister whistling across the horizon and through the broken window. Flashes of light accompanied the concussion, and moments later more light flickered from inside. Soon the flashes of light became flames and the billows of teargas smoke became blooms of black smoke. A fire raged inside. If the suspect remained, he would be consumed by it. I readied myself in anticipation of his exit.

Suddenly, a figure appeared in the doorway, a silhouette against a fully-engulfed inferno. The figure raised a pistol and began shooting in all directions. I heard bullets whizzing past us, and then the sounds of bullets striking my sedan were accented with the popping sounds of the windshield being hit. A barrage of gunfire from all directions answered. Josie and I fired our pistols until they were empty. Gunfire continued. While replacing an empty magazine with a loaded one, I thought again about the rifles and wished we had them. I glanced over to see Josie coming back up on target. Calm, deliberate. Badass. She was back in the gunfight.

As I came back up on target, I saw the figure retreat into the flames and disappear. The gunfire persisted for a brief moment before silence fell upon the night and the sounds of crackling fire and a distant helicopter were all that could be heard. Flames shot through the roof of the garage and reached high into the sky, popping and snapping against the black sky. Our faces glowed from the heat.

The fire department was held at the outskirts while the building burned to the ground. It was not worth risking their lives to allow them in. Though it seemed impossible that the suspect had survived, all precautions would be adhered to until it was proven that he was deceased.

As dawn came, the building only smoldered. We were thankful that the fire had been contained to the detached garage and had miraculously not spread to the home. The helicopter was long departed, but we remained, as did the SWAT team members. It was the calm after the storm, the eerie feel of reflection that follows deadly encounters. The adrenaline dumps we had each experienced would drain us of our energy, if only for a few moments.

We held our positions and waited until it was light enough to see the charred remains of the structure from a distance. Only after seeing no movement or signs of life for another half hour, the SWAT team formed a squad and a search for the suspect began.

Josie and I folded into our seats and laid our heads against the rests and waited. Floyd soon joined us, climbing into the back seat, grumpy that he had missed the action.

"You guys suck."

A BODY WAS RECOVERED FROM THE CHARRED DEBRIS OF A GARAGE THAT, for the last seven years, had served solely to house a 1939 Ford coupe owned by World War II Veteran James L. Borgstrom. His grandson, Roland, had been willed the treasured car. As a child, Roland had ridden in the coupe with his grandfather through the streets of New Hope, Pennsylvania, along the canal, over the Delaware River, out through the countryside where wild flowers covered the hillsides and ferns carpeted the mystical, dark woods. On a few occasions, he had accompanied his grandfather on the forty-mile trip north to Philadelphia. Roland recalled many of the trips he'd made in the classic automobile, and he recalled bringing the heirloom home in an enclosed cargo trailer after laying his grandfather to rest in 1996.

Roland had moved to Los Angeles to be a police officer in 1971. Like his father and grandfather before him, he had served his country with the United States Marine Corps. As a rifleman in the 2nd Battalion, 1st Marines, he'd served in Vietnam, surviving a thirteen-month tour that took him to the streets of Hue City where Marines fought house to house and many did not come home. But he had survived Vietnam and he had survived twenty-six years as a cop on the streets of Los Angeles. He reflected on it all as he stood stoically at the edge of his property, peering toward the burned shell of the old Ford with eyes that seemed to see something or someplace far away from where he stood.

Beyond the smoldering remains of the classic coupe, in the furthest corner of where the structure had stood, lay a pile of burned flesh and bone with skeletal fingers clutching a pistol, its chamber and magazine as empty and finished as the man who had died holding it.

Roland Borgstrom didn't have many words for the detective who walked him to the edge of the demolished garage and stood with him while he appraised it. He didn't share his memories of his grandfather that the coupe always evoked, and he didn't reveal the flashbacks of war sparked by the sight of a charred man huddled in the corner with his gun. Nor did he disclose the reason that he missed all of the action and drama, having spent last night and most others for the past two months with his wife of more than three decades who was fighting terminal cancer at the USC Medical Center.

When he had seen enough, he thanked the lady detective and disappeared into the home that stood unharmed just twenty feet away.

———

"How'd he take it?" I asked, when Josie returned to the car. I was waiting with the air-conditioner running and the visor down as my sedan baked beneath the mid-morning sun.

She closed the door and slid her sunglasses into place. "Surprisingly well. Unemotional, really. I guess whatever old heap burned up in that garage must not have had much sentimental value. The sight of a dead man may have stunned him into silence. I guess most people go a lifetime without seeing something like that. But, he's a nice old man, the type that seemed supportive of law enforcement. He asked if any officers were hurt and shook his head sadly when I told him about Morgan being shot. That was about it. I've got his name and phone number. He said call his cell if we need anything, he won't be home much the next week or so."

"Oh? Is he staying somewhere else because of this?"

"He didn't say. Probably headed to Palm Springs or Florida, playing golf or doing whatever old men do."

"Must be nice to be retired, not have a worry in the world. Even your garage burning down can't dampen your mood."

"Someday," she said, "we may be so fortunate."

I drove slowly through the maze of detective cars, patrol vehicles, fire department and coroner's office personnel, making our way back to the command post.

"I think we've done all we can do here. I don't know about you two, but I could use some breakfast and then a few hours of sleep."

"And beer," Floyd said.

Josie quietly said, "Works for me."

WHEN I RETURNED HOME WITH A FULL BELLY AND HEAVY EYELIDS, I WAS greeted by two shopping bags blocking my front door, one of which had an envelope protruding from the top. I recognized the writing on it as Katherine's. The bags would no doubt contain the few items left at her home over the last few months: casual attire, workout clothes and running shoes, a toiletry bag, a few paperback novels—Connelly, Block, and Leonard—and a couple of ball caps with various insignia including the Homicide Bureau logo and bulldog mascot on at least two. There might have even been returned gifts: a gold sheriff's star necklace, a ladies Homicide Bureau sweater, a pair of silver hoop earrings from Tiffany's. I didn't know.

I stepped around the clutter and let myself into my apartment, closing the door resolutely behind me.

34

"We put the 'fun' in funeral."

It was how Lupita Rosas described her duties as the primary funeral planner for the department, assigned to Sheriff's Personnel. It wasn't that Deputy Rosas was uncaring or cold-hearted; she, like all cops, had learned to remove the emotion from a horrible job in order to survive. After eight years of working the streets, first as a patrol deputy and then undercover in the Narcotics Bureau, she'd seen her share of death and destruction and had attended more than her share of cop funerals. Some of those funerals had been for deputies whom she had personally known. There had never been any 'fun' in those, and there never would be. But after a few brushes with death herself, and now a baby on the way, *Lupe* had sought a position on the department that better fit the life of a young mother. At least for now.

She hated it. How do you console a grieving mother while peeling her away from the casket in order to adhere to a schedule? She had practiced saying to the parents that she felt their pain, but she didn't. She knew it and so did they. How could anyone who hasn't endured such pain know what it's like to lose a child? Soon, she knew, her belly would reveal that she was expecting a child. She would no longer be able to hide it, or her glow, while trying in vain to console a grieving mother.

But Lupe embraced the assignment for its schedule, and each day she arrived determined to make the best of it. Few people knew of the work that went into planning and coordinating department funerals. It was behind-the-scenes type of work, a production of sorts. She was an event planner with a gun.

"The guy was killed in a motorcycle accident in Malibu," she snapped into the phone. "No, look, he was off duty. This is a simple Wedding Package C, rice for the birds and a flower bouquet type of funeral. Church to dirt in thirty. I'm getting my nails done at four and my baby shower starts at five. Believe me, I'm going to keep it on a tight schedule."

She hung up and looked at her partner, Tracy, a civilian who handled much of the clerical duties associated with the assignment. "These deputies and their fucking Harleys, Trace, are driving our stats through the ceiling. Someone needs to invent training wheels for the goddamn machines so that these middle-aged men stop tipping over in the canyons."

Tracy shook her head without so much as a grin. Lupe hardly noticed. "Now Forest Lawn wants to push our services to Monday, saying Saturday is too busy with visitors for them to shut everything down for a cop funeral. You heard me tell him, it ain't a cop funeral, for the love of Christ, it's a funeral for a cop. I swear these people take the fun out of this job."

"What's wrong with Monday?" Tracy asked, her words slow like her movement.

Lupe stopped what she was doing and looked at Tracy for a long moment. "You know I don't like working Mondays."

"But if—"

Lupe hated Mondays and took most of them off. From her years working Narcotics, she had built up a large bank of "comp" time on the books. Her husband worked Gangs and had Sunday, Monday, and Tuesday off, and Lupe enjoyed the lazy Mondays while the rest of the world revved up for the week.

"We're not rearranging a funeral that's a week out. Everything else is set."

There were different arrangements depending on the circumstances of the death. A variety of packages, something for everyone. No group rates, Lupe would joke.

Line of Duty Deaths are what Lupe referred to as the Wedding

Package A. These funerals are what most people imagine when they hear of a police funeral. But these enormous spectacles were only for deputies who were killed while performing their duties as law enforcement officers, whether they were on- or off-duty at the time. *Active Sworn Deaths* include natural and accidental deaths, and even suicide. This might be a B package, or it might be the C. It just depended on the circumstances, and the identity of the deceased. *Active Civilian Employee Deaths* would also fall under the B package, though if the deceased was a VIP, they'd bump it to a B+. Family Member Deaths were solid C packages.

Line of Duty Deaths were the worst. Almost unbearable.

Lupe and Tracy would together oversee the publication of a deputy's death. They would assist the family with preparing the funeral notice and selecting a church, mortuary, and cemetery. The two would be responsible for coordinating the use of the Honor Guard, the bagpipers, and the bugler. They'd notify Aero Bureau who would assemble a team of helicopters and their pilots for the funeral flyover. If the twenty-one-gun salute didn't get you, the flyover would. Lupe and Tracy would liaise with other agencies who planned to send representatives and executives. They would inquire with influential politicians to determine who planned to attend, and who wished to speak, and what, if any, accommodations would be required. They would touch base with Employee Support Services, the Chaplain Corps, the Financial Counseling Team, and the Family and Children's Support Group.

And they would do all of this *With Dignity and Honor*, their official unit motto.

Her claim to fame was burying Buckwheat. Lupe would gleam as she told friends while sipping wine that indeed, she had single-handedly planted the Little Rascal. Lamont Grant was his true name, an actor who had played the role of Buckwheat as a child. He had gone on to become a minister, and he had been a reserve deputy for twenty years when he passed away from natural causes. He got the B+ package, and the undersheriff attended along with two county supervisors and a handful of mourners. Lupe arranged for the color guard and the 21-gun salute, which may have bumped it to an A- package; she wasn't sure. But Tracy flipped when she returned from vacation. "Girl, no you did not!" Lupe would smile and put a little more energy in her work while Tracy pouted, having missed out on burying Buckwheat.

Lupe grabbed another ringing phone, glancing at her watch as she did. "Employee Services, Deputy Rosas." After a brief moment, she glanced at Tracy with a look that indicated bad news was on the other end of the line. "Uh-huh, yes, yes. Okay." Lupe pulled a sheet from her drawer and started filling in the blanks.

When she placed the phone in its cradle, she looked up to see Tracy's eyes glued to her. She was waiting for the details; she would already know the story.

"Line of duty," Lupe said softly, "Compton."

Tracy just shook her head. Lupe had no idea how many deputies Tracy had helped bury in her many years of working at the unit, and she didn't know what toll it took on her. But Lupe knew the toll this case would take on her, personally, as she was familiar with the name she had written on her sheet, and she couldn't stop staring at it.

Lupe's husband was a gang detective who frequently worked in the City of Compton and its surrounding jurisdictions. He, and all of the other cops on those streets, would now go through the range of emotions, from anger to sorrow to guilt, and back to anger. They would renew their resolve to make the streets safer for the good citizens held hostage in their cities by the gangsters that plagued them. Lupe would watch as her husband increased his workouts, hit the bag a little harder, ran a little farther, and left the house each afternoon with darker eyes. And she would unconsciously rub a hand on her stomach while silently praying for his safety.

Lupe wiped at a tear forming in the corner of her eye and forced her mind to shift to the business at hand. The grim business of burying cops.

A WEEK LATER I SAT ON MY COUCH WATCHING THE NEWS, A COLD BEER within arm's reach.

I had stopped attending cop funerals after attending my first cop autopsy. Enough was enough; I could only bear so much weight. As a young cop, I went to all of the funerals of our fallen brethren. Like most cops, I kept a designated uniform for funerals and interviews. It was free of the wear and tear that my daily uniforms endured, and tailored for a sharp appearance, like a uniform one might wear for an inspection, if our department did such a thing beyond your days at the academy. Everyday uniforms, on the other hand, were tailored to allow room for a protective vest beneath the shirt, and flexibility in the pants. On the day before the funeral, I would polish and shine my badge, nameplate, and the snaps and buckle of my gun belt. Leather shoes with a high shine would replace the semi-polished boots I normally wore while working patrol. My badge would be adorned with a black band across it to signify the mourning of a brother. The small elastic band had been used more than I ever could have anticipated on the day I raised my hand and took an oath to serve with honor.

When I first promoted to station detectives, I could still wear that special uniform, and unfortunately, I still had to on several occasions. Eventually, I would attend the funerals in a suit, as the years and miles and decreased physical activity managed to shrink the uniform. When I promoted to Homicide, I immediately found myself involved in the case of a murdered deputy sheriff. I attended the autopsy, and as I stood tableside watching a colleague dissected, I made the decision then and there that I would no longer attend the funerals of fallen comrades, unless—God forbid—it was that of a close friend.

But I couldn't help but watch the news the evening after they buried Thomas Johnson. The camera filmed from a hillside in Los Angeles that offered a view of downtown and the city that sprawled beyond it, to the south where he had shed his lifeblood a week ago this day. The procession of hundreds of black and white cars with flashing lights of red and blue stretched as far as the cameras could film. A thousand mourners crowded the hillside and stood solemnly under a peaceful blue sky as a flag was folded, and a husband, father, and son, waited to be lowered into the earth. A formation of helicopters shattered the silence. Every wet eye behind sunglasses watched as a lone bird peeled away from the others. Seven riflemen aimed at the heavens and fired their rifles three times each on command. And as the echoes of gunfire and plumes of smoke hung in the air, a lone bugle cried the melody of taps while tough men choked back tears, or they didn't.

35

Three months passed before the preliminary hearing was held for the man who had been charged with the first-degree murder of Deputy Thomas Johnson. Cameras crowded the steps of the Criminal Courts Building on Temple Street in downtown Los Angeles. A team of prosecutors, assigned to the Crimes Against Peace Officers Section of the Los Angeles County District Attorney's Office, prepared for a long and arduous legal battle, one for which they would seek the death penalty against Juan Hector Machado. A long list of witnesses was expected to be put on record at this early hearing. The prosecution's strategy was to memorialize the testimony and cross-examination of some of the witnesses who might not be available for trial several years down the road, due to the vulnerable nature of their lifestyles. Junkies, gang members, and a prostitute who carried the AIDS virus were among them. Other witnesses, such as the partner of Deputy Johnson, would be called to testify before a courtroom packed with supporters. This would be no ordinary preliminary hearing, and it would go on for several days.

Josie and I sat sipping coffees in the living area of a hotel suite while waiting for Lynette Luna to emerge from her room. Josie had spent the night with her, sleeping lightly on the couch where we now sat. It was between the entrance door and the room where Lynette was secured. I had dropped the two of them off at the hotel after returning from the airport where Lynette had arrived on a flight from New Mexico. Las Cruces is where Lynette now lived, courtesy of Los Angeles County tax payers.

Lynette, standing five feet, four inches tall and weighing just over a buck, emerged from her room with a smile on her face. Steam followed her from the doorway as she continued brushing her black hair that was long and straight and still wet from her shower. She wore jeans and a tight white tank top, accentuated by silver bracelets, rings, and large hoop earrings. When she finished brushing her hair, she slipped into a button-up blouse that would cover many of her tattoos and scars left from years of intravenous drug use. She was dressed up as if headed to family court.

I stood and waited while Lynette sorted through her purse, placing her hairbrush, a mirror, a lipstick, a package of cigarettes, a lighter, two packs of gum, and a variety of cosmetic containers therein. Josie stood waiting near a window that overlooked a parking lot where four men in jeans and loose-fitting shirts that concealed firearms sat in a variety of unmarked cars, providing security.

"Are you ready for this?" Josie asked, stepping to the witness and placing a soft hand on her shoulder.

She smiled and picked up her purse. "I've never been readier for anything in my life."

The night before, she had remarked that her life had been given to God, and it was His to take when He was ready. She was clean, sober, and no longer selling her body in order to support a heroin habit. The AIDS virus she carried was controlled by drugs and monitored by physicians, and she lived in a place where her background was a mystery to her neighbors and her future was as bright as it had ever been. "He saved my life," she had said, speaking of Deputy Johnson who had been gunned down before her weary eyes.

He hadn't physically saved her life, but his dying had changed hers forever. Lynette knew the killer. She had known him most of his life. She was watching him before the cops arrived and knew he was up to something, and she watched in horror as he shot the deputy and fled, somehow managing to escape a hail of bullets. Lynette had also known the deputy, as he had contacted her many times. On a couple of occasions, he had arrested her for drug possession. He had always been fair, kind, and professional; she would never forget his smile or his bright blue eyes. That night, when the gunfire had stopped, she heard the wailing of Deputy Johnson's partner. Those sounds and the image of the young black deputy cradling the dead cop had been seared into her mind. She didn't hesitate to do what she never would have considered doing before, and what most others in her community would not do: she came forward with a name, a statement, and a promise to tell the truth, the whole truth, and nothing but the truth. She had said, "What do I have to lose? I'm living with a death sentence now. For once in my life, I'm going to do the right thing."

I held the door for them, switched off the light, and hung a sign requesting housekeeping. It would be a long week for the two ladies who would be holed up in the modest room.

The first witness to be called for the people's case in chief was Deputy Roger Nelson. I stood against the back wall while Josie sat with Lynette six floors up, waiting in the prosecutor's office. I would send her a text when it was time for her to testify. Deputy Nelson took the stand in uniform. For the first time since meeting the young man, I was disappointed in him. Every cop knows that you can appear for court in uniform or a suit, but a suit is preferred for trials and all cases of importance. Though this was only the preliminary hearing, it was of the utmost importance, and it would be viewed as such by the nation, since the media would televise much of it.

He was sworn in and seated at the witness stand. The judge watched him closely, and I couldn't help but wonder if the judge was also thinking the man should have worn a suit—or at least a long-sleeved, Class A uniform complete with a tie. The prosecutor began with the basics. State your name for the record. Please tell the court your occupation and assignment. And on the night of September 18, 2018, were you so assigned. "Yes."

"And on that night, were you dressed as you are today, wearing a uniform with a badge and patches that clearly identify you as a deputy sheriff for the County of Los Angeles?"

I wondered if the prosecutor had told him to wear a uniform for effect.

Because the prosecution was seeking the death penalty, it would be important to establish that there was no doubt that the killer knew that the two men who confronted him that night were deputies. Still, he could have worn a long-sleeve Class A, what we'd refer to as an interview and funeral uniform, not a short-sleeve everyday uniform shirt with no tie.

"Yes, I wore this uniform that night."

The prosecutor paused, and I knew why. The testimony could be construed as the deputy stating that he wore that actual uniform, not merely a uniform similar to that one. Small details matter in cases that would later be reviewed by a variety of jurors and justices in the decades to come.

"You mean, Deputy Nelson, that you wore a uniform similar to what you are wearing here today?"

"No sir. I mean I wore this uniform."

A hush fell over the courtroom; not a murmur nor rustle could be heard. The prosecutor looked to the table where one of the homicide investigators who handled the case sat as his designated investigating officer. The detective shrugged.

"The exact uniform, Deputy Nelson?"

"Yes sir."

After a moment: "How can you be sure, Deputy Nelson, that it is the same exact uniform you wore that night?" the prosecutor asked tentatively.

Nelson looked down and picked at the front of his uniform while speaking softly into the microphone before him: "There are still stains from my partner's blood on both the shirt and pants." He looked up, wetness filling his eyes. The judge looked away. The prosecutor looked down at his notes. Sniffles penetrated the otherwise silent room. I blinked violently against the flood of emotion. I pictured the deputy cradling his dead partner in the manner that Lynette had described to us and would soon be testifying to.

Soon, the courtroom became restless and the judge asked the prosecutor to continue, and he did. Nelson walked the court through the actions of the night leading up to the pedestrian stop of Deputy Johnson's killer, Juan Hector Machado, known as "Apache" in his neighborhood. Deputy

Nelson testified that he and his training officer, Deputy Johnson, knew Apache from previous contacts, and they knew him to be affiliated with a local street gang whose members were known to control drug sales in the area. The gang controlled their turf through violence and intimidation. Deputy Nelson and his partner had made numerous arrests of the various members of this gang, and based on their training and experience, coupled with the defendant's furtive movement upon their arrival, they believed him to be involved in criminal activity. They stopped and exited their patrol vehicle in order to detain Machado, who turned and fired his weapon at them both. His partner was struck by gunfire and went down quickly. Nelson returned fire as Machado ran into the night.

The prosecutor used the remainder of the morning session to fill in details with Deputy Nelson. After the noon break, the defense had its first crack at the young deputy. A black attorney leaned on the podium and smiled when he greeted Deputy Nelson, who smiled and greeted him likewise.

The defense attorney began, "Deputy Roger Nelson, huh?"

Both of them smiled as if there were an inside joke of which I—and most others in the courtroom—was unaware. Nelson replied. "Yes sir."

"Not *the* Roger Nelson, I presume."

Still smiling: "No, sir."

"Just to be clear," the attorney said, "and for the record, you're not *Prince*, right? The popstar icon whose real name is Roger Nelson?"

"*His* name is actually Rogers Nelson," Deputy Nelson replied, emphasizing the S. "But to answer your question, Counselor, no, I am not Prince."

Nelson's eyes met mine as I stood in the back of the courtroom. I suddenly realized who he was, and gratitude washed over me. I understood now why his eyes and smile had seemed familiar to me, and why he had assured me we had previously met. He had made it out. He had survived living in the various foster homes scattered throughout rough neighborhoods and mean streets, and he had become a man, courtesy of the United States Marine Corps. I was proud of him, and elated for him, and thankful that there had been at least one happy ending to an otherwise tragic story of life on the streets in South Los Angeles.

I thought about his testimony, how after the suspect had fled and the shooting had ended, how Deputy Nelson—*Prince*—had sat cradling his dead partner as he waited for help. I pictured the scene as I had seen it that night, dark and eerie, deep in unfriendly territory. I thought about the tears in his eyes as he spoke of his bloody uniform, and I imagined him taking steps to preserve that blood, instructing the cleaners to never remove it from his shirt. He probably hadn't worn it since that night, and he would probably never wear it again. Maybe for the trial, or when he watched from the audience as Machado would be walked into the chamber decades later for his execution. And as all of these thoughts rattled around in my head, profound sadness grew inside me, and I asked myself, had he really made it out?

Then I thought about why we were here this morning. I dwelled on the thought, repeating it silently, and, without realizing it, allowed the words to cross my lips in a whisper: "Why the hell are we even here?" A reporter who stood nearby stared at me for a long moment before returning to his pad of paper. I shook myself, mentally. After pondering it for several moments, I reasoned that we are here for a good goddamn reason. That we do the job for the Princes of the world, those for whom there is hope, those who can be saved. Saving a life or seeing someone make it out was the only reward, the only prize received for doing a tough, dangerous, and otherwise thankless job.

Of course Deputy Nelson had made it out. Even though he chose to work in the same dangerous streets he had survived as a child, and in doing so, he would face the same challenges, traumas, and heartbreaks as each of us who choose the badge, he had made it out. He had defeated the odds and for whatever reason, he was back. Probably to make things better.

This was only the natural order of things, and I had to accept it. I was no longer a street cop, but having been one for a lot of years had shaped me into the man I now was. It had educated me, hardened me, and at times it had left me with a broken heart. The young deputies will learn from the old bulls, and they will carry on the traditions and the memories of their predecessors with great reverence. It was now their responsibility, their job. Prince was part of it, and I was proud that he was.

My job was to arrive at times like this and do everything I could to send murderous sons of bitches like Apache to Death Row.

Nelson was stepping down, and the judge announced we would resume testimony at nine-thirty tomorrow morning. The spectators began shuffling toward the doors, crowding past me. I made eye contact with Prince from across the courtroom again, and I knew. He had made it. We had both made it.

36

After driving Josie and Lynette back to the hotel and securing them for the evening, I pulled out of the parking lot in my Crown Vic with a nod to two deputies who sat in a parked car watching the building. I had done their job before becoming a homicide investigator, and I didn't envy their assignment. It would be a long night and most likely there would be no action or activity of interest. But every moment they would be prepared for the worst, and it would wear them down. Tonight, and over the years.

Hitting the freeway gave me a feeling of freedom. Until tomorrow morning, I was free of responsibility. I had been taken out of the rotation for callouts, as my partner and I were solely responsible for seeing to our witness and having her available for court until she was dismissed. The wind rushing through my open window seemed to cleanse me of the day's memories and nudge me back to Katherine and my pile of returned property with a note I still hadn't read. The sedan had heard my thoughts and automatically veered us toward Sierra Madre where Moby would be waiting to pour me a cold one, or two. Over drinks I'd ponder the Katherine situation but skirt around some of the harsher truths that Floyd had pointed out. *I got scared. I allowed this to happen.* No, I made it happen. I pulled back and away and left her with no choice but to realize what a mistake she had made getting involved with someone like me. Was it her, or was it me? It didn't matter.

I parked at the rear of Buck's and had just shut off the engine when my cell phone vibrated in my pocket. It was Floyd.

Excitement surrounded his words. "Hey, Dickie, are you headed back to the office?"

"No. Why?" I sensed that my cold beer would be delayed.

"We have a problem."

"No, you have a problem. I'm out for the week on this prelim, the Johnson case. We have a witness from out of state we're babysitting, so I am therefor unavailable."

"Yeah, well, you might reconsider when I tell you where me and Mongo are headed."

I stared off across the parking lot. A couple approached the door to Buck's and went inside, the sounds of music and chatter fading as the door closed behind them. Floyd was baiting me. He knew I wouldn't say no to anything that fit into the categories of excitement, danger, or challenge. He would make me feel needed, maybe ask my opinion on something and then say I should come have a look, lend my expertise. I wondered if they had caught a murder and he was headed to a fresh crime scene. I didn't know. I didn't even know which teams were currently on call, because it didn't matter to me; I was out of the rotation. I had to have a witness in court tomorrow morning, and by God, I would, come hell or high water. Not even another bizarre, twisted, convoluted case that promised hours of Floyd entertainment and sleep deprivation could entice me away from a cold beer and a night to myself.

Unless.

Floyd, never one for patience, interrupted my contemplation: "Come on, Dickie, get crackin'. Meet up with us at the office and we'll roll together. You don't have anything better to do."

He hung up. For a long moment I gazed through the open window, silently cursing him while shaking my head. Katherine's note that had been left on my step sat next to me on the seat, beckoning. Maybe its contents would help me choose: cold beer or Floyd? I picked it up and tore open the flap.

Dear Richard,

    I truly regret having to address this with you in a letter, but . . .

I dropped the letter and its envelope on the seat. There was no sense in reading on; the opening words removed any doubt I might have had.

I cranked the motor and jerked the shifter into drive. Somebody was dying to meet me.

THE COLOR DEAD

A Dickie Floyd Detective Novel

Danny R. Smith

I sat anxiously with Esmeralda, the mother of Josefina Sanchez. An awkward silence hung between us as I fussed with the hat I held in my lap. Josie's mother sat picking at the fabric of the oversized chair that swallowed her frail body. A clock ticked slowly against the wall. The pool filter hummed outside the open patio door. I glanced quickly through the living room window at the sound of a passing vehicle, as did Esmeralda. The car passed, and both of us returned to waiting in silence. I drew a deep breath and let it out slowly, easing some of the tension. Esmeralda sighed, seemingly her way of expressing similar disappointment. Her thoughts were likely no different than mine, only in Spanish. My bilingual skills were limited to the few basics: *alto*—stop, or more accurately, halt; *manos arriba*—hands up; *muerte*—death. Hopefully none of those words would be needed in my limited communications with Josie's mother. When I first arrived, I had smiled at the small woman with graying hair, and asked where Josie was: *"Donde esta Josie?"* Esmeralda, her small dark eyes showing fear and concern, had shaken her head and shrugged. *"No sé."* She didn't know.

Like many cops, I was quick to assume the worst. Josie was missing, so something terrible had happened to her. My experiences had conditioned me to think that way. But I had also been trained and conditioned to never give up, so I forced myself to see my partner alive and well. There had to be a reasonable explanation of her absence.

Josefina Sanchez had been a deputy sheriff for twelve years. She had survived three shootings and dozens of altercations. She knew the streets, and she knew the hustlers, gangsters, and junkies who roamed them. She had put countless bad men away, and she had even put some down. Josie was a cop any other would be proud to have as a partner. It wasn't as if she was the vulnerable type, and her personal lifestyle wasn't the type to put her at risk. As far as I knew.

Though two things did bother me: Josie and I had picked up a new murder case three days ago, one that had *bizarre* written on it from the start. It was a case of a gunshot victim found in the mountains near rural Gorman, the last stop headed north through Los Angeles County. Gorman felt more like an outpost in Wyoming than a sheriff's substation in southern California. When we were given the assignment, I had frowned at Rich Farris who was manning the desk and had dispatched the callout. "Gorman?" I questioned. "Are you shitting me, Rich?" After Farris explained the basics of what he knew—a man was found in the woods with a single gunshot wound to the chest and a rifle at his side—I had said, "Rich, this sounds like a suicide to me, or an accidental death. Maybe a hunting accident?"

Farris said he had thought so too, at first. Rich had been at Homicide a long time—several more years than I had—and he had handled scores of suicide cases in which men had taken their pistols and even rifles out to their favorite hunting or camping grounds and sat down beneath the shade of a large oak or pine for last moments of reflection before taking their own lives. He said, "When's the last time you saw a dude off himself standing up?" I hadn't. For whatever reason, people didn't want to fall, once dead. They'd sit beneath a tree, behind the wheel of a car, or on their favorite sofa or chair, or maybe they'd lie down in bed. But rare was the case of the man or woman who put a bullet through their own power plant while standing upright, thus allowing their dead bodies to fall to the floor or ground. Even the newly departed seemed hesitant to take a fall.

What bothered me most about the case and Josie's absence was a comment she had made after we had wrapped up Thursday evening and driven back into civilization. Josie had asked if we would be going back up to the mountain over the weekend, and she seemed puzzled that I had suggested we take the weekend off and start back up on Monday. It hadn't sounded good in my head when I said it, and it tasted sour coming out of my mouth. But we were scheduled to be off for a three-day weekend, and there was no immediate workable information that needed to be pursued right away. The captain had been complaining about overtime again, and I didn't care to give him more to gripe about. So, I had thought, why not take a weekend off? I suggested to Josie that we let the case sit for three days, handle the detail we had been asked to deal with Sunday evening for another detective on an unrelated case, and then we'd get back to the new murder Monday. The murder on the mountain. Josie had frowned and questioned, "On a fresh case? We're going to just park it?"

The question I had now was would she have taken it upon herself to work the case over the weekend without me? I didn't think so, yet there was a possibility she had. I had told her to enjoy a few days off, and I'd pick her up from her home on Sunday at five.

I glanced at my watch, looked through the front window toward the quiet street, and then my eyes slowly drifted back to the anxious mother.

The second thing that bothered me was how little I actually knew of Josie's personal life. She was private, even after six months of partnership, careful to guard against revealing much of her life outside of the job. Was she seeing someone? If so, had she been having trouble with him? Or her? Jesus, I didn't even know whether she was straight or gay. Not that it mattered, but it accentuated the point that was troubling me: I knew almost nothing of my partner's personal life. Floyd and I had had no secrets when we were partners, and probably still didn't.

I forced myself out of my naturally pessimistic thought pattern and considered the fact that she may have just gone away for the weekend without telling anyone. It was a question I'd have to ask Esmeralda. But how?

I glanced at my watch again, and only five minutes had passed. I had been waiting for more than an hour now, and I needed to do something other than sit here and worry. I stood up from the couch and paused, searching my brain for the Spanish translation of "Excuse me." Esmeralda waited, watching, seemingly knowing my thoughts. I nodded, smiled, held up my index finger and said, "*Momento,*" and walked outside.

Under the bright sunlight, I put my ball cap on and then thumbed my phone to life and called Floyd. I waited impatiently as the call went unanswered and was eventually picked up by voicemail. I disconnected and called again. Same result. I shoved the phone in my pocket, removed my hat with one hand and wiped dampness from my forehead with the other. An airplane passed overhead, inbound to LAX, I assumed, as I caught a glimpse of it against the late afternoon sun to the west. I shifted my weight from one leg to the other, antsy, my mind racing as I fought to control my emotions. Not being able to get ahold of either of my partners—my new one, Josie, or my old one, Pretty Boy Floyd—threatened to send me over the edge. For a brief moment, I pictured them somewhere together, living it up, a quiet barroom or maybe a Jacuzzi.

Through the open front door I could see that Esmeralda had left her chair. She was probably in the kitchen making something to eat. That's what Mexican women of her generation did at times of peril; they fed you. They fed everyone. The more people they could feed, the more content were their lives. You'd never see them partaking, only providing. Nurturing. Mothering. God bless them all.

I sent another call to Floyd's phone and was startled when it was answered. "Hold on," a woman snapped. It was Cindy, Floyd's wife, but she wasn't her usual friendly self. I waited and listened to the sound of a slider being opened and the faint sound of a boy's voice. I then heard Floyd. His voice was distant at first but seemed to draw nearer. I pictured Cindy walking the phone to him, my old partner standing at the barbecue, a meat hook in one hand and a can of beer in the other. The uniform of the day would likely include board shorts, flip-flops, and a cowboy hat, no shirt. Never a shirt. He'd have wire-rimmed mirrored circles covering his eyes, something Elton John or John Lennon might wear on stage, something he had grabbed at the market when he picked up a box of beer and two bags of ice. He'd be contented in his haven, his private retreat from the world, all the peace and quiet a man could want right in his own backyard.

"What's up Dickie?"

Floyd hovered a meat hook over a sizzling tri-tip while sipping his beer and watching his son run toward him. The kid suddenly jumped into the pool not far from where he stood, tucking himself into a cannonball mid-flight. He landed with a whoosh, and water sprayed across Floyd's back, cooling his shoulders. He jolted and thrust his beer toward the sky, cat-like instincts saving it from a wave of water.

"Cody, not in the shallow end, bud," he said flatly.

Cody went under, headed to the other end, a skinny porpoise gliding effortlessly through the crystal-blue water. Like his father, he had taken to the water early in life and spent hours every week swimming laps for exercise.

"Little shit," Floyd mumbled, smiling as he swigged his beer and watched the boy turn at the far end of the pool, still not coming up for air.

Cindy appeared at the slider, her blonde head and tanned shoulders squeezing through the small opening. She swatted at a fly and spoke as if it was urgent. "How much longer on the meat?" she asked.

Floyd regarded the slab of beef smoking on the grill. He dropped the curved part of his meat hook from a couple inches above the center of the four-pound tri-tip. It had no bounce, which indicated it was far from finished. He glanced at his watch and turned back to his bride. "Fifteen, maybe twenty minutes. I don't know."

She waved her hand at another flying intruder and disappeared, the glass door hitting hard in its frame.

"The hell is your problem," Floyd said at the closed door. He took another drink of his cold beer, and it felt good going down. He cherished his days off, though few they were nowadays. That was the life of a homicide detective.

"Dad, watch this!"

He looked in time to see Cody launch himself from the top of the slide and into the water, foregoing the slow ride down.

"For fuck's sake," Floyd said, before the boy surfaced.

The sound of the slider drew his attention again, and he turned to see his wife approaching with his cell phone held out toward him.

"What's up?"

She didn't answer. She handed him the phone and turned to walk away. Floyd let his eyes settle on her ass as she did, and he smiled and took another swig of beer. If there was one thing he loved, it was a nice ass. If there were two things he loved, it was a nice ass and cold beer. If he had to list three things, he'd add a medium-rare steak. It was a perfect day, he thought, until his attention turned to the screen displaying "Dickie Cell."

"What's up, Dickie?"

He listened while watching Cody climb out of the pool, the young man's eyes upon him. Nearly a teenager now, the kid watched him closely at all times. Cody emulated him in many ways and cherished the time they had together. Floyd knew this, and he could see the look of concern in the boy's eyes each time he took a business call at home. Many times, the conversation would result in a change of demeanor, and then attire, followed by a hasty departure in the county car. Floyd always felt guilty when it happened.

Dickie said, "I need your help, partner."

"What's up?"

"Josie."

Floyd waited a moment, his eyes on Cody who now stood nearby toweling off. He knew the boy would be taking in every word, wanting to know the details. He turned back to the barbecue and dropped the hook on the slab of meat again.

"What about her?"

"We were supposed to meet at five. I have no idea where she is."

Floyd set the hook down at the side of the barbecue, picked up his beer and took a swig before speaking. "Well, it's not my turn to watch her, Dickie. Cindy won't allow it. Not that I wouldn't—"

"I'm at her house. Her mother is worried."

"Whose house?"

"Josie's. Her mother lives with her, and from the best I can get—because wouldn't you know it, she only *pinky panty*—Josie didn't come home last night."

Floyd mumbled, "Jesus, dude. So you want me to come *pinky panty*; that's where this is going?"

"You speak it better than me."

"Dickie, you can't order tacos in Spanish. Why don't you call Miguel, or Joe the Mo, one of them assholes who gets paid to *habla*? I'm fu—" he glanced at his son "—I'm in the middle of cooking a tri-tip."

Dickie said, "Dude, I've got a bad feeling on this."

"You always do," he said, though he could hear the concern in Dickie's voice.

"But I also don't want to blow this up just yet, get others involved, just in case I'm wrong."

Floyd considered it a moment. "You think she's gone missing? What, like she's been kidnapped?"

"Yeah, something like that."

Floyd took in a deep breath and let it out slowly, thinking about the situation. The situation with Dickie and the situation at home, his son watching, hoping no doubt that he wouldn't leave, and his wife already pissy about God knows what.

"Dude, she's single. Come on, man, she probably spent the night somewhere, know what I mean?"

"Yeah, maybe."

"I mean, maybe give it some more time, a few more hours?"

"Yeah, fine. I'll just sit here with her mom and hope she comes home."

Floyd noted the tone. Disappointment. Irritation.

"Jesus, man."

"Plus I need to get down to Orange County, take care of Lopes's informant. That's why I was picking up Josie."

"Okay, okay," he said, motioning for his son to step closer. Floyd picked up the meat hook and handed it to Cody. "Watch the meat, little man."

He could hear Dickie still talking on the phone, ". . . get more information from the mom, and maybe toss her room, see what I can figure out about her personal life. The woman's a complete mystery to me."

"Settle down, Dickie, I'm on my way. Text me her address."

Floyd disconnected and held his son's gaze but for a moment. He glanced at his watch and made a mental note of the *time of notification,* grabbed his beer and polished it off as he headed for the house. He set the empty can on a poolside table before pulling the sliding glass door open and pushing through the drape on the other side.

Cody said, "Are you leaving?"

He paused in the doorway and looked at the kid once more. "I won't be long, buddy."

Floyd started for his room, ignoring his wife's admonishment about leaving the door wide open behind him.

Within minutes Floyd had changed out of his board shorts and into a pair of jeans and a buttoned short-sleeved shirt. It was his day off; he wasn't putting on a suit. He detoured to the back door, flung it open again and called out to his son: "See ya later, meatball. I promise I won't be long." The boy's shoulders sagged in apparent disappointment, and his mouth turned down in a pout.

Leaving the door open, Floyd turned to find Cindy waiting behind him, her hands on her hips and eyes narrowed. He leaned in to kiss her goodbye, and she turned to offer a cheek.

"What's up your ass?"

"Nothing."

Floyd didn't have the time nor inclination to play the game she might have expected as a result of her terse response. The game where he would ask again what was wrong, and she would continue to deny that anything bothered her, and they would go back and forth in that manner until she gave him both barrels, providing a list of all that was "up her ass." He grabbed his gun and badge from the top of the refrigerator and without looking back, said, "See ya tonight." He left the front door standing open.

Shades on, Floyd wheeled his county car from the driveway and took off down the street, smiling broadly at the brunette across the way who stood in shorts and a t-shirt, watching him leave. Her husband hadn't been home for a few weeks, and Floyd wondered if they were separated. The thought occurred to him he should find out someday, just in case she needed anything. It would be the neighborly thing to do.

As he merged onto the freeway, Floyd kept one eye on the road and the other on his phone. He had put Josie's address into a mapping program that would tell him the fastest route, the shortest route, and where to watch out for hazards and the highway patrol—one and the same in Floyd's mind. Once the address was programmed, he thumbed his ETA into a text message to Dickie, and watched impatiently, waiting for a response. *Delivered*, showed on the screen. After a moment, *Read*. "Attaboy, Dickie. Come on." There, the three dots danced on his screen, showing him Dickie was typing something. But then they stopped. And started. Stopped. "What the hell? Come on, Dickie." He hoped for more information, an update, anything.

He placed the phone in its cradle on the dash. The screen darkened. Floyd reached over and touched it to bring it back to life. The cycle continued: Dots. No dots. Dots. Finally, a thumbs up emoji. "Jesus Christ," Floyd said.

He turned on the radio, unable to contend with the silence that came with being alone. Floyd pictured his old partner, Dickie, sitting at Josie's house. It was probably quaint, and her mother likely wore a dress and tennis shoes, frail hands clutching a handkerchief. He had never met her, but he had met many like her. The mothers of wondrous Latinas. Dickie probably sat with his hat in his hands, turning it while massaging its brim into shape, anxiously awaiting his partner.

He glanced at the phone again. Nothing.

Floyd replayed the conversation they had had while he was out back cooking, and the more he replayed it in his mind, the more he felt the urgency taking hold. Or maybe it was that he had shifted gears and was now in work mode. Game time. Helmets and shoulder pads, time to light something on fire and cause a wreck. He cracked a grin at the thought, remembering those words spoken by his high school football coach.

As he sailed along, his mind drifted back to Cindy and the look she had given him, and the avoidance of a goodbye kiss. Floyd again wondered what it was that had been up her ass, and dismissed it as most likely having something to do with a hormonal imbalance.

Floyd touched his phone again to bring it to life. Still no messages. Restless, he thumbed over to emails and began scanning through the numerous unread messages that appeared, while sailing along the I-5 doing seventy. But dodging lousy drivers didn't provide enough activity to keep Floyd entertained, and the emails soon bored him as well, so he returned to wondering what might have happened to Josie, if anything. He smiled at some of the ideas that followed, picturing Josie at various undisclosed locations enjoying herself in the way that a smoking-hot single woman might. Dickie was just wound too damn tight, he reasoned, settling into his seat and wondering if this would be all for naught, a dry run. He didn't care; it was an excuse to get out of the house for the night. He'd miss Cody, but Cindy he could do without until she managed to unfuck herself.

I love staying connected with my readers through social media and email. If you would like to connect, find me on BookBub, Amazon, Goodreads, Facebook, Instagram, and Twitter. You can also sign up for my newsletter and receive bonus material, such as the action-packed short story, Harder Times.

As a newsletter subscriber, you will receive special offers, updates, book releases, and blog posts. I promise to never sell or spam your email.

Danny R. Smith

Dickie Floyd Novels

Dickie Floyd Detective Novels

- A GOOD BUNCH OF MEN
- DOOR TO A DARK ROOM
- ECHO KILLERS
- THE COLOR DEAD

SHORT STORIES

- In the City of Crosses - A Dickie Floyd Detective short story
- Exhuming Her Honor - A Dickie Floyd Detective short story
- Harder Times: A Cop Goes to Prison - Not a Dickie Floyd Story - Free to Newsletter Subscribers, visit dickiefloydnovels.com

Danny R. Smith spent 21 years with the Los Angeles County Sheriff's Department, the last seven as a homicide detective. He now lives in Idaho where he works as a private investigator and consultant. He is blessed with a beautiful wife and two wonderful daughters. He is passionate about his dogs and horses, whom he counts among his friends.

Danny is the author of the *Dickie Floyd Detective Novel* series, and he has written articles for various trade publications. He publishes a weekly blog called The Murder Memo, which can be found at dickiefloydnovels.com.

He is a member of the Idaho Writers Guild and the Public Safety Writers Association.

45734798R00151

Made in the USA
Lexington, KY
19 July 2019